MORE THAN FRIENDS

Acclaim for Erin Dutton's Work

"*Designed for Love* is…rich in love, romance, and sex. Dutton gives her readers a roller coaster ride filled with sexual thrills and chills. *Designed for Love* is the perfect book to curl up with on a cold winter's day."—*Just About Write*

"*Sequestered Hearts* is packed with raw emotion, but filled with tender moments too. The author writes with sophistication that one would expect from a veteran author. …A romance is about more than just plot and character development. It's about passion, physical intimacy, and connection between the characters. The reader should have a visceral reaction to what is going on within the pages for the novel to succeed. Dutton's words match perfectly with the emotion she has created. *Sequestered Hearts* is one book that cannot be overlooked. It is romance at its finest."—*L-word Literature.com*

"*Sequestered Hearts* by first time novelist, Erin Dutton, is everything a romance should be. It is teeming with longing, heartbreak, and of course, love. …As pure romances go, it is one of the best in print today."—*Just About Write*

In *Fully Involved* "…Dutton's studied evocation of the macho world of firefighting gives the story extra oomph—and happily ever after is what a good romance is all about, right?"—*Q Syndicate*

With *Point of Ignition*… "Erin Dutton has given her fans another fast paced story of fire, with both buildings and emotions burning hotly. …Dutton has done an excellent job of portraying two women who are each fighting for their own dignity and learning to trust again. The delicate tug of war between the characters is well done as is the dichotomy of boredom and drama faced daily by the firefighters. *Point of Ignition* is a story told well that will touch its readers."—*Just About Write*

Visit us at www.boldstrokesbooks.com

By the Author

More Than Friends

by

Erin Dutton

2013

This Trade Paperback Original Is Published By
Bold Strokes Books, Inc.
P.O. Box 249
Valley Falls, NY 12185

First Edition: February 2013

CREDITS
Editor: Shelley Thrasher
Production Design: Susan Ramundo
Cover Design By Sheri (graphicartist2020@hotmail.com)

Acknowledgments

The past year while writing and editing this book has been an absolute roller coaster. As always, professionally, my thanks go to Shelley Thrasher, my amazing editor, for guiding me and teaching me. To Radclyffe for publishing my work and for your lessons on craft, which I hope have deepened this manuscript. And to the rest of the staff at Bold Strokes Books, for all you do behind the scenes.

But even more so, this time I owe some personal appreciation. To my family, I love you and wish I could be there for every moment. To my friends, who have listened when I needed to talk, and made me laugh when I wanted to cry. And to Christina, you are my constant and my comfort. You make everything better.

Dedication

For Christina—My best friend and the love of my life

CHAPTER ONE

2 15B, I've got one not stopping. Eastbound on Shelby, passing Sixth." Evelyn Fisher nearly shouted into her radio in order to be heard over her siren. She split her attention between the red sedan in front of her and the upcoming intersections, always watching for any other vehicles pulling out in the middle of her pursuit.

Her sergeant acknowledged her transmission and gave his permission to continue the chase. She never lifted her foot off the accelerator. Two other patrol cars pulled up behind her as she allowed a quick glance in her rearview mirror before returning her attention to the red Nissan Altima in front of her.

As the suspect vehicle slowed to round a corner, the passenger-side door popped open and one of the occupants jumped out. He hit the ground, barely able to regain his footing, then took off.

"Passenger just bailed." The voice of one of her fellow officers crackled over the radio. "Male, Hispanic, white T-shirt, blue jeans." The description was succinct in order to not tie up valuable airtime on the channel.

As the lead car, she stayed behind the sedan, confident that one of the units behind her would pick up the passenger. The officer in the second car called out the street names as they wove through the neighborhoods just east of downtown Nashville.

The organized cadence of the vehicle pursuit dissolved into the transmissions from the officers chasing the passenger on foot.

"I lost sight of him, behind the houses over here."

"Dispatch, see if we can get aviation."

"The Altima just went in the park. Driver's looking for a place to bail."

"Somebody hold back and seal this entrance. Maybe we can trap him in the park."

"The passenger is in custody."

Evelyn could feel the barely contained energy as officers keyed up one after another, but despite the seeming chaos, every person, from the dispatcher to the officers in the field, played their part in the fluid choreography. She concentrated on the vehicle in front of her, tracking every turn and assessing the danger to innocent bystanders as they careened over the narrow roads.

"Almost there," she muttered. "Just a little farther."

The suspect was clearly familiar with the large park as he took another quick turn toward the softball fields. But staying inside the park allowed more time for her colleagues to seal off the limited exits. At these speeds, their sergeant had to be close to calling off the pursuit. If they didn't contain this guy before then, they might have to let him escape.

As they rounded the next corner, she flicked her eyes up ahead and smiled. A patrol car sat waiting for them to approach. "Gotcha. Where are you going now?"

Almost as if reacting to her words, the driver wrenched the wheel to the left and tore through an open field. When she followed, her tires rebelled at the lack of asphalt, spinning and shredding the grass beneath them. Apparently having the same problem, the driver stopped abruptly and jumped out of the car. She slammed her car into Park and shoved her own door open. She shouted for the suspect to stop and get on the ground. Knowing he wouldn't comply, she sprinted after him.

He was fast, but, even with the cumbersome gun belt jangling at her waist, she was faster. In seconds, she was within steps of catching him, as he raced toward a vacant softball field. She groaned when he vaulted the chain-link fence, but she flung herself over it, too. Chatter echoed from her shoulder mic as another officer called out their position. Backup was behind her somewhere, and if she could just catch this guy, her fellow officers would be with her in seconds.

The suspect cut left toward the woods, but the sudden move slowed him down just enough. She pushed a little harder, her thighs burning in response. With three long strides she was on him, tackling him. He grunted as she landed on top of him, but he didn't stay stationary long. He flipped onto his back and threw her free. Before she had time to react, he landed a punch high on her cheek, and pain shot through the left side of her face. When he tried to scramble to his feet, she caught him. He swung at her again, but she avoided the blow and landed one of her own.

She'd managed to pin him to the ground and pull one of his arms behind his back when several other officers surrounded her. One of them grabbed his other arm, while another pressed a large hand against the back of his head, forcing his face into the grass. She secured the handcuffs with a satisfying series of clicks, then stepped back.

"215B, suspect is in custody," she said into her radio between panting breaths. She bent at the waist and braced her hands on her knees.

Two officers hauled the suspect to his feet. She straightened and clapped one of the officers on the shoulder. "Thanks, Jeb."

"Nice catch," Jeb Riggs said, his eyes shining with the same adrenaline that sang through her body.

"You okay, Fisher?" Sergeant Eddie Stahlman asked as he reached her side.

"Yeah, I'm good."

"How's your face? You need an x-ray?"

"No, sir." She glanced at the suspect, knowing he was within earshot. "He doesn't hit that hard."

"Okay. Then you're feeling well enough to write reports." He smiled when she winced. Between the original traffic violations, the pursuit, and the charge for assaulting an officer, she'd be filling out reports for a couple of hours.

"Yes, sir."

"Bring your car around to the ball-field entrance. Riggs will search him for you."

She jogged back to the field where she'd left her car and smiled when she saw a familiar face. Kendall Jarvis rested against the quarter panel of Evelyn's patrol car, her hip canted and her hands slung over the heavy gun belt at her waist.

"Hey there, hotshot." Kendall swept her blue eyes over her now-dirty uniform. "Playing linebacker again?"

"Yeah, something like that." Next to Kendall's perfectly styled spiky blond hair and crisply pressed uniform, she felt even more disheveled.

"Are we still on for tonight?"

"Absolutely. I'll definitely need a drink after this shift." Every Friday night, she met Kendall and her girlfriend, Melanie, at a bar downtown to decompress from the work week. Sometimes she took a date, but more often, like tonight, she wouldn't.

"Just make sure you clean up first. Melanie's going to have a fit when she sees you."

She swiped at the grass and mud smearing her navy-blue polyester pants, but those stains would require more than the brush of her palm. She shrugged. "I've got clothes in the car. I'll shower at the station."

"It's not your clothes I'm worried about. It's your face."

She opened her car door and slid behind the wheel, then pulled the rearview mirror around and studied her already-swollen cheek. Her skin was bright red and would soon turn into a nasty bruise. "She's seen worse."

Over the years, Melanie had seen a number of bumps and bruises. Of the two, Kendall had a quicker temper, but neither of them shied away from getting physical when the job demanded it.

She rolled the window down and swung the door shut. "See you later," she called as she maneuvered carefully back onto the asphalt.

When she stopped in front of the ball field, Jeb led the handcuffed suspect to her car. The guy glared at her, but Jeb caught the look and his big hand tightened visibly around the man's upper arm. He winced and glanced nervously at Jeb. She smiled. She'd seen that expression on more than one suspect's face. At six foot five inches, with a solid build, a natural scowl, and a military haircut, Jeb rarely had to get physical to gain submission.

"Hey, Fisher, I got you a present." He held up a small-caliber handgun encased in a plastic evidence bag. A smile softened the hard lines of his face, and his thick black brows lifted.

"Where'd you find it?"

"Your buddy here had an ankle holster."

"Thanks, man." She nodded and took the bag.

Part of her assigned district contained an interesting mix of refurbished historic homes owned by artsy types. But more than half of her area was known for drug activity. She'd found guns on suspects before, but like every other time, she forced herself not to think for too long about what could have happened if he'd gotten his hands on that gun while they struggled on the ground. She chose not to concentrate on things she couldn't control and, instead, focused on the training, strength, and instinct she'd accumulated in the past decade on the job.

Evelyn pushed through the door of the Third Street Bar and blinked as her eyes adjusted to the dim interior. She didn't need to make out the faces around her to locate her friends. She wove through the tables in the center of the room to their usual booth in the back.

The waitress arrived at the same time she did, so she ordered a beer, then slid into the bench opposite Kendall and Melanie.

"Hey, guys."

"What happened to your face?" Melanie asked.

She silently cursed the pendant light hanging over their table. A shower after her shift had eliminated the mud and grime, but scrubbing her face had only made the blossoming bruise stand out even more. "You didn't tell her?"

Kendall shrugged.

"What happened?" Melanie repeated, moving from her side of the booth to Evelyn's. When she didn't make room, Melanie shoved against her shoulder until she relented. She turned away, but Melanie grasped her chin and forced her head around. Melanie's green eyes raced over her face, assessing the damage.

"It's just a black eye. No big deal." She minimized the injury, despite the painkillers she'd downed after her shift. When Melanie pressed against her cheek, she flinched. Melanie's eyes narrowed, but she lightened her touch.

"Did you get it looked at?"

She pulled her chin away. "Of course not." She glanced at Kendall. "Would you tell her it's nothing, please?"

"Mel, leave her alone," Kendall said halfheartedly.

Melanie shook her head. She caught a wave of honey-brown hair as it fell in front of her face and swept it behind her ear. "You two are just alike."

Evelyn forced a smile and leaned back in her seat. She and Kendall had been friends for five years, since being assigned to the same precinct, and she both admired and respected her. But she didn't like being so dismissively compared to Kendall. From her tomboy adolescence to her years as a female police officer, she had grown used to people making assumptions about who she was. But she expected Kendall and Melanie to see her as an individual.

Melanie returned to her side of the booth, but before she could slide into the seat, Kendall exited.

"Gotta pee," she said as she brushed past Melanie. "Order me another drink if she comes back around."

"Just one more, okay? It's been a long day. I'm ready to get home and crawl into bed." Melanie had spent the entire day in the unusually warm fall sun trying to finish a big landscaping project. If she hadn't been on such a tight deadline, she might have cut her crew loose early. Instead, she made sure they drank plenty of water and took adequate breaks under the nearest shade tree.

"Do you have your next job lined up?" Evelyn asked.

She nodded. "I start at the new site bright and early tomorrow."

"Saturday?"

"It's the only time the owner could meet with me to approve the final plans. We've been through several drafts trying to incorporate everything he wants."

"We could have canceled tonight."

"I'm okay. I squeezed in a nap while I waited for your shift to end." As soon as she'd gotten home that evening, she'd jumped into the shower, dancing beneath an icy spray that brought up goose bumps. Then, since Kendall and Evelyn didn't get off work until eleven, she lay down, intending to close her eyes for only a minute, and awoke an hour later.

"Do you ever wish you could turn down the pain-in-the-ass clients?"

"Any work is good work these days." Her landscaping company had a loyal customer base, but she hadn't totally escaped the effects of a bad economy. She had four crews that handled the regular maintenance that her current customers required. But the requests for elaborate new designs had fallen off enough that she and her guys could personally handle each one.

Tomorrow she would start installing a custom design at a home still under construction. The owner, a prominent local physician, wanted the grounds to appear finished and well-manicured before he moved in. Between trying to accommodate his design ideas and keep the feel of her own concept, she had also been coordinating with the building contractor in order to properly time the start of her work. She enjoyed beginning a new project and found satisfaction in seeing a raw piece of land and imagining how she would transform the space.

The waitress returned and Evelyn ordered another drink for each of them.

"Are you sure you should be drinking?" she asked after the waitress left.

"Why not?"

"Could you have a concussion?"

"Mel, it's a black eye—not even the first one I've had. I don't have a concussion." Evelyn punctuated her words by lifting her bottle and draining it.

"Okay." She raised her hands in surrender but let her irritation show in her voice. "I worry about you and Kendall. And I won't stop just because you both want me to."

"I don't expect you to change. And I appreciate your concern, but I can take care of myself. Believe me, this guy wasn't that tough. And I had plenty of backup." She smiled. "Then, when I put him in the cell at booking, I apologized for hitting him back, so all the guys in there with him now know that he got *his* shiner from a woman."

Melanie's nervousness over the injury eased as they laughed together. Evelyn's black eye *was* minor, and fussing over her wouldn't make her take it any more seriously.

Kendall had been on the force for three years already when they'd met. Kendall had expected her to understand what dating a cop would entail, but she'd been unprepared for the seed of fear every time Kendall came home a little late. Early in their relationship, she'd freaked out the day a client had casually mentioned that she'd just seen breaking news of a bank robbery where an officer had been hurt, even though the targeted bank was nowhere near Kendall's sector.

Over the years, she'd learned to cope, or at least not to get her feelings hurt when Kendall dismissed her concern. Kendall's commitment to her job helped make her the woman Melanie had fallen in love with. And she tried to remember that every time the fist of worry gripped her heart.

But she had also decided not to harden herself too much. If Kendall and Evelyn wanted to stay in such a dangerous profession, they would just have to put up with her occasional overbearing concern. Usually, her attention was wasted because they always sided with each other against her. Though they thought they were skilled at deceiving her, she often knew when they'd had a tough call. Kendall came home ready to fight after a bad shift. Evelyn hid her damage much more adeptly. Sometimes, she saw the stress of the job in the stiffness of Evelyn's shoulders or the tight line of her mouth.

Tonight, Evelyn had let her long, dark hair fall in loose waves around her face, probably in an effort to conceal her bruise. And she had no doubt that Evelyn had rifled through her locker at the precinct searching for makeup that would cover the evidence. If she'd thought she could get away with it, she probably would have worn sunglasses into the bar as well.

Melanie had resigned herself to being on the outside of that part of their relationship. But she could admit to being jealous of the bond they shared. Sometimes she resented the fact that Kendall would always keep a part of herself from her—a part she shared only with Evelyn and her fellow officers.

❖

"Football still on for Sunday?" Evelyn asked as she paused next to her sleek black coupe.

"Absolutely." Kendall punched Evelyn's upper arm. "See if you can cover up that bruise. Richard's bringing his cousin and I hear she's cute. We don't want her to think you're some kind of barbarian."

"Yeah, okay." Evelyn lowered herself into the car. "See you guys later." She closed the door and started the car. The dark window tint hid her from view as she zipped toward the parking-lot exit.

Melanie pulled her keys from her pocket and disengaged the locks on her truck.

"Want me to drive?" Kendall asked.

"I've got it." She climbed into the big Dodge. Her pickup didn't represent her in quite the way Evelyn's sport car fit her. She viewed her vehicle as a necessary convenience, given her frequent need to haul supplies. On occasion, she drooled over a hot little convertible, but she couldn't justify the payment on an extra car that neither of them would drive very often.

"You know Evelyn hates when you try to fix her up," she said as Kendall settled into the passenger seat. She turned out of the parking lot and headed toward their house.

"Did she say that?"

"Not specifically. But I get the impression—"

"Whatever. If I see a hot chick, why shouldn't I try to get them together? She'll thank me someday when I introduce her to her soul mate. Hell, a few have been so hot, she should have thanked me even though they didn't work out."

"Yeah. Are you living vicariously through her?"

"Now why would I need to do that, when I've got my soul mate right here?" Kendall laid her hand on Melanie's thigh.

She glanced down, then over at Kendall. The words were perfect, but sometimes Kendall seemed to say what she thought Melanie expected to hear. Though she couldn't put her finger on why, they hadn't been connecting for over a year now. They'd talked about what might be the problem and vowed to try harder, each saying she would put work aside and make time just for the two of them. But before long they fell back into the same pattern.

Soul mate. She remembered a time when she wouldn't have questioned using such a phrase to describe her relationship with Kendall. When they'd first started dating they planned for a future, growing old and retiring together. Now, when their schedules were so misaligned that they hardly spent any time together, she had trouble bringing that long-term vision into focus.

"Melanie? Where did you go?"

"I'm sorry. I've been distracted today."

"Not just today." Petulance colored Kendall's tone.

She scrubbed a hand over her face and concentrated on the road in front of her. Arguing wouldn't get them anywhere, so she ignored Kendall's comment. She couldn't handle another conversation that led them in circles. Hopefully they were just going through a normal cycle that long-term partners experienced and would figure out how to pull themselves out of it.

CHAPTER TWO

"Hello, anyone home?" Evelyn called as she opened the front door to Melanie and Kendall's ground floor apartment and went inside. The living room was empty but had obviously been arranged for the party. An assortment of folding chairs clustered among the couch and loveseat, each one angled toward the television over the fireplace.

"I'm in the kitchen."

She followed Melanie's voice and found her peering inside the oven. The countertop was already littered with "football food": a tray of veggies and dip, two bowls of chips, and cocktail wieners in a spicy sauce.

"Early as usual." Melanie glanced up and smiled.

"Hey, I don't want to miss anything," she said as she eased past Melanie on her way to the fridge. She slid a six-pack of beer into an empty space on the top shelf. "That smells awesome. What is it?"

"Buffalo-chicken dip." Melanie pulled a casserole dish from the oven and set it on top of the stove. "Kendall is on the patio checking on the grill."

"I'll say hi in a minute. First, can I help you with anything in here?"

"Will you grab the fruit out of the fridge?"

Evelyn pulled out three plastic containers full of cut fruit.

Melanie slid a divided serving tray across the counter. "You can set it out on there."

They worked quietly side by side; she arranged the fruit and Melanie prepared a cheese-and-cracker plate.

"How's the eye? You've got some nice shades of purple and yellow going on there." Melanie's casual tone sounded forced.

She paused and raised an eyebrow. "I'm surprised you don't want to inspect it."

"I do. But I'm not going to."

"Good." The entire side of her face had throbbed that first morning. Then the pain subsided, but a sickly rainbow had spread across her cheek and around her eye. Melanie's lips were pressed together, but she didn't speak. "It's fine, Mel. It's a two-day-old bruise. It looks a lot worse than it feels."

Melanie nodded.

She sighed and touched Melanie's shoulder. "But thank you for being concerned."

"Okay. I'll let it go."

"I've heard that before." She meant her comment in a teasing way, but Melanie froze and her demeanor changed right away. Her back stiffened, and the tiny muscles around her eyes and mouth tightened. "Hey, it's okay. I know it's hard to see anything marring this gorgeous face," she said, hoping to reverse whatever had just changed the mood in the kitchen.

Melanie met her eyes and she was surprised to find the remnant of hurt, before the tension in her expression eased. She smiled, albeit slightly awkwardly, then bumped her shoulder against Evelyn's and resumed work on the snack trays. Evelyn watched her for a moment longer. Though she nodded along when Kendall complained about Melanie's motherly concern, she kind of liked knowing that Melanie cared. Melanie had always been touchy about what she called their "tough-guy acts," but had she been more edgy lately?

While she was still debating whether to ask her what was wrong or just drop it, Kendall came through the back door.

"The ribs are almost done." She stopped and gestured to Evelyn's Patriots jersey. "Oh, come on. Did you have to wear that thing?"

"Yes." Evelyn grinned.

"We're watching the Titans play the Colts."

"But the late game is the Patriots and the Jets, and I plan to stick around for it."

Kendall faked a stern look. She'd guessed that Evelyn would want to stay and watch the late game. But she couldn't miss the chance to tease her about her favorite team. "Says who? The invite was for the Titans. We may not want to watch the Pats game."

"Oh, what? You have better plans?" Evelyn glanced at Melanie, then back at Kendall with a wink.

She blushed, but not for the reason Evelyn probably assumed. She couldn't remember the last time she and Melanie had made love. Weeks? Months? And when they did, their interaction lacked passion and she was left feeling even more disconnected. When she met Melanie's eyes, she saw her own sorrow reflected there. "Whatever. Watch your damn game, but you may be alone on the couch."

"Yeah? What about Richard's cousin. Maybe she'll watch it with me."

"I bet she will," she said, relieved for the subject change.

Evelyn laughed. "Why do you do this? You know these fix-ups never work out."

"Because I'm bound to get it right someday. Besides, if I didn't force you to go out, you'd happily turn yourself into a hermit."

"I'm not a hermit."

"Uh, you are—a little," Melanie said.

Evelyn glared at her. "You're not helping."

"I'm not saying there's anything wrong with that."

"Oh, no." Evelyn wagged her finger at Melanie. "No backpedaling now. You've picked your side."

Kendall broke in. "Just promise me you'll give Richard's cousin a chance."

"Okay. Damn it. I'll give her a chance."

The doorbell rang and she smiled, knowing Evelyn would have to paste on a fake smile and make nice for the next several hours. Someday, she'd find the perfect woman for Evelyn, but for now she was operating under the theory that quantity could beget quality. Fixing Evelyn up with every available lesbian she met could only increase the odds that one of them would be the right one.

❖

Thirty minutes later, Kendall and Melanie's apartment was filled with football fans. Melanie threaded her way between them, offering to refill drinks. When she reached the kitchen, she checked the levels of the snack trays. She'd just dumped another bag of tortilla chips into a bowl when she heard a voice close to her ear.

"Sit down and relax, Mel. Everything is taken care of." Evelyn leaned over her shoulder to survey the counter full of food.

She turned and Evelyn took a step back. "I just want to make sure everyone has enough to eat."

"The game is about to start. Let people fend for themselves."

"I'll be right there."

Evelyn shrugged as if she knew distracting Melanie from her hostess duties was a futile effort. She stepped toward the door to the living room but stopped when Kendall entered escorting Richard, their neighbor from two doors down, and another woman.

She bore some resemblance to Richard, having the same pale complexion and prematurely gray hair. But her silvery strands had obviously been enhanced at the salon. She scanned the room, then stopped when she saw Evelyn. As she purposely raked her gaze over Evelyn's body, interest flooded her eyes.

Evelyn's faded jeans hugged her narrow hips, but the over-sized Patriots jersey hung on her shoulders and gave little clue as to what lay underneath. The woman's eyes lingered predictably on Evelyn's face, taking in her high cheekbones, smooth olive skin, and almond-shaped eyes the color of rich chocolate. Evelyn was endearingly unaware just how gorgeous she was, but Melanie had watched several women fall for her exotic features.

"Hey, we were just looking for you two. This is Richard's cousin, Tiffany." Kendall touched the woman's shoulder. If she'd witnessed Tiffany cruising Evelyn, she gave no indication. "Tiffany, this is my girlfriend, Melanie, and this is Evelyn."

"It's nice to meet you." Now, Tiffany made eye contact with each of them.

"Welcome, Tiffany. Make yourself at home," Melanie said.

"Yeah, and if you need anything, just ask Melanie." Evelyn dropped a hand on Melanie's shoulder and grinned at her.

"Funny," she murmured.

"You're a Patriots fan, huh?" Tiffany asked, her gaze on Evelyn's chest.

"Afraid so," Evelyn said with a shrug.

"Hmm. I suppose that's not a deal breaker."

"Good to know." Evelyn smiled.

They made polite small talk for several minutes, then drifted toward the living room to claim seats.

"You coming, Mel?" Kendall asked as the kitchen emptied.

"Yeah, I'll be right there."

"It's almost kickoff."

She smiled, knowing that seeing the kickoff was much more important to Kendall than to her. For Kendall, the opening minutes of the game were a ritual, as were the closing ones. No matter how wide the point spread between the two teams, she never left a game early. "Go ahead. I'll just be a second."

Melanie lingered in the kitchen for several minutes, then grabbed a fresh beer from the fridge and stepped through the threshold to the living room.

She paused and leaned against the doorjamb as her friends erupted into cheers for the kickoff return. Kendall and Evelyn slapped each other's hands in an enthusiastic high-five. Titans football was a tradition in their house, through good seasons and bad. Today, it seemed, things were already going well for the home team.

Kendall looked over and gave her a grin and a thumbs-up. She smiled back, trying to ignore the ache in her chest. Moments like these made it hard to think about letting go. She had watched more football games with Kendall than with anyone else. If they split up, who would fill her living room on Sunday afternoons? She couldn't ignore the fact that she'd been asking herself questions like these more and more often lately.

❖

"Richard told me that you and Kendall are cops?"

"Yeah." Evelyn nodded. She recognized Tiffany's tone and knew immediately where this conversation was headed.

"So you've got a badge and handcuffs?" Tiffany's creamy complexion showed only a few lines around her mouth when she smiled broadly. She focused on Evelyn's face, obvious interest in her pale-blue eyes.

Evelyn smiled grimly—so predictable. She fought a full-on grin when she caught Melanie rolling her eyes. Melanie often teased Kendall about how the uniform multiplied her attractiveness to some women. The guys called women like Tiffany "badge bunnies." Evelyn didn't like the term, but, she had to admit, the quality wasn't exclusive to straight women.

In the beginning, dating a cop was thrilling and they all thought they wanted to play with the handcuffs. But she didn't find handcuffs sexy, especially when she considered the kind of scumbags she slapped them on every day. In fact, if she ever did relent and fulfill a request to try them on, she'd need to use a good dose of disinfectant spray first. Eventually, most women grew bored when they realized her job wasn't as exciting as they'd anticipated, and if they had nothing else in common the relationship fizzled like a spent sparkler.

"What do you do, Tiffany?" she asked, trying to shift the focus from her job.

"I'm a dental assistant."

"That's interesting."

Tiffany smiled. "No. It's not. But thank you for saying so. It's mostly sticking my hands into people's mouths or handing the dentist instruments all day. But it pays the bills and that's all I require from a job. I get my thrills in my personal life."

"Yeah? Where do you find your thrills?" It could be a loaded question, but considering they were in mixed company, she hoped Tiffany would take it as intended.

"Downhill mountain-bike racing."

"Now *that* is interesting and unexpected."

"I love the adrenaline rush and the physical challenge."

"Are there places around here to do that?"

"East Tennessee has some great locations. Around Nashville, it's mostly just trail riding. But I train here during the week, then head east on the weekends to find steeper terrain. I save up my vacation so that in spring and summer, I can travel to competitions. Strictly amateur." Tiffany's eyes danced as she talked about racing. She had such expressive eyes, every ounce of her obvious passion for her hobby reflected there. Perhaps Evelyn had been too quick to judge. Maybe Tiffany had more layers after all.

"Wow. That's very cool."

"Do you ride?"

"Um—it's been a while." She didn't even own a bike. "But they don't say it's like riding a bicycle for no reason, do they?"

Tiffany smiled. "We should go sometime."

"Sure."

"How about next weekend?"

"Yeah. That sounds good." She glanced at Kendall, but her attention was riveted on the game. Did she and Melanie still have those bikes in storage?

"Don't look so nervous. I'll take you on a novice trail."

"Novice? Yeah, that sounds about right." Given her profession, she was no stranger to adrenaline, but the thought of hurtling down a mountain on two wheels and praying she wouldn't snag a stray tree root didn't exactly appeal to her. However, she hadn't had a personal life lately, so she vowed to give this fix-up a chance.

❖

Melanie closed the door behind the last of their guests. She yawned as she turned off the outside light and flipped the deadbolt. She'd enjoyed seeing everyone, but now she couldn't wait to slide between the sheets and close her eyes.

On her way to the bedroom she paused in the doorway of the kitchen. Kendall stood at the sink, rinsing and stacking dishes.

"Leave those. I'll finish them tomorrow," she said.

"I'm almost done." Kendall didn't turn around.

"Are you coming to bed?"

"Not yet," Kendall said tersely.

"I told you to go without me if you wanted to." She didn't wait for a response before she headed for the bedroom. A few of their friends had stayed to watch the beginning of the late game and then gone to a sports bar downtown for the second half. Kendall had wanted to go but declined when Melanie said she'd rather stay home.

"Did I say anything?" Kendall called as she followed.

"You didn't have to. I could hear the attitude in your voice."

"I asked you to go with me. I wouldn't have had fun knowing you were here alone."

"I would have been here sleeping. I worked all day yesterday, and we both have to work tomorrow. I didn't want to go out drinking." After ensuring her alarm clock was set, she folded back the comforter.

"We're not eighty years old, Mel. We could have left as soon as the game was over."

If they had gone to the bar with the others, they would have had too much beer and stayed too late. The occasional Hangover Monday had been okay when she had an office job. But she didn't like football enough to spend tomorrow fighting nausea and fatigue while doing manual labor. She wasn't even sure she liked their friends *that* much. That's why she'd hosted the party for the early game.

Kendall went to the bathroom and closed the door firmly behind her. Melanie stared at the door, fighting an irrational desire to escalate this into an argument out of pure frustration. Instead, she strode to the dresser and pulled out a pair of boxers and a T-shirt. She changed and climbed into bed. As she lay down and rolled away, she heard the bathroom door open.

The mattress moved as Kendall got into bed, and then the bedside lamp clicked and darkness shrouded them. When they'd first got together, giddy with new love, they'd said they wouldn't go to bed angry. Even if they'd argued, Kendall would lie down and gather her against her chest and kiss her. Now they rarely went to bed at the same time and often shared only a quick peck before rolling away from each other.

❖

Evelyn dropped her gun belt as she walked through the door to Kendall and Melanie's apartment. She tugged her shirt free of her waistband as she crossed the living room. Kendall and Melanie each occupied one end of the sofa, their legs outstretched toward the center. They moved their feet just as she plopped down between them.

"Hey, moneybags," Kendall said.

"Not hardly. But it wasn't hard labor for the money." She had been working a few extra jobs lately. Companies sometimes hired commissioned police officers to provide security or direct traffic. She had spent the past three hours sitting in her car blocking traffic for a construction company doing road repair. It was boring as hell, but texting Kendall and flipping through the magazines she'd brought along had eventually helped her pass the time. She almost felt guilty for how little she had to work to get paid, but they didn't want her to do anything else.

"You gotta take those jobs where you can get them. It beats standing in the middle of an intersection directing traffic in the pouring rain."

Evelyn nodded.

"So, how was your date with Tiffany?" Kendall asked.

"Eh, not so great." She propped a foot up on the coffee table.

"Boots off my table." Melanie poked her thigh with her toes. She sighed heavily in protest, but she lowered her feet to the floor. "What happened?"

She shrugged. "Nothing really. We went bike riding. She's nice enough. But we just weren't compatible."

"Sexually?"

"Kendall." Melanie scolded her.

"What? It's possible. I mean, I've heard that Ev is a stud in bed, but—"

Evelyn laughed. "Yeah? Where did you hear that?"

"Oh, what's her name?" Kendall grinned and snapped her fingers in the air as if trying to recall the tidbit of information. "Oh, yeah, Jennifer Prince."

A wave of heat blazed across her face, but there was no point in denying it. "Well, she would know."

Jennifer Prince, a downtown bicycle officer, was just a friend, except for one night in a bar when "Drunk-Evelyn" flirted shamelessly and admitted how much she'd admired the way Jennifer's muscled legs looked in her department-issue shorts. A couple hours and three times as many drinks later, she'd discovered she liked the feel of those thighs and calves wrapped around her.

The next morning, they'd talked and decided that, though they'd both enjoyed the previous night's activities, they had no interest in dating one another. Jennifer was hot, but she was a control freak, and Evelyn didn't want to be micro-managed. Her pride had only stung a bit when Jennifer told her that she liked her women more femme. She wasn't that butch, but she'd never be described as girlie either, rather somewhere in the middle. Regardless, they had resumed their friendship with very little effort or awkwardness, just a shared memory of a good time.

"Seems like you've got a thing for women and bicycles," Melanie said.

"Purely coincidence," she said.

"So it's not going anywhere with Tiffany?" Kendall asked. She shook her head.

"Do you think she feels the same way?"

"Yeah. She said she liked me but couldn't see us together long-term."

"Could you?" Melanie asked, her face soft with compassion.

"No."

"Hey, it's her loss," Kendall said with a dismissive wave. She'd known after watching Tiffany and Evelyn interact during the football game Sunday that her latest fix-up wasn't successful. "She was a ditz anyway."

"I appreciate you saying that, but she really isn't. I'm not upset about Tiffany. I mean—not her specifically. I just want—aw, hell, I want what you guys have."

Ouch. Kendall lifted her gaze and, even in the dimly lit room, she saw her own grimace mirrored in Melanie's features. Kendall hadn't revealed their relationship problems to Evelyn, and she didn't think Melanie had either. It wasn't that she *couldn't* talk to Evelyn; they shared nearly everything else. But she didn't display her feelings readily.

Besides, she didn't want her own frustrations to color Evelyn's friendship with Melanie. Rather than put Evelyn in the middle, she kept her concerns about her future with Melanie to herself.

"Ev, no relationship is perfect. And you certainly shouldn't idealize ours." Melanie's voice carried a heavy weight of sadness and maybe a little regret.

"You know what I mean. I want forever. I want to be deliriously happy." She chuckled. "Who doesn't, right?"

"Yeah, who doesn't," Melanie murmured.

Kendall's heart ached, knowing that she no longer made Melanie deliriously happy, assuming she ever had. She could vow once more that things would be different, say that she would try harder. And she wanted to. She wanted to believe she could change what she now dreaded was the inevitable. Someday, possibly soon, Melanie would break her heart, because she couldn't bear to do it herself.

CHAPTER THREE

Melanie rolled over and looked at the clock for the third time in an hour. She sighed and flopped onto her back. Beside her, Kendall stirred, mumbling but not waking. She could sleep through the house falling down around them.

Melanie lay there for a minute more before she decided she wasn't going to sleep again. She folded back the covers and slipped from bed. She didn't need a light to navigate around the bed, across the room, and into the hallway. When she reached the living room, she clicked on a floor lamp in the corner.

As she looked around the room, she studied each item she and Kendall had purchased together. That vase, the photo frame made from reclaimed barn wood, the collection of DVDs. The thought of disentangling the history they had here made her sad. How would she know when it was time to let go? She'd been waiting—for what she wasn't sure. A sign, maybe, some moment of clarity. Was the flash of guilt she'd felt when Evelyn said she aspired to a relationship like theirs enough? If only Kendall had cheated or lied, her decision would be easy.

She laughed, short and harsh, at the direction of her thoughts—wishing for infidelity so she could be spared the hard choice. But she wouldn't be granted an easy out. Yes, they had problems, but she never questioned Kendall's loyalty.

So how long should she wait? What could prompt her to take the next step—the one she'd been dreading, the one she'd been putting off? Kendall's parents had split up when she was seven years old, and she had never forgiven them for giving up on each other. And though she and Kendall didn't have any children together, Melanie knew Kendall's strong commitment to their relationship was connected to her disjointed childhood. She wouldn't be the first to surrender. Though she was certain Kendall knew—had known for some time—that neither of them was happy, she would most likely place the blame on Melanie's shoulders, at least initially.

"What are you doing up?"

Given the path of her thoughts, hearing Kendall's familiar voice sliced through her heart. "I'm sorry if I woke you." She turned. Kendall's hair stuck up except on the right side, where she usually slept; there it had flattened against her head. She looked adorable, like the woman Melanie had fallen in love with seven years ago. That realization made it even more difficult to admit those feelings had faded to friendship.

"You didn't. But I rolled over and realized you were gone."

Melanie's stomach twisted. She didn't think Kendall intended her words to have a double meaning, but she felt their foreshadowing keenly.

"Kendall, I…"

Kendall tilted her head to the side, confusion then concern sliding across her face. "Is something wrong?"

"No. Yes." She drew a slow breath as Kendall crossed to sit beside her. What was she waiting for? There would be no perfect time, only the ever-growing knot in her stomach and a million reasons to put off what she should do, for both of them. She closed her eyes, unable to look at Kendall when she forced out the words. "I can't do this anymore."

"What?"

She didn't repeat herself. Kendall's inquiry was only a stall—her brain trying to delay the pain for her heart.

Finally, Kendall shook her head. "We're just in a slump—"

"No, Kendall. We've been saying that for too long. It's not a slump anymore. Something is wrong." She opened her eyes, but when she saw the heartbreak on Kendall's face, she wished she hadn't.

"Maybe we just need more time." Kendall's eyes filled. The veneer of Melanie's control threatened to shatter. "I can't, Mel—you're my best friend."

She wanted to take it back, pretend she hadn't said it. They had been hurtling toward this moment, but somehow that knowledge didn't blunt the blow. Instead, she said, "I know, honey. But we deserve more."

Kendall lifted her eyes to the ceiling as if she could find some solution there.

Melanie took her hand and their fingers naturally intertwined, as they had been doing for seven years. Tears stung her eyes when she realized that this might be the last time they touched each other this way. "It's time, Kendall."

Kendall nodded slowly. "I know." Her voice cracked and she coughed out a sob.

"I'm so sorry." She moved to gather Kendall in her arms, but she jerked away and stumbled to her feet. She fled down the hall toward the bedroom.

Melanie stayed on the couch, uncertain what to do next. Would Kendall try again to convince her that they could work it out? If she did, could Melanie stick to this decision? She leaned forward and rested her elbows on her knees, fighting her rising panic. She'd been barely twenty-six when she and Kendall got together. If she'd had any idea who she was back then, she certainly wasn't the same woman now. Now, her identity felt so wrapped up in who she was with Kendall. Who was she without her?

❖

Kendall paced the bedroom, fighting the suffocation rising in her throat. Melanie's words played on a loop in her head. *I can't do this anymore. Something is wrong.* She'd had similar thoughts but always had been able to excuse them as the growing pains of a long-term relationship. Hearing Melanie say the words with such resignation and finality ripped something inside her.

She drew short panting breaths, nearly hyperventilating. What was supposed to happen now? Certainly they'd had fights, but she'd never actually envisioned them *here.* She couldn't think, couldn't even find room to *feel* while surrounded by the home they shared. She grabbed a backpack from the closet, jerked open a drawer, and shoved a fistful of clothes into the bag.

As she strode down the hallway, she steeled herself against seeing Melanie. But the pain hit her like a two-by-four as she descended the stairs and saw Melanie sitting on the couch cradling her head in her hands. She summoned anger in order to resist the urge to comfort Melanie, when what she really wanted was to hold her and tell her they could fix whatever was wrong. This situation was Melanie's fault and she refused to feel sympathy for her.

She looked away in avoidance but in her periphery caught the motion of Melanie raising her head. She shoved her cell phone and wallet into her pocket, then picked up her keys.

"What are you doing?" Melanie stood and moved toward her. Kendall forced herself to concentrate on frosting over her pain before she raised her gaze. She guessed she was successful when Melanie flinched and took a step back as their eyes met.

"Leaving. I'll come back for more of my things later while you're at work."

"You don't have to do that. I—I can sleep in the guest bedroom and we'll figure things out in the morning."

She shook her head. "I need to get out of here."

"Kendall, it's," Melanie glanced at the mantle clock, "three a.m. Where are you going?"

"I don't know." *What do you care? Does it matter anymore? Do I matter?* She wanted to fling the words at Melanie as if she could also hurtle the pain away.

"This is as much your home as mine."

"I can't be near you right now," she snapped. Melanie flinched again, as if she had struck her. And for a moment she wished for the relief of such a physical reaction. But, dark as her emotions might be, she would never raise a hand to Melanie.

Instead, she headed for the front door. When Melanie whispered her name, she froze and let the soft cadence of Melanie's voice wash over her, allowing herself this one last bit of warmth. She wanted to turn and run into Melanie's arms. But sadly, she couldn't remember the last time she'd sought shelter there. They'd grown further apart than she'd even realized.

Straightening her shoulders, she made herself move through the door and took a tiny bit of pleasure in slamming it hard behind her.

❖

Evelyn stepped out of the shower, toweled off, then slipped on a thick, white robe. She wound her hair up inside another towel. She'd watched the sunrise while running five miles. In the early hours, autumn gave ground to the impending winter. Later the air would be warmer and humid, but as she ran, she pulled the crisp, cool air into her lungs. She liked starting her days with the endorphins from a good run still pumping through her system.

Ever since middle school, she'd risen early, often before her parents began getting ready for work. She would shower and dress for school, then go downstairs and pack a lunch for her father. Later, she'd discovered that he didn't even like peanut butter and jelly, but he had dutifully carried that brown paper sack out the door every morning, stopping to kiss her before he went.

During high school, she joined the cross-country team and dedicated her mornings to training. No matter the weather, she logged several miles, followed by a quick session on the weight bench her father set up in the garage. She'd reached an age where time with her friends replaced time spent with her family. She wouldn't have admitted it then, but she enjoyed the mornings when her father joined her for her workout.

The current state of their relationship made the memory of those mornings even more valuable. She loved her father. But it had been many years since she'd been able to enjoy the simplicity of her childhood adoration. These days, her family and professional lives intertwined more often than she would like, and she and her father were always on opposite sides.

Her morning ritual no longer included sloppily crafted PB and J. She lifted the protein shake from the counter beside the bathroom sink and took a large swallow. The thick, strawberry-flavored liquid washed away her nostalgia.

She loosened the towel and tugged a brush through her damp hair. As she crossed toward the closet, she heard the doorbell. She grabbed some sweats and a T-shirt and pulled them on as she headed for the front door.

She glanced through the peephole, then swung the door open. "Kendall? What are you doing up and about so early?"

"I—I've been driving around." Kendall's monotone response and the unfocused look in her eyes caused Evelyn to study her more closely. Her hair was disheveled and her worn sweatshirt didn't really go with her khaki slacks, as if she'd thrown on her clothes with little regard for style.

"Come in." She stepped back and waited until Kendall moved inside. She took her arm and steered her to the kitchen table. "Coffee?"

Kendall nodded numbly.

"Did you sleep last night?" Kendall looked ready to crash. Evelyn opened her single-serving machine and popped Kendall's favorite-flavored coffee inside.

"Not much."

"So, what's going on?"

"Melanie and I are splitting up."

"You had a fight? What about?"

"We didn't really fight. She just told me she wanted to break up."

"You should apologize, even if you don't think you were wrong."

"I'm serious."

"Whatever it is you'll work it out." Melanie and Kendall didn't have a tumultuous relationship, but any long-term couple had their little blowups.

"It's beyond that."

Evelyn studied her. The agony etched on Kendall's face backed up her words. "What happened?"

Kendall shrugged, but the nonchalant gesture contradicted the quiver in her chin. "She said it was time."

"What the hell does that mean? Something specific must have happened to spark this."

"No. Nothing."

"You fought—"

"No."

"What was she pissed about?"

"Evelyn, no," Kendall barked, then took a deep breath. "She wasn't pissed. She was—resigned. This has been coming on for some time now."

Shaking her head, she sank into the chair across from Kendall. Kendall and Melanie belonged together. Yet Kendall sat here telling her that Melanie had ended it.

"When things settle down, you'll talk to—"

"She's right, Evelyn. We're basically roommates these days. It's over." Kendall's eyes filled and immediately spilled over, as if saying the words pushed her across a boundary she'd been clinging to.

Evelyn stood and circled the table. Kendall started to cry just as she put her arms around her. She couldn't say anything to comfort Kendall, but her mind raced ahead to where she would seek answers next.

❖

"Open up, Mel. I saw your truck. I know you're in there."

Melanie had known who pounded on her door even before Evelyn shouted. Despite Kendall's assertion that she didn't know where she'd go, Melanie suspected she would eventually end up at Evelyn's.

After Kendall had left, she'd curled up on the couch and let go. She'd pulled a blanket over herself and cried, as if releasing her tears could also purge her heart of the grief and guilt. When she'd finally quieted, her throat felt raw and her eyes swollen, but her emotions remained.

She wasn't ready to deal with Evelyn yet and debated not answering the door, but Evelyn probably wouldn't give up. Unfortunately, she couldn't let her continue to yell and wake her neighbors. So she stood and used the few steps to the door to compose herself, pushing back her shoulders and taking a deep breath. She glanced in the mirror in the hallway as she passed. She didn't have time to fix the mess her face had become, but she swiped at her cheeks and straightened her hair anyway. Evelyn barely waited for the door to open completely before she strode inside.

"What's going on? I just spoke to Kendall and she's a wreck. She says you two are splitting up."

"It's complicated." She turned away.

"Relationships are complicated." Evelyn rolled her eyes. "Or so I've been told." She skirted the coffee table and blocked Melanie's path back to the sofa. Melanie changed course and avoided eye contact. "What happened?"

"Nothing. I mean, nothing specific." She picked up a stack of mail off the foyer table and began to flip through it. Though the task occupied her hands, she stared unseeing at the envelopes in front of her.

"You don't just end a seven-year relationship for no reason, right? Come on, Mel. What happened?"

"I don't want to talk about it right now."

"You don't—Kendall's at my place crying her eyes out. Tell me—"

"It's really not your business, Evelyn."

"The hell it isn't." Evelyn ripped the stack of envelopes from her hand and tossed them on the counter behind her. "You guys are my closest friends." Evelyn took her by the shoulders and guided her to the couch, then sat down on the edge of the coffee table facing her, their knees nearly touching.

She met Evelyn's eyes and choked back a sob. She looked away, unprepared for the compassion so at odds with the harshness of Evelyn's tone. She took a deep breath. "We'd been holding onto something that was no longer there."

"You can get counseling."

"We tried it once." She heard the echo of failure in her own voice.

"What? When?"

She shook her head. "It doesn't matter, it didn't work."

"Maybe if she knows it's her last chance, Kendall will try harder this time."

"It's not—she didn't—" Therapy had been Melanie's idea, but she hadn't expected to feel so uncomfortable. They would talk to someone and fix their relationship, or so she'd thought. But they couldn't find a solution by talking to a stranger about the intimate details of their life together. Or maybe she just didn't want to accept the answers she'd discovered. Though she didn't want to discuss this, she also couldn't let Evelyn blame Kendall. "Counseling didn't work—for me, Ev. This was on me."

"You can try again."

She surged to her feet. "Seven years. Do you think I'd just let that go without being sure?" She sighed. She'd rehearsed that conversation with Kendall dozens of times before getting up the nerve to initiate it. But she hadn't thought about how difficult talking to Evelyn might be.

"We lost touch. I mean, I know the relationships in those romantic comedies she loves so much are fiction. But do you think the passion can last?"

"So this is about sex?"

"Not sex. Well, not just sex. Intensity, maybe. Kendall and I had become little more than friends. We could barely summon the energy to argue anymore."

"You—uh—you said not just sex. Kendall said something similar. I didn't know you guys were—um—"

"Incompatible?" Melanie forced a smile. "I can't remember the last time we were intimate."

"Geez."

"Yeah. More than you wanted to know about us, huh?"

"I'll say."

"It wasn't always like that. In the beginning—" Her face suddenly flushed with embarrassment when she realized how much she was revealing. She clenched her hands together until her fingers ached. "I'm sorry. I'm sure you don't want to hear about this."

"Not in detail, no." Evelyn covered her hands. "Are you sure about this?"

Evelyn's eyes mirrored Melanie's own grief, and emotion strangled any response she might have had. She nodded.

"Are you—um—is there someone else?"

"Wow. Kendall didn't even accuse me of cheating." She pulled her hands free and leaned back.

"I didn't mean—I'm just trying to understand what happened and why now."

"I've always been faithful, and if we'd stayed together I would have continued to be. But fidelity isn't enough, Ev. I want her to be happy and I want to be happy. I want to be wanted—desperately. God, does that just make me sound like a pathetic romantic?"

"Not at all," Evelyn said quietly.

"I'd convinced myself that couples were supposed to mellow into friendship—that it happened to everyone. But I just couldn't shake the feeling that I need something more. Besides, that wasn't our only issue. We barely see each other. I work all day, and by the time she gets home from work all I want to do is go to sleep."

"We bid for shifts every year. She's got enough seniority to get day shift."

"I know. But she didn't."

"That doesn't make sense. If she knew you were having problems, she should have…"

Melanie winced, knowing exactly the memory Evelyn's mind had grabbed hold of. Once, last year, Kendall had told Evelyn she was thinking about bidding a different shift. Evelyn shot the idea down immediately without asking about Kendall's motivations.

"She never told me." Guilt washed over Evelyn's features.

"It's not your fault." She and Kendall had talked extensively about the proposed change in shift, but in the end Kendall wouldn't commit. She clung to her routines, both personally and professionally. Evelyn's objection had been a convenient excuse, one of many. But she'd grown tired of excuses when she barely got to see her girlfriend. Just once, she wanted to come first.

"Why didn't you tell me? I know, this is about you guys, not me. But neither of you let on that things had gotten this far."

"I'd been telling myself my unhappiness would pass, that it was a phase. And I didn't want to put you in the difficult position of choosing sides. I still don't." As close as they both were to Evelyn, Melanie believed some things should stay between them as a couple.

"Is there anything I can do for you?"

She shook her head.

Evelyn looked as if she wanted to say something more, but she didn't. Instead, she stood. "I'm sorry for barging in so early. But Kendall was so upset I kind of freaked out." She backed toward the door and Melanie followed.

"It's okay. You were concerned for Kendall, I get it."

Evelyn lowered her head and fished her keys out of her pocket. "I'm sorry you guys are going through this. You'll call me if you need something?"

"Of course."

Again, she felt like Evelyn wanted to say something more, but she held back. After a moment of awkward silence, Evelyn nodded and opened the door.

Melanie suppressed the urge to call her back inside and ask her to stay. Though she should be alone, to work through her feelings, she'd rather plop down on the sofa with Evelyn and find a good movie to distract herself for a few more hours. But Evelyn worked with Kendall and Kendall was at her house right now. Even if they didn't ask her to choose sides, by default, the decision was made. Her friendship with Evelyn was just one of many things that were about to change drastically.

CHAPTER FOUR

G ood morning," Evelyn called as she pushed open the front door.

"In the kitchen."

Evelyn followed the sound of Kendall's voice, surprised to find her there. The past several mornings she'd returned from her daily run to find Kendall still moping in bed. Today, she stood in front of the stove, spatula in hand. She flipped several pancakes and then turned to Evelyn. "Breakfast?"

"I can't eat anything that heavy after a run." She inhaled the smoky scent of bacon and couldn't resist snatching a piece from the plate.

"Pancakes?"

"No, thanks." Knowing the punishment her stomach would inflict if she indulged, instead she took a container of Greek yogurt and several fresh strawberries from the fridge. "Looks like you're feeling better." She watched Kendall pile four pancakes onto a plate and saturate them in syrup. "Got your appetite back, huh?"

"I guess so." Kendall shrugged as she slid onto a stool next to the island.

"Will you be ready to run with me tomorrow morning? I could really use the workout." Their competitive natures fueled them when they exercised together. She mixed sliced strawberries into her yogurt and then leaned against the counter opposite Kendall.

"I see no reason to get up at five a.m. if I don't have to." Kendall shoved a forkful of pancake into her mouth, chewed quickly, and swallowed. "There's a reason I work second shift, you know."

"Yeah, what is it?"

"What?"

"Why do you work evening shift? You and Melanie could have been on the same schedule if you'd gone to days."

Kendall shoved her plate away and stood up. "I thought you went over there last weekend to talk some sense into her, but apparently you've been listening to her bitch about me."

"I just asked a question." She clamped down the urge to remind Kendall that she'd been listening to her complain about Melanie as well. Kendall had called in sick to work and sulked for the past four days.

"Oh, come on, those words were right out of her mouth."

"She wasn't bitching about you. She talked about her reasons for doing what she did. I listened, yes, because I'm trying to be a good friend to both of you."

"Yeah, well, I have my reasons, too. I worked days when I was in training and hated it. I don't like getting up early, and I hate making bullshit reports all shift. That's all they do on days, and you know it. So what good is there in Melanie and me spending more time together if I'm miserable half the time? I would never ask her to change her career to make me happy."

"I'm sorry. I know this is a tough time and I don't want to add to your stress." She didn't have any right to judge how Kendall was handling her relationship. She certainly wasn't an expert on keeping a girlfriend.

Sometimes she wished she could go back to men, though she knew plenty of lesbians who would judge her for such thoughts. Her relationships with the men she dated until her junior year in college had been easy. She had no problem fulfilling the physical requirements, and they expected very little from her emotionally. Then she'd met Colleen. Colleen was older, a graduate student, and unabashedly driven. She'd fallen head over heels. She'd never felt anything nearly as intense and, while not ready to label herself as lesbian, she couldn't deny being at least bisexual.

When it ended, she tried to convince herself she'd been attracted to Colleen not *because* she was a woman, but in spite of it. She started dating men again, but once that part of her was awakened, she was unable to stop the flashes of awareness when she encountered a lesbian or the sparks of attraction when she developed a crush on a female classmate. She could still appreciate an attractive man, but when it came to relationships, she wanted to be with a woman.

Her relationship history was still a disaster—short-lived love affairs that burned out once the sex was no longer exciting and regular. She couldn't always blame the other woman, but she didn't shoulder all of the responsibility either. Still, she expected things would change when she met the right woman. She hoped her grand romance, her love-at-first-sight-across-a-crowded-room moment was still out there.

For now, she intended to support Kendall through this breakup.

"Are you going to work today?" She didn't think their sergeant would buy illness as an excuse for too much longer. And she hated the evasive answers she recited when the other guys kept asking after Kendall's health.

Kendall shrugged. "Stay home with me. We'll catch a movie or something."

"Can't." She snagged another piece of bacon from the plate Kendall had pushed away. "I have court, two cases in General Sessions. Actually, I have to get ready soon so I can go in early. You have to go back eventually. Tuesday is as good a day as any to make a fresh start."

"Maybe tomorrow—"

"Nope. Today." She took Kendall's hand and guided her from the stool and down the hallway toward the bedrooms. "Maybe work will help occupy your mind for a while. It can't be good to spend so much time alone. I'm giving you a few more hours for this pity party, and then I expect you to take a shower and get your butt to the precinct. I'll meet up with you when I get out of court."

She nudged Kendall in the direction of the guest bedroom, then went to her own room to get ready for work.

❖

Melanie hefted several patches of sod from a large pallet at the edge of the driveway. She crossed the lawn to the end of a completed row, passing two other members of her team on the way, and placed the new pieces, carefully adjusting the seams. As she returned to the pallet, her mind began to wander to Kendall but she snapped it back. She wondered how Kendall was coping but had decided not to call or text. Though their relationship had been nearing an end, she had been the one to sever their lifeline and now she had to give Kendall space.

In the meantime, she distracted herself by working. She labored alongside her crew, digging trenches, running wires for landscape lighting, and laying sod. By the time she went home each night, her shirt soaked through with sweat and streaked with dirt, she had only enough energy left for a quick shower before she crawled into bed. The grueling pace meant she would finish this job several days ahead of schedule. She'd promised her crew a long weekend before they headed to the next site.

"Take a break, guys," she called after they'd emptied another pallet of sod. She pulled a bandana from her back pocket and wiped her forehead, then grabbed her water bottle and took several long swallows.

Leaning against the door of her truck, she surveyed today's progress. The lawn sloped gradually down from the front of the house, giving way to a circular drive and a gated exterior. Her crew had added several walkways connecting the house, the four-stall garage, and the driveway. At the owners' request, they'd installed an opulent fountain in the middle of the drive. The gold-gilded cherubs spewing water into the center of a round pool would not have been her choice for the space, and she still winced when she looked at them. But accepting the piece afforded her the luxury of a large budget and free rein over the rest of the yard. She'd worked in the sculpture as well as possible, distracting from it with gorgeous, elegant flowers and carved marble benches.

"It's really shaping up," Lucas, her most trusted employee, said as he came to stand next to her. "Other than that god-awful fountain, I mean."

She laughed. "It really is horrible."

"Money doesn't buy taste." He shrugged and tilted his water bottle.

Eight years ago, when she left her desk job to start her own business, Lucas was one of the first two men she hired. The other man had left within a year, but Lucas proved to be loyal and hardworking. Because he was twenty years old, she hadn't expected a long-term commitment when she'd hired him. But he proved eager to learn and, with a new wife and a baby on the way, he needed the job. Now, she could confidently hand him the reins on almost any project.

Since then she'd added nearly a dozen men to her landscape crews, as well as an office manager so she wouldn't end up behind a desk full-time again. Still she spent at least two days a week in the small office she leased. Her office manager, Roberta, handled the billing and assigned crews to routine-maintenance accounts. But Melanie met with prospective clients and approved all new projects.

"Everything okay, Boss?" Lucas asked.

"Yeah, sure."

"You're not wearing your ring." He nodded at her left hand. The light strip where her gold band used to rest stood out against her otherwise tanned skin.

"No. I'm not." She'd felt strange removing the ring and had worn it for several days after the breakup. But seeing it on her finger had only made her sad, so she'd tucked it away in her jewelry box.

"What happened?"

"We split up."

"If you want to talk…"

She shook her head. "I just need to work."

She and Lucas couldn't be more different, yet she considered him a friend. He was a country boy, raised on a farm with traditional Southern Christian values. He'd admitted shortly after she introduced him to Kendall that he'd never been around an openly gay person before. He struggled with how her lifestyle fit into his religion, but he accepted and respected her. Over the years, they'd worked closely together and she liked to think she'd broadened his view of how God created people. Conversely, he taught her a great deal about how strong faith could be.

Last year, when he and his wife had divorced, she had supported him as best she could, letting him adjust his hours so he could pick up his son and listening when he needed to vent. She knew she would have his ear now if she needed it, and she trusted him to keep her business private. But she couldn't talk yet, not without crying.

She hated walking through the house and seeing Kendall's things, but it just didn't feel right to box them up, and Kendall hadn't contacted her regarding what she would do with them. Instead, she found excuses to be out of the house, working late and running imaginary errands. But nothing completely distracted her from the mess her life had become.

She still believed ending their relationship would eventually prove best for both of them. But knowing that didn't change the fact that she was now in her mid-thirties, alone, and with all of her previous plans for her future blown to hell. Maybe eventually "starting over" would sound promising—full of positive possibilities—but for now, all she could think about was how much she missed her old life, her old routines, and their friends, specifically Evelyn.

❖

Evelyn entered the courtroom and strode to the front. She pushed through the swinging gate and joined several other officers sitting behind the prosecutors' table. One officer was engrossed in a paperback book, and two others appeared occupied with their phones. She dropped into a chair next to a familiar face.

"Hey, Princess," she said. On the outside, Jennifer Prince was all girl and made no secret of just how high-maintenance she could be, which was why she'd earned the nickname in the academy. The instructor had coined the not-so-imaginative take on her last name the very first day in his attempt to break her down. But she'd proved to also be extremely tough and had soared through the challenge of the police academy.

"Hey, Fisher. How've you been, babe?" Jennifer winked and her belly fluttered. Something about a beautiful woman winking at her always got to her. Jennifer was one of those women who didn't seem to notice the effect she had when she tossed her chestnut curls, beamed a dimple-revealing smile, or casually touched an arm while she spoke. She was a natural flirt, which is what had made it easy for Evelyn to cross a line with her.

"My day just got a little brighter. How are you?"

"Not bad. I've been seeing someone new."

"Yeah? Is it serious?" Evelyn kept her voice down, conscious not only of the other officers around them, but the defendants and their families occupying the rows behind them.

"There's definite potential."

"Good for you. We should have lunch one day and catch up."

"Absolutely. I always have time for you." Jennifer smiled. "Hey, I heard about Kendall and Melanie. How's Kendall doing?"

"Ah, she's a bit of a wreck, but she'll get through it."

"How long were they together?"

"Seven years."

"Wow, an eternity."

"Yeah. I've never known them separately. It's weird."

They fell silent as the seats around them filled. The prosecutors entertained a line of defense attorneys, brokering last-minute deals for their clients. When the judge took the bench and the clerk read through the names on the docket, those who'd reached an agreement would enter their pleas and sign the appropriate paperwork. The remaining defendants waited their turn for the preliminary hearing to determine if probable cause existed to bind their case over to the grand jury.

Just as everyone else had settled down, the heavy door at the back of the courtroom swung open. The man who entered had carefully cultivated his appearance, from his towering height to the breadth of his shoulders, all wrapped in a dark suit custom-tailored to appear distinguished but not too expensive, alluding to stability. He'd selected the wire rims on his glasses specifically because they didn't obscure the one touch of softness in his appearance— big, brown, trustworthy eyes. He strode to the front of the room, emanating the prowess that earned him his hourly fees.

He still knows how to make an entrance. Nearly every head turned as he passed. His smug smile seemed to encompass every one of them.

"Hey, isn't that your—"

"Yeah." Evelyn reluctantly made eye contact with her father. He raised his chin in greeting and she nodded in response.

He pushed through the swinging gate and turned left, heading for the defense table on the opposite side of the room.

"Damn, he's intimidating," Jennifer whispered.

Evelyn was relieved when the court officer ordered them to stand and announced the judge's name. She didn't want to talk about how impressive her father was. She'd grown up in awe of his obvious power and confidence, until she was old enough to understand exactly what a defense attorney did. The biggest argument she'd ever had with her father had come on the day she'd told him she'd applied to the police academy instead of law school. Until then, he'd believed she would eventually join his firm.

"Be seated."

She sank back in her seat and listened for the names of her defendants. When the clerk finished reading the docket, neither of her cases had pled, and what was worse, her father represented the defendant in her first case. She shifted, pushing against the bulky gun belt around her waist, and attempted to get more comfortable. She'd be here most of the morning.

CHAPTER FIVE

A re you just now getting out of court?"
      "Yep. And I hadn't even left the parking garage when
dispatch sent me this call." Evelyn climbed out of her patrol car and
glanced at the house in front of her, checking the address against
the one on the laptop screen in the car. Kendall, her backup, had
pulled up just before her.

"Well, at least you'll have fat overtime on your next check."

She nodded. Sitting around in court all day had exhausted her,
and now she had to endure the rest of her regular shift.

"What's wrong? You seem a little edgy."

"Eh, my dad."

"He was in court?" Kendall winced. Evelyn had watched
him cross-examine Kendall once, and he didn't give her any slack
either.

"Yeah."

"How is Charles W?" Kendall asked, making her usual joke
about his penchant for introducing himself as "Charles W. Fisher."

"Same as always. He is who he is and I'm not changing
either."

"Did something happen today?"

"No, we didn't even speak, except when I was on the stand."

"Unfortunately, he really is good at what he does."

"I know." His questions were always on point and delivered
with just the right amount of respect and skepticism.

"So, what's the score now?" Kendall asked.

"What?"

"You keep a running tally every time you're in court with him, right?"

His criminal-trial record was beyond impressive, and he was a pro at winning juries over. But she had inherited his trustworthy smile and usually felt she could hold her own against him. *Against him.* Despite knowing that they were both simply cogs in the gears of justice, she couldn't help making their encounters personal.

"Forget that. Let's go find out what they're fighting about this time." She forced her attention back to her current situation—one she could do something about.

Today wasn't the first time they'd been to this particular residence. The husband and wife who lived here argued often, which usually resulted in one of them calling the police. Today it was the wife. But when police officers arrived, neither would make a statement against the other. If they got physical, they were careful about it. She hadn't seen a mark on either of them yet, and until she did, she couldn't do anything to force prosecution.

Kendall nodded and opened the chain-link gate leading to the residence in question. Aside from the bright-red front door, the small, square house wasn't different from any of the other houses on the block. But before they could reach the front porch, that very door flew open and a harried-looking woman hurtled out and stopped when she saw them. She wore fuchsia fuzzy slippers and a flowing nightgown covered in huge, obnoxiously bright flowers. She shook one fist in the air while clutching the neck of a broken wine bottle in the other.

"Where have you been? I called fifteen minutes ago."

"What's going on today, ma'am?" Kendall asked. She stopped at the bottom of the porch steps, leaving plenty of room between them and the woman.

"Other than the piss-poor response time of the police? If I'd been shot in the street, I would have been dead before you got here."

Evelyn bit back a snarky response. She'd heard this twisted logic before and had long ago given up explaining just why this woman would not have been left to die in the street while the police ate doughnuts down the street.

"Where's your husband tonight?" she asked, ignoring the rest of her tirade. If the woman complained to the department, their response time would be investigated. The department didn't have enough officers to answer every call immediately, so incidents were prioritized and that meant some people had to wait. She had no doubt that's what had happened in this case. Neither of these two admitted to physical injury, and despite the bottle in the woman's hand, she hadn't mentioned any weapons on the phone, so some high-priority calls had been dispatched first.

"He's inside. On the kitchen floor where I left him."

"What happened to him?" When the woman tightened her grip on the bottle, Evelyn rested her right hand on her gun. "Ma'am, I need you to put down the bottle and stay out here with my partner while I go inside and check on him."

She nodded and set it down in a nearby rocking chair. Evelyn met Kendall's eyes in silent communication, and at her slight nod, they both moved forward. Kendall steered the woman toward a chair on the other side of the porch, and Evelyn continued through the front door.

Her hand still on her gun, she scanned right to left as she passed through each room. An overturned chair and broken vase on the floor indicated a struggle in the living room. She stepped over a lamp lying across the doorway, and the broken bulb crunched under her boots. A fixture in the next room provided enough light that she didn't have to use her flashlight. A picture hung askew in the hallway leading to the back of the house. She saw no effort to hide the obvious physical struggle here. The couple had apparently crossed a line this time.

She found him unconscious, in the kitchen, on his side, wedged between the counter and a battered dinette table. After a quick glance around the room, she bent and felt for a pulse. Satisfied that he was alive, she grabbed her radio and asked dispatch for an ambulance and a domestic-violence detective.

"Fifteen to thirteen." She called Kendall using their unit numbers.

"Go ahead."

"He's got a head wound and there's some broken glass that looks like a match to that bottle on the front porch. Hold what you have until we get DV out for pictures." She chose her words carefully, knowing that the wife was within earshot. She doubted the woman was dangerous to anyone except the man currently incapacitated in front of her, but Kendall would take her into custody just in case.

"Ten-four."

She pulled on a pair of latex gloves, then grabbed a towel from the counter and pressed it to the gash on his head.

When paramedics arrived a few minutes later, she was still crouched there and had gotten little more than a moan from the patient. She waited until one of the medics nodded and placed his hand over the towel she held; then she stepped back and moved out of their way. Judging from the vitals and comments they called to each other over his prone body, his condition was stable.

She found Kendall in the front yard, returning from securing the wife in her patrol car.

"He'll survive," Evelyn said.

The medics wheeled a stretcher carrying the husband out of the house and toward the ambulance. His wife watched wistfully through the car window as they passed. When she called out that she loved him, Kendall shook her head.

"We'll be out here again in a few weeks."

Evelyn snorted. "Welcome back."

"Yeah, thanks."

"Seriously, how's it been?"

"You were right. I needed to stop wallowing and get back to it. It's just—everything's changed and I can't seem to fix it. Did I tell you Melanie texted me?"

Evelyn shook her head.

"I thought maybe she wanted to work it out. But turns out she just wanted to talk about splitting up the furniture—like I have anywhere to put that stuff. I'm living in your guest room. Then she starts in about separating the bank accounts and won't I be glad to have my share of our savings. She's so fucking ready to move on. I don't think she's even upset about all of this."

"Of course she is." She recalled the sadness in Melanie's eyes when she last saw her.

"She's got a funny way of showing it."

"Not really. Everything you said sounds just like Melanie."

"Huh?"

"She's a planner, Kendall. Occupying her mind with what she needs to do next is her way of dealing with all of this. She needs to feel like she's *doing* something to move the situation forward."

"Well, she can't make me move forward." Kendall looked over her shoulder at the woman sitting in her patrol car. "Will you go by there with me tomorrow before work to pick up some stuff?"

Something about people now negotiating their breakups through text message made Evelyn sad. Even relationships were becoming far too impersonal.

❖

"Hi," Melanie said somewhat breathlessly as she opened the door to Kendall and Evelyn.

She hadn't gone this long without seeing Kendall since they'd first started dating. Their few attempts at communicating had ended with Melanie feeling guilty, then trying to convince herself she shouldn't. Kendall seemed to still hope she would change her mind about the breakup and she didn't want to encourage that, but they had to have a certain degree of interaction until they sorted everything out.

And she wasn't heartless. Certainly she still cared about her. Kendall looked tired and Melanie wanted to smooth away the smudges of fatigue around her eyes. But it wasn't her place to offer comfort. And despite the remorse she felt for causing Kendall such distress, she didn't have a trace of regret for the decision she'd made. As soon as their personal business was separated, she planned to keep her distance, hoping a clean break would help them both heal.

"I'm here to pick up some things." Kendall's cool tone indicated this was not a social call.

She stepped back, waited until they came in, then closed the door behind them. As they passed, she noticed the familiar spicy perfume she would forever associate with Kendall.

"Hey, Mel." Evelyn followed Kendall inside, though she looked as if she would rather be anywhere else. She barely made eye contact and had her hands shoved so deeply in her jeans that Melanie was surprised they hadn't bored holes in the pockets. Melanie longed to calm her obvious worry as well.

"I was hoping you would come over when we can sit down together and talk. We should go over the finances in person," Melanie said.

"I'm on my way to work. I don't have time for that today."

"But you assumed I would have time for you to just show up without calling?" Irritation overshadowed her compassion.

"What? I'm supposed to call before coming to my own home now? Besides, I didn't think you'd be here."

"I had a meeting with a client this morning and dropped by for lunch. I was just about to head out to the job site."

"Well, I don't need your help packing anything, so you're free to go."

"I talked to the apartment manager about switching the lease into my name."

"Why do you automatically get the apartment?"

"You haven't said you wanted it. If you do, I'll start looking for another one."

Kendall looked around, disdain painting her features. "I don't."

Melanie sighed, exhausted with Kendall's passive-aggressive game.

"I'm going to wait outside," Evelyn blurted into the tense silence.

"You don't have to."

"I want to. Let me know when you're ready to start packing things in the car." Evelyn didn't wait for agreement before she crossed the room and headed out the front door.

"Fine. I won't be long." Kendall strode toward the bedroom.

After Evelyn left, Melanie followed Kendall and picked up the thread of their previous conversation. "I'm just trying to figure out what the next step is, Kendall. We need to make some practical decisions, and I'm not sure how long we should wait." More than anything, she needed the closure of disentangling their lives.

"Keep the money, Melanie. All of it." Kendall took a suitcase down from the closet shelf and opened it on the bed. She opened a drawer and emptied it into the bag, seemingly with no regard to the actual contents.

"We saved that money together. It's half yours and you are going to take it."

"No. I'm not."

"You are. I won't have you telling everyone I left you with nothing."

"What difference does it make? *You left me.* Whether it was with nothing or with everything makes no fucking difference."

Melanie's body went cold and her limbs felt weak, but she stood her ground. "If you need to make me the bad guy, go ahead. But there were two of us in the relationship. The fault isn't mine alone."

"Don't you have someplace to be?" Kendall didn't look up from her packing.

Melanie stared at her a moment longer before leaving the room. She continued straight through the living room and out the front door.

After taking three quick steps into the middle of the breezeway, she spun around. Evelyn leaned against the wall, one ankle crossed over the other, fiddling with the stem of her sunglasses. She looked up, and the sympathy in her soft brown eyes diffused Melanie's anger. She drew a deep breath and released it slowly.

"I'm sorry if we made you uncomfortable," she said quietly.
Evelyn shrugged.

"I guess this is weird for all of us, huh?"

"Yeah, I mean, I've heard you guys argue, but I always knew
you would work it out."

"Not this time, Ev. I'm sorry." Strange as it sounded, she did
feel as if she owed Evelyn an apology as well—as if Evelyn were
the child of their broken home.

"How are you?" Evelyn asked as she took a step closer.

"I'm okay. I just—" She stopped, uncertain how to proceed.
She wanted to talk to Evelyn but didn't want to put her in an
awkward position.

"What?"

"I have a lot to adjust to right now."

Evelyn touched Melanie's arm. "Why didn't you tell me you
guys were having problems? I don't expect Kendall to talk to me
about her feelings. But you—all of the times I've opened up to you
about my girl trouble—"

"I know." She nodded. "You're right. We went from being
happy to being in a rut so gradually, I didn't notice until it was too
late to recover. Then I guess I didn't want to admit we'd failed."
She never had trouble sharing her feelings, but this time—this
failure made her want to draw tightly inside herself. Kendall was
her first serious girlfriend, and for a long time she'd thought she'd
be the only one.

"I put you guys on a pedestal as an example of my ideal
relationship."

She mentally added another casualty to her recent actions.
She'd shattered not only her own world, but Kendall's as well. And,
without even realizing it, she'd first let Evelyn harbor illusions
about their "perfect" partnership and then torn those illusions apart
with one decision.

"We didn't belong there. I don't even know what an ideal
relationship is." She had to believe that after the emotions cleared,
they would realize this was best for all of them.

CHAPTER SIX

I have a date," Kendall announced as she and Evelyn walked together through the cafeteria-like line at their favorite meat-and-three place. Once a week, they ate there during their shift and indulged in the rich Southern cuisine. "Do you think it's too soon?"

Four months after her split with Melanie, she still sometimes had trouble not thinking of them as a couple. But in that time, she'd taken steps toward moving on. She'd managed to get the rest of her things from the old place and rent a condo in an affordable neighborhood not far from Evelyn's. Surprisingly, decorating it by herself brought feelings of satisfaction and pride along with the expected tingle of loneliness.

She'd spent her first holiday season without Melanie in seven years. She had resisted the urge to text Melanie on Christmas and New Year's Eve. And she'd finally stopped checking Melanie's Facebook page—well, she'd cut it down to once a week.

"I don't think there's a timetable for these things. If you're ready, then it's been long enough. Where'd you meet her?" Evelyn asked, after pointing out her choice of vegetables to the woman behind the counter.

The woman holding a spoon of green beans seemed too interested in their conversation, so Kendall waited until they'd both paid and settled at a table to answer. "I met her on one of those online sites."

Evelyn laughed.

"What? I don't want to date anyone I already know. The police department can be so—incestuous. And it's exhausting to think about meeting someone in a bar and trying to figure them out. On the Internet, they spell it all out for you. Sure, most of it may not be true, but I can hope for a while until I meet them and find out they have some major personality flaw or a huge wart, or a—"

"Hey, slow down. I'm just surprised. I didn't know you were thinking about getting back out there, let alone putting your profile online."

"I didn't either. But it's pretty clear Mel and I aren't reconciling." The Web site required an active account before allowing users to browse available women. So, on a whim one night last week, while tipsy, she'd set up her own profile, intending only to see what kind of women visited those sites. She'd nearly forgotten about it until, a few days later, she received e-mail notifications that a couple of women had viewed her profile and "smiled" at her, whatever that meant.

"Good for you. What's the plan?"

"We're meeting for dinner. Someplace bright and public, you know, in case she's a murderer or has a scary ex-con boyfriend."

"That sounds like a good plan."

She shifted in her seat and bent her head closer to Evelyn's. "I haven't been on a first date in seven years."

"Nervous, huh?"

"You could say that. But right now I'm more concerned with just putting myself back out there." The woman she planned to meet tonight seemed nice and, if her profile was accurate, she was cute and they had shared interests, but she didn't let her expectations get too high. "I just hate the awkwardness and uncomfortable silences that go with a first date."

"You're looking at it all wrong. Think about the possibilities. Right now, there's potential. You could have a great first date. And if not," Evelyn shrugged, "you meet someone else and have another one. Nothing lost."

She teased Evelyn. "So, I should just become a player?"

"I'm not saying that. But maybe just don't take things seriously right now. I know you, Kendall. You want to be in a relationship. You like being taken care of and having someone to dote on."

She nodded.

"I have no doubt you'll find that again. But it doesn't have to be right now. You have your own place for the first time in a long time, so enjoy being alone. And if you meet some cool people in the process, that's great."

"You're right. But hey, you're still there for me when I need a wingman, right?"

Evelyn grinned, knowing Kendall was only half joking. "Absolutely."

They finished their lunch with light conversation and made plans to get together late Saturday morning for breakfast and a postmortem of Kendall's date. They'd established the tradition years ago after Evelyn had a particularly tragic one. This would be Kendall's first time on the other end of the meal.

As they walked out the front door, Evelyn's phone buzzed and she pulled it free from the holster. When she saw Melanie's face on the screen, she switched it to her other hand, facing away from Kendall.

But she didn't need to make an excuse to take the call, because the dispatcher's voice came across the radio requesting Kendall to back another officer on a disorderly person.

"I'll catch you later," Kendall said after acknowledging the transmission.

"See ya." Evelyn slid behind the wheel of her patrol car and answered her phone. "Hey, how are you?"

"I'm sorry to bother you while you're working. But that's actually why I'm calling. One of my clients had a break-in and the theft included some stuff from one of my trailers. It's down on Riverside Street, so I thought since it's in your district—"

"Absolutely. Give me the address." She grabbed a pen and small notepad and jotted down the location.

"Thank you. I'll meet you over there."

❖

Evelyn pulled her patrol car to the curb behind Melanie's truck and surveyed the house in front of her. Several large trees shaded the small bungalow. Like every other place on the block, the owner had painted the exterior and trim in bright contrasting colors. But the attempt at individuality somehow made them all look the same.

She hit the button on her laptop computer that indicated to dispatch that she was on-scene and unavailable for calls, then climbed out of the car. Melanie stood in the driveway next to a white utility trailer.

Evelyn waved and warmth spread through her chest when Melanie smiled. She circled the car and headed down the walk toward her without hesitation. It had been too long since she'd seen Melanie.

When she reached the driveway, Melanie rocked forward on her toes, then back again, and Evelyn realized she'd just stifled the urge to hug her. Melanie's eyes shifted briefly down her body then back to her face. Kendall didn't like to be hugged in public while in her uniform. Evelyn didn't remember ever actually agreeing with her, but she also couldn't recall a single time when Melanie hugged her while she was dressed for work either.

"Hey, Mel."

"Thanks for coming down."

She examined the broken padlock that hung lopsided in the hasp of the trailer door. "Is this your trailer?"

Melanie nodded. "They broke a window in the back door of the house and got inside, too. The owner is pretty wound up. He's inside." Her eyes held an apology for the attitude Evelyn was about to get from the property owner.

If Evelyn looked between the two houses across the street, she could see several known drug houses. She already knew what to expect when she went in to make this report. This guy wasn't the first to purchase and renovate a historic house only a few streets away from a high-crime area. The neighborhood would eventually change, slowly becoming more upscale, safer, and trendy. But the first wave of buyers should expect to make these repeated calls for police assistance.

"I'll start with him, knock out his report, then we'll do yours."

"Let's go inside and I'll introduce you." Melanie led her up the front steps. She pulled open the screen door and called out to the owner before entering.

They passed through the foyer and rounded the corner into an open living room lit by work lights on tripods in each corner. A beefy man with a shaved head wedged a crowbar into a piece of molding around the hearth. The muscles of his shoulders flexed against his sleeveless shirt as he worked it until the strip of wood came free with a resounding pop. In the silence that followed, Evelyn's boots echoed on the dulled hardwood floor.

He straightened and turned, still holding the pry bar. His eyes dipped to the silver nameplate on the right side of her chest, obviously taking note of her name in case she didn't handle the issue to his satisfaction.

"Paul Baxter," he said, as he bent and leaned the bar against the wall.

"I understand you had a break-in last night, Mr. Baxter." She used her most professional tone. "Was it the back door?"

"Yes. I'll show you."

As he strode across the room, Melanie tilted her head indicating she would be outside, and Evelyn nodded.

"Are you doing all the work yourself?" she asked as she followed him. She hadn't seen evidence of any other workers in the house.

"Everything inside. I'll need to contract out some projects outside. And of course, I hired your friend out there to do the flowers."

She didn't like the dismissive way he talked about Melanie's work, as if it was as simple as sticking some plants in the ground.

But she didn't comment, focusing instead on the broken pane in the door where the suspect got in. "Do you know what time this took place?"

"I worked late, left about ten, and discovered the broken window at six a.m. Neighborhood thugs, no doubt."

"Did anyone see the suspects?"

"If they did, they're not talking to me. But I'm an outsider around here. So that's how it usually is, isn't it?" She almost expected a nudge and a wink along with this statement.

"Overnight—it's not uncommon to not have witnesses. Most people are asleep, and only your closest neighbors might have heard breaking glass, anyway. Have you touched this door or the frame at all?"

"No."

She made several notes regarding the forced entry and called dispatch to request a crime-scene tech for fingerprints. When the dispatcher responded "I'll put you in line," she knew the few officers covering the county must be backed up with calls. She advised Mr. Baxter about the wait time and told him what to do in the meantime.

When she finished taking his report, she went outside to find Melanie. The front yard was empty, so she circled to the back. Inside the privacy fence, which last night had helped shield a thief at work, she discovered a hidden garden. Lush green plants, accented with brightly colored flowers, lined the walkway. Shoots of new vines crawled up a lattice archway, and she could imagine how beautiful the area would be as the plants matured.

An outdoor sofa and chairs circled a fireplace and created a quaint conversation area steps away from the back door. She spotted a few well-hidden path lights and suspected there were a number more she didn't see that would adequately light the walk at night.

"How do you have this much color so early in spring?" she asked when she saw Melanie kneeling next to a flower bed situated inside a bend in the path.

"We had such a warm winter that things are coming up and flowering earlier than usual. Some of our plants are local, but some come from even warmer climates. As long as we don't get another hard frost, this stuff will be okay."

"So you're taking a chance?" She recalled a few years ago when it had been warmer than usual and the trees had all budded, but then temperatures dropped for about a week and killed most of the greenery.

"Yes. If it freezes, I'll have to replace some of it, but he wants it done now so we'll risk it."

"Well, it's beautiful."

"Thank you." Melanie stood and swiped her hands across the thighs of her well-worn jeans, leaving smears of dark soil. "But Lucas gets most of the credit. I've started letting him take on some of the design work. He's really very talented."

"He certainly is. Does Mr. Baxter know that *a man* did most of his design?"

"I don't know. Why?" With the back of her still-dirty hand, Melanie pushed at a wisp of hair in her face. When the stubborn strand fell back down, Evelyn moved forward, intending to help her. But Melanie grabbed it and shoved it behind her ear, leaving her standing a little too close for casual conversation.

"Um—no reason." How had she never noticed the dark ring around the grassy green of Melanie's irises?

"Okay."

She took two steps back, restoring comfortable space between them. "He just strikes me as a bit of a chauvinist."

"I got that from him, too."

"How bad were you hit last night?"

"I've got a list out front by the trailer."

"Okay, great. Let's go out there." She wanted to escape the intimate backyard and return to the very public front of the house. Perhaps that would keep her from noticing how Melanie's perfume mingled with the earthy smell of the soil she'd had her hands in.

❖

"Thanks again. I know I could have just called dispatch, but—"

"It's no problem. That's what friends are for."

Melanie nodded, trying to ignore the twinge of bitterness in response to Evelyn's words.

"Hey, what's wrong?" Evelyn touched her arm. "What's going on?"

"Is that what we are? Friends?"

"Of course."

"I—uh—I just—since the split, I feel like you took her side." Did she sound petty? She'd tried to ignore the feeling that all of their former friends had dropped her, Evelyn among them. Other than a few texts inquiring after her well-being, she hadn't seen or spoken to Evelyn in a couple of months.

In truth, many of their friends had been Kendall's friends when they got together. Melanie had been working so hard to build her business when they met that she hadn't had much time for socializing. Maybe she felt Evelyn's absence even more because they'd grown close to her together. She and Kendall had been together for two years already when Kendall and Evelyn started working together.

"Mel, no. It seemed like she needed me more. You—you're strong."

"Maybe not as strong as you think." Perhaps she should have been more honest in her replies to those texts. Instead, she'd answered with a generic reassurance that she was okay.

"You always seem to hold everything together. Hell, Kendall would have been lost without you, and, at times, I'm pretty sure I would have, too."

"Sure, the little stuff, I can handle. But we're talking about the end of a seven-year relationship. Do you really think I didn't fall apart just as much as she did?"

"I'm sorry, Mel. I know it has to be hard for you, too."

"I'm working through it. This is what happens when people split up, right? Their friends take sides."

"I'm not taking sides."

"But you're naturally going to be closer to one of us than the other. It's okay, I understand. You have more in common with Kendall."

"Jesus, Mel, she was sleeping in my guest room. What was I supposed to do, invite you over for coffee?"

She pressed her thumb and forefinger to her forehead, over her eyes. "No. Of course not. I'm sorry."

Evelyn sighed. "Don't be sorry. You're not wrong, I should have called you."

She shook her head. She hadn't intended this to be a pity party. "It's in the past. Bygones and all. I don't know if Kendall and I will ever be able to be friends."

"Sure you will, that's what lesbians do," Evelyn joked.

She smiled. "Maybe. But either way, I hope you and I can still be in each other's lives." She didn't know how not to put Evelyn in the middle to some degree, but she couldn't just concede Evelyn's friendship. So she said exactly what was in her heart. "I miss you."

When she met Evelyn's eyes, she relaxed a little. Evelyn's brows drew up over her velvety brown eyes and she realized that no matter what had happened with Kendall, she hadn't lost her friend.

The front door of the house banged open and Evelyn's gaze shifted quickly toward the sound. Paul came out carrying an armload of scraps and headed for the construction dumpster nearby.

"I should get back to work." Evelyn handed her a card, her tone professional in case Paul overheard, but her expression held friendly familiarity. "There's your report number. Wait a day or two for it to be processed, and then you can go down to records and get a copy."

"Thanks again." She followed Evelyn down the drive and paused beside her car.

Once inside the car, Evelyn rolled down the window. "It was good to see you."

"You, too."

"Hey, are you busy tomorrow night?"

"No."

"I'm meeting some of the girls out at the bar. You should come with me."

"I don't think so. Kendall and I aren't ready to hang out yet, even in a group."

"Kendall—won't be there. Don't you need a night out of the house?"

Maybe she could use a little distraction. And going with Evelyn could help ease her back into the social scene. She'd have a few drinks and let loose a little, and if she had a few too many, she could trust Evelyn to take care of her.

Chapter Seven

"Wow, it really has been a long time since I've been out dancing."

Evelyn laughed. A dance mix set a pulsing rhythm for the flashes of strobes and laser lights that cut through the smoky air. "Yeah, it's not Indigo-Girls-wannabes playing lesbian dive bars anymore."

"Shit, I don't want to do this again." Melanie looked as if she might bolt.

"Hey, hey, come on." She grabbed Melanie's hand. "You don't have to frequent the clubs. But for tonight, let's just go with it." She spotted Jennifer over by the bar, so without waiting for a response, she pulled Melanie behind her as she wove through the crowd.

"Hey, Jenn. You remember Melanie."

"Yeah, right. How are you?"

"I'm good."

"Have you been here long?" she asked. Judging from the glassy, unfocused look in Jennifer's eyes, she was quite a few drinks ahead of them.

Jennifer slung her arm around Evelyn's shoulder. "Not too long. But I've been waiting for you." Jennifer poked her shoulder a little too hard. She caught Melanie's amused, questioning look and shrugged.

"Where's your new girl? I want to meet her."

"She's not coming." Jennifer waved a hand in a sweeping gesture. "Apparently she didn't think we were exclusive yet, and she has a date tonight."

"Oh, honey, I'm sorry. But if you want to be exclusive you could just tell—"

"Come dance with me." Jennifer grabbed her hand and pulled her into the gyrating throng.

As soon as they reached the dance floor, Jennifer pressed close to her, rolling her hips against Evelyn's. Evelyn backed up, but she bumped into someone behind her. She turned far enough to make eye contact and offer an apologetic wave. Jennifer molded to her and wound her arms around her neck.

"Jenn, what are you doing?" She had to lean close to Jennifer's ear in order to be heard over the music.

"Just dancing, baby." Jennifer pressed her lips to the side of her neck. When Jennifer touched her tongue to the sensitive area below her ear, a swift surge of heat flushed her body.

She protested weakly. "Sure feels like more than dancing."

"Feels good, hmm?"

It really did. Her recent dry spell, coupled with Jennifer's blatant sex appeal, had her libido primed and firing. But when Jennifer slid her hands down the front of Evelyn's shirt, she caught her wrists before she reached her breasts. Under her fingers, Jennifer's pulse beat as rapidly as Evelyn's. If she was interested in casual sex tonight, this would be the perfect scenario. Her history with Jennifer would eliminate any potential misunderstandings about the level of intimacy between them.

"Jenn, wait." Her brain won over the arousal beginning a slow pulse in her blood. She took a step back, still holding Jennifer's wrists. "You're drunk and your feelings are hurt. You should figure out what you have with this new girl."

"She's out with someone else."

"But you don't want her to be, do you?" Jennifer shook her head petulantly, and Evelyn had to smile at how adorable she looked. "Then don't use me as an excuse to tank it. Because we both know that this," she released Jennifer and gestured between them, "isn't going anywhere."

"When did you get so honorable?"

"Hmm, I don't know." She'd never thought of herself as particularly *dishonorable*. Had she been perceived that way? She didn't screw around with attached women, but she didn't necessarily get attached herself. "Good luck, Jenn. I hope things work out for you." She smiled before she turned away.

Melanie had settled at a table on the edge of the dance floor, and Evelyn cringed when she realized Melanie had a perfect view of what had just transpired with Jennifer. The only thing worse would be if Kendall were here to bust her balls about messing with Jennifer again.

"Evelyn, so help me," Melanie began talking as soon as she reached her side, "if you leave me here to sleep with Jennifer Prince—"

"I'm not leaving."

"Really?"

She nodded.

"Impressive."

"What?"

"She was all over you. And you're here with me. You have some kind of willpower."

"Nah, been there done that," she said with a fake leer as she slid into the seat next to Melanie. Then she smiled genuinely. "She's got a girlfriend." She looked at the crowd of women around them and didn't see a single one worth turning her attention away from Melanie. "But what about you? See anything that interests you?"

"I'm not ready."

She shrugged. "When you are, let me know. I'll fix you up with someone."

"No way. All your friends are cops. When I do start dating again, I won't be seeing any police officers."

She pressed her lips together tightly and nodded, trying not to take the bitter edge of Melanie's tone personally. Given the demise of her relationship, Melanie's reluctance to date another police officer didn't surprise her. "It's settled then. Tonight is about having fun, not hooking up."

"I'll drink to that." Melanie lifted her beer bottle and touched the neck of it against hers.

So they drank. Melanie already knew most of the other girls they were meeting out, Evelyn's co-workers. A couple of them, having heard about Kendall's breakup and trying to be friendly, bought a few rounds. And Jennifer even rejoined them and sent her an apologetic smile, presumably for her behavior on the dance floor. Evelyn nodded in return and gestured toward an empty seat at their table.

After another beer, she switched to water. This was Melanie's night to cut loose, and she wanted to be a sober, safe ride for her. While she enjoyed her tapering buzz, she watched Melanie chat with the others. She couldn't remember having been in a social situation like this with just Melanie. When Kendall was around, her outgoing nature commanded more attention, and Melanie had always been in the background, seemingly content with her role as Kendall's loving partner.

But tonight, she watched as Melanie's warmth charmed several of the women who had probably barely noticed her before. When Melanie was ready, she wouldn't have any problem finding someone new to date—cop or no cop.

❖

"We're home," Evelyn said as she pulled into a spot in front of Melanie's apartment building.

"Your home?" Melanie mumbled, her words slurred into each other.

"No, yours." When Melanie didn't move, Evelyn got out and circled the car. She opened Melanie's door and caught her as she leaned too far out and nearly lost her balance. She wedged her shoulder under Melanie's arm and circled her waist tightly.

Melanie cooperated, wrapping her arm around Evelyn's shoulders. As they headed toward the apartment, Melanie rested against her and they walked in stride together. Maneuvering to Melanie's door was easier than she would have thought.

"Got your keys?"

"In my purse," Melanie answered, but she made no move to retrieve them.

Evelyn shifted until she could slip Melanie's purse off her shoulder, then dug through it until she found her keys. The second one she tried allowed the knob to turn.

"Are you coming in?" Melanie said, her voice husky from the alcohol and the smoke in the bar.

As Melanie draped against Evelyn, her fingers rested against Evelyn's neck, toying with the collar of her shirt. Her body reacted to Melanie's suggestive tone and her soft touch, but she mentally chastised herself. Melanie was drunk. Though it wasn't fair that she should have to turn down two beautiful women in one night, she refused to give permission to her reckless libido. Melanie was definitely off-limits, so she'd already passed up her only viable chance to get laid tonight. But she'd rather be here with Melanie than anywhere else.

"Let's get you inside." She shoved the door open with her foot.

Melanie stumbled in ahead of her, leaving her keys hanging in the doorknob. Evelyn pulled them out and closed the door behind her. She would just make sure Melanie was okay. Then she'd leave.

By the time she dropped Melanie's purse and keys on the hall table, Melanie was well into the apartment. She found her in the bedroom, shoving pale-green and lavender decorative pillows from the bed onto the floor.

"I can't sleep in this sweater." Melanie pulled it over her head, then reached behind her and flicked open her bra. When she pulled it off and tossed it onto the dresser, Evelyn forced herself to turn away.

"Okay." She drew the word out, trying to keep the image of Melanie's full breasts from imprinting itself in her mind. She jerked open the nearest dresser drawer, muttering to herself, "T-shirts. Where are the T-shirts?"

"Second drawer down," Melanie answered.

She grabbed the first one she saw, spun back around, and froze. Melanie stood in the middle of the room, making no effort to cover herself. Only the tan lines on her biceps and her rosy nipples broke up the creamy skin of her torso. When Melanie started working at the fly of her jeans, Evelyn threw the shirt at her on her way out of the bedroom. "I—uh—I'll give you some privacy."

As she wandered through the apartment, giving Melanie time to change, she noticed things missing. Picture frames, a lamp, Kendall's favorite chair, all things that now resided in Kendall's new condo. Their absence left deep shadows.

Over time, Melanie would probably bring in new things to fill those spaces, or maybe when the lease expired, she'd move someplace else entirely. Tonight, Melanie and Kendall had both taken steps toward adapting to their new lives.

Kendall's social nature helped her cope. She was always the first one to chat up the new rookies on their shift. And her return to dating hadn't surprised Evelyn anymore than Melanie's reluctance to do so. Melanie needed time to think, to reflect, and—she would say—to process.

Evelyn sat down on the sofa and swept a hand over the cool leather. Countless nights, she'd hung out here with the two of them. She hadn't expected the adjustment to be so polarizing for her. Initially, she'd rushed to defend Kendall because she'd seemed so broken right after the breakup, but tonight she'd seen vulnerability in Melanie as well.

She'd been concentrating so much on each of her friends that she hadn't given much thought to how the change would affect her. She hadn't considered the void their former relationship left in her life. Maybe Melanie and Kendall's breakup had been more stressful for her than she thought. Perhaps that's why she'd had a lapse back there in the bedroom.

For a moment, when Melanie had taken off her sweater, she'd seen Melanie as a woman—not as Kendall's girl. And when Melanie reached for the fly of her jeans, the jolt of arousal that shot through her had been dulled only by the wave of guilt that followed. She'd always thought Melanie was beautiful, and maybe she'd even had a bit of a crush on her. Who wouldn't? Melanie was amazing.

But Kendall was like a sister. By extension, shouldn't the sledgehammer of arousal Melanie's breasts inspired feel incestuous?

She shook her head. Nothing had happened that she needed to feel guilty about. Stress and the unfamiliar feeling of socializing with Melanie alone had caused all this craziness in her head.

She sighed. She'd go tuck Melanie in, then head home. Certainly, she'd feel more able to cope once she'd gotten some rest. She went back down the hall. The bedroom door was open a crack and she paused outside, listening for sounds from within. She knocked softly and didn't hear a response, so she eased the door open.

"Melanie," she said quietly.

Melanie came out of the bathroom wearing the T-shirt Evelyn had tossed at her. Beneath the hem, her firm thighs were bare. Melanie yanked back the comforter and flopped onto the bed.

"Okay, it's bedtime." She eased the sheet over Melanie. "Sweet dreams, I'll call you tomorrow." When she turned to leave, Melanie rolled over and caught her hand.

"Stay."

"Mel—"

"Please." When Melanie tilted her face, the bedside lamp illuminated the loneliness in her eyes.

She sighed, climbed onto the bed next to her, and stretched out on her back. She'd stay until Melanie fell asleep.

"Thank you," Melanie whispered, as Evelyn switched off the lamp.

Melanie moved closer and rested her head on her shoulder. In the darkness, she pretended not to notice that Melanie's arm lay across her stomach.

❖

Evelyn slammed her hand down on the nightstand, but the blaring sound of her alarm clock didn't stop, and her fingers encountered only smooth wood. She opened her eyes and stared across the surface of the nightstand at Melanie's clock, several inches past where hers should have been sitting. She stretched and turned off the alarm. Over her shoulder, Melanie still slept soundly.

She rolled to her back and shoved a hand through the front of her hair. She'd slept in her clothes, and the sheet was twisted and tangled around her waist. She slowly worked herself free, trying not to wake Melanie.

"Oh, hell," she groaned. She had to meet Kendall in thirty minutes and pretend she hadn't slept next to her ex all night.

Melanie murmured and shoved her arm farther under her pillow. A strand of hair fell across her face and Evelyn gently swept it back with one finger. She didn't want to hurriedly throw her clothes on and scramble off to breakfast. She wanted to stay.

The guilt that followed in the wake of that thought compelled her off the bed—quickly. She strode across the room and studied herself in the mirror, finger-combing her unruly hair. Her clothes were a lost cause, but she kept an extra pair of jeans and T-shirt in a backpack in her car. She never knew when she might draw a special assignment with vice that required civilian clothes.

"Hey," Melanie said from behind her, her voice rough with sleep and last night's activities. "You stayed."

"Yeah. I did."

Melanie propped herself up on her elbow and rubbed her eyes. "Thank you. I'm sorry you had to babysit me last night."

She sat on the edge of the bed. "Please, I had a good time. How are you feeling this morning?"

Melanie winced. "Uh, hung over. You?"

"I'm good." She'd stopped drinking well before she'd have to worry about a hangover. "I'm sorry, I have to go."

"Are you sure? I could make you breakfast."

Evelyn laughed, a short bark born mostly of the awkwardness of the situation. "I'm—um, supposed to be meeting Kendall in twenty minutes."

"Post-date breakfast?"

Shit.

"You didn't have a date last night."

She stood quickly, searching for her shoes. Before she could string together an explanation that wouldn't be a lie, Melanie spoke again, quietly.

"Oh. I see." Melanie's expression filled with pain and she wanted to erase it.

"Mel, I—"

"Please, don't." Melanie held a hand up. "I don't want to make you feel you have to lie to save my feelings."

She sighed and sank back onto the bed. Melanie scooted up until she leaned on the headboard. She let her head fall back against the wood with a dull thud, but she didn't speak. Evelyn remained silent as well, not sure what to say—what Melanie would want to hear right now. So she covered Melanie's hand with her own, and when Melanie laced their fingers together, she held on, not caring that she'd be late.

"I'm trying not to ask you when she started dating again," Melanie said after several minutes of silence.

"Last night was the first."

"I guess four months is long enough."

"Are you having second thoughts?"

"No. I can't say I don't miss her at times, but when you spend so many years with someone..."

She nodded.

"The separation was the right thing to do. But I hadn't thought about how I'd feel to hear she was going out with other people."

Melanie smiled, but the usual spark didn't light her eyes. "It's partly ego, I guess. I'd like to think I'm hard to get over."

"You were. But I get it. You don't want her to be miserable but not necessarily happy either." She squeezed Melanie's hand.

"Exactly." Melanie squeezed back, then released her. "Go. You'll never make it there in twenty minutes."

"You okay?"

"I'm fine. Thanks for making me go last night." Melanie slid out of bed and followed her to the front door. "And for seeing that I got home safely. I needed to let loose, and knowing I could trust you to take care of me really helped."

She stopped in the doorway. "I'll call you later?"

"Absolutely."

Evelyn tightened her hand on the door casing. Melanie was beautiful, sitting there in her soft T-shirt with her sandy hair falling around her face in sleep-mussed waves.

"I uh—better go. Kendall will be waiting." She heard the tremor in her voice and forced herself to say Kendall's name aloud, to remind herself who Melanie was.

CHAPTER EIGHT

G ood morning."
"Sorry I'm late." Evelyn slid into the booth across from Kendall and wrapped her hands around the warm porcelain mug in front of her, glad that the trend toward disposable cups with plastic lids hadn't reached their favorite coffee shop. The neighborhood place, little more than a long Formica counter and a few booths, had survived the influx of gourmet chain shops, so far.

"I ordered coffee, but I didn't know what you wanted to eat."

Evelyn nodded, and as if on cue the server approached. She opened the menu and ordered the first thing she saw.

"Steak and eggs, huh? Are you hungry?" Kendall asked.

"Apparently." Her usual breakfast of a hard-boiled egg and wheat toast would be like an appetizer compared to what she'd just asked for. "How was the date?" She jumped right in, hoping to find normalcy in conversation.

"Not bad. She seemed nice and down-to-earth."

"Are you going to see her again?"

"Maybe."

"That doesn't sound very promising."

"It's not meant to be. I'm definitely not looking for anything serious. And I was pretty up-front about that, so I don't think she expects any more from this than I do. "

"That's understandable, and good that you were honest about it. Was she cute?"

Kendall smiled. "Yeah, she was. And easy to talk to."

"Did you kiss her?"

Kendall didn't answer, but the rush of pink up her neck revealed the truth.

"So, how was it?" She felt awkward asking, having always been on the other side of the inquisition.

"It was—strange. I haven't kissed anyone but Melanie in— hell, I'm tired of thinking about Melanie. I want to talk about something else."

When the server set a large plate of food in front of her, Evelyn decided to dig in and enjoy the indulgence. Her stomach growled in response to the enticing aroma of the steak, eggs, and mound of hash browns heaped on her plate. She shook steak sauce over the entire plate and picked up her fork.

Kendall narrowed her eyes. "You look like you slept in those clothes. Or maybe they spent the night on the floor at some hottie's house."

"What? No." She glanced down. Her jeans were clean and the T-shirt was pretty wrinkled from being folded, but it was passable.

"So you slept in your own bed last night, and you still look like that?"

"Hey."

"Seriously? You just dragged details from me and you're going to hold out on me now."

She shrugged. "There's nothing to tell. I met Jennifer and some of the other girls out at the bar. I overslept this morning and just threw on some clothes to meet you." Technically, that was true, but she had more to tell in her effort to remain fair and neutral. "Melanie came out for a few drinks, too."

Kendall jerked her eyes up from her plate. "Yeah?" She seemed to press the stilted word through thinned lips.

"I ran into her when I took a break-in report for one of her clients. So I talked her into going out with us."

"Good. I'm glad." Kendall rolled her shoulders, as if forcing herself to relax.

"You are?"

"Sure. She's probably been overworked these past few months and needed to unwind. You looked after her, right? You didn't let anyone hit on her?"

"No one bothered her."

"Yes." Kendall nodded, her mood obviously shifting. "This is actually a good idea. She gets to go out and you take care of her."

"She can take care of herself." She wouldn't let Kendall make her responsible for Melanie's social life.

"I know. She's a smart girl. But you've been out there, Ev. You know what some of those women in the bar are like. I hate to think of her with one of them."

She recalled how Jennifer had come on to her and didn't want Melanie dealing with such aggression either. But given the direction of her thoughts last night, could she truly separate herself from the lecherous women that concerned Kendall?

"Hell, I hate just as much to think of her with someone nice and settled and sane, too."

"I don't think you can win on this one. You're not going to like whoever she dates, and she won't like who you see. That's part of breaking up, right?" She sopped up steak sauce with the last bit of her toast and shoved it in her mouth.

Kendall nodded. "So I'll just keep going out on dates until it starts to feel okay again."

"Yep. And if you need anything, I'm here for you, buddy." *Assuming I can figure out how to stop lusting after your ex.* When the server laid the bill on the table, she picked it up. "Starting with breakfast." She pulled out her wallet and counted out enough cash to cover the total and a generous tip.

Melanie shook two aspirin into her hand, then downed them with a large swallow of orange juice. Hopefully, the pounding in her head would ease soon so she could peel herself off the couch and get some much-needed housework done. The headache and a dry mouth were apparently the only repercussions for her over-indulgence the previous night. She hadn't been drunk in years, and while she didn't recommend it as a means for solving problems, she didn't regret it either. She hadn't set out with that goal, but the more she relaxed and enjoyed the night out with Evelyn and her friends, the easier the drinks went down.

Maybe after the stress of the breakup, she deserved one night of letting loose, and today she'd return to reality. She had already planned to take today off work in order to catch up at home. While she waited for the aspirin to kick in, she settled on the end of the couch and picked up a notepad and pen from the coffee table and began making a to-do list.

At the end of her list she made a note to call her mother and schedule lunch one day next week. Last year, she never would have thought she'd have to vie for a spot on her mother's busy social calendar, but now she welcomed making the call.

Her father had passed away three years ago after a prolonged illness. And her mother, suddenly without the distraction of caring for him, had tumbled into depression. She wouldn't leave the house unless Melanie or her sister dragged her out. Her health began to decline, until Melanie worried she might be burying her soon as well.

Her mother's wake-up call had come when one of her friends lost her husband as well. She'd set aside her own grief to help her friend cope. They began going to senior outings together. Amazingly, when seeing someone else in the same situation she'd been in, her mother could so clearly find the solution. Six months ago, she'd said she was ready to sell the house and get an apartment in a senior community. Before long, she was involved in a regular schedule of activities and outings with other residents.

Melanie was happy that her mother remained active and busy, but lately she'd been missing both her and her father. Since her breakup with Kendall, she'd been incredibly nostalgic, desperately recalling happy memories from her childhood to help alleviate her own loneliness.

At times, she and Kendall had talked about having a child, both saying they wanted to start a family "someday." And though they hadn't taken definitive steps in that direction, she had believed it would eventually happen. At thirty-three, she had plenty of time before panic was warranted, but the years had a way of slipping away, as they had done while she and Kendall were together. And by the time she met someone new, reached the "planning for the future" stage, and got ready to have a child, several more years would likely pass.

Sighing, she pushed off the couch, determined to distract herself with activity. She strode to the bedroom, grabbed an armload of clothes she'd sorted from the hamper, then dumped them in the washer. While waiting for the laundry, she decided to get to work cleaning the kitchen. Once she started, she found an uncharacteristic need to scrub every surface and rearrange the items on her countertop. Did the spice rack look better in the corner, or should it be closer to the stove for convenience? Should she keep the bright-green tea kettle even though she rarely made tea, just because she liked the pop of color it added to the sleek black lines of her stovetop?

By the time she'd emptied the jumbled mess her Tupperware cabinet had become, she'd finally driven her concerns about the future out of her mind. Organizing the many containers and their lids of varying sizes became her main goal. This time, she vowed she would keep them orderly, even though she knew the promise was hollow. In a few months, she would once again be sitting on her freshly cleaned kitchen floor surrounded by more plastic food storage than one person ever needed.

After she finished her chores, she called her mother, who surprisingly was free for dinner. Neither of them felt like cooking, so they settled on a restaurant and she offered to drive. She puttered around the house a bit more, then showered and changed before heading to her mother's apartment.

She'd just pulled into a spot in front of the building when her mother came out of the breezeway walking with another woman. As they reached the edge of the sidewalk, her mother took the other woman's arm, guided her across an expanse of grass, and helped her settle onto a wood-framed swing.

After a few more words, her mother straightened and headed for her truck. Melanie had often marveled at how many years her father's illness had seemed to steal from her mother. The lines on her face had deepened, and she'd stopped coloring her hair, letting the artificial light-brown give way to gray. But living here might have restored some of that time. She seemed better able to balance helping some of the older residents with household chores or errands without losing herself in the process. Here, she flourished by being needed, while cultivating her own interests as well.

"How've you been, dear?" her mother asked as she climbed into the truck. She leaned across the wide center console and patted Melanie's hand. Her eyebrows peaked in concern and she seemed to be searching Melanie's face for signs of wear.

"Fine." Melanie drew her hand back. Then, to avoid offending her mother, she acted as if she'd needed to do so in order to shift.

How much time had to pass before people stopped looking at her with the sympathy she didn't feel she deserved? She hadn't been dumped; she'd been the one to end it. She shouldn't get sympathy for pain that basically had resulted from her own decisions, should she?

"Are you getting by okay?"

"How do you mean?"

"Without Kendall's income?"

"Yes, Mom." Melanie nodded, not surprised that her mother's initial concern was financial. For over forty years, her mother had been the homemaker in a rather old-fashioned marriage. Her father's insurance had left her comfortably taken care of, but not extravagantly so. Never having worried about money issues, after his death, she had thrown herself into learning every aspect of her financial situation. Consequently, she'd also become more concerned with how well Melanie and her sister planned for their futures.

"Perhaps when your lease is up, you'll want to consider moving to a smaller apartment."

"Mom, I'm fine. I don't need to move." She liked the open floor plan of her apartment and had no desire to confine herself to a more cramped space. In fact, since Kendall had taken her workout equipment from the third bedroom, she had begun to think about fixing it up as a guest room so the futon in the office could stop doing double duty.

"You could get a little place on your sister's side of town. I'm sure she would like to see you more often."

"We see each other plenty. Besides, she's never home either." As a regional sales manager, her sister traveled at least two weeks out of every month. Her husband spent nearly as much time on the road, but, if fifteen years of marriage was any indication, it worked for them.

"Are you dating again, yet?"

"No."

"I heard Mr. Rubio's daughter is single again. Would you like me to get her number?"

Melanie smiled. Her mother had adjusted well to her coming out while in her twenties. She'd simply made the transition from trying to find her a nice young man to a young woman. She had earned a reprieve during her years with Kendall but apparently now was once again fair game. Mr. Rubio from down the hall was the only other resident in her mother's building who admitted to having a gay child.

"What? She's running the family dry-cleaning business. You could do worse."

"I'm sure she's lovely. Although Mr. Rubio is in his eighties, so unless he had her late in life, she's probably in her sixties."

"I hear about women having sugar daddies. Can't it be the same for gay women?"

"I don't want to be the kept woman of a dry cleaner, Mom." Melanie struggled to keep the laughter out of her voice.

"Now you're making fun of me." Her mom's smile suggested that she'd been teasing.

"I'm not. Let's just put the dry cleaner on the back burner for now. If I change my mind about her, I'll let you know. I'm really not thinking about dating right now." She steered her truck into the parking lot of the restaurant and chose a spot near the door.

"It's natural for you to miss Kendall. But working all the time isn't good for you."

"I know," she replied automatically, and when her mother's expression changed to disbelief, she went on. "I did miss Kendall a lot, at first. I still do, often. But she's not what's stopped me from dating. I haven't been alone in a long time. Now that I am, I don't feel an overwhelming urge to throw myself into a new dynamic with another person." Searching for the right words, she turned in her seat and met her mother's eyes. "I can hardly remember the last time I made a decision without thinking about how it impacted someone else. I want to do that now. I want to do things that make me happy, perhaps selfishly, but I think it's my right."

"What if Miss Wonderful comes along while you're figuring yourself out?"

She sighed. "If I promise that, if someone comes along that I can't live without, I will give her a chance, can we stop talking about this and go inside and eat? I'm starving."

"I suppose that's the best I'm going to get out of you, so, okay."

She smiled, knowing that they hadn't truly dropped the subject. But as they walked inside, her mother began talking about her upcoming bus trip to the Mississippi casinos. Maybe Melanie would give her a twenty and ask her to play the slots for her.

Chapter Nine

J arvis, Fisher, you're on enforcement tonight," Sergeant
Stahlman said. "Get with the motors supervisor and see
where they want to concentrate."

Kendall managed to keep her groan inside. Some officers
jockeyed for the special assignment, welcoming the chance to
escape answering calls and dealing with the public. But she didn't
like the constant traffic stops and writing tickets for moving
violations. She didn't mind working with the motorcycle officers;
they were a cool bunch of guys. But she'd much rather get a night
with the crime-suppression unit. At least they got to look for guns
and drugs.

Across the table, Evelyn slouched in one of the yellow, hard-
plastic chairs that had been there longer than both of them. She
twirled a pen between her fingers and, when she met Kendall's
eyes, she winked. Evelyn didn't share her disdain for an evening
of enforcement. Being in a uniform made Evelyn happy, no matter
what task she was given.

Sergeant Stahlman finished his briefing and excused the shift
to hit the streets. She and Evelyn headed for the parking lot. A
group of guys clustered around a row of white Harley-Davidson
motorcycles parked next to the curb. They all had the same
swagger, walking like they'd just spent hours in the saddle. They
resembled a motorcycle gang, dressed alike in Ray-Bans and navy

uniforms, their pants tucked into calf-high boots meant to keep errant hems away from moving parts.

"All right, guys. What are we getting into tonight?" Evelyn asked as they approached the group.

"Seems we've got a problem with speeding on our interstates," one of them said.

"Surely not," Kendall shot back sarcastically.

"Let's ride, fellas," the supervisor, a seasoned sergeant who had spent most of his tenure in motors, called as he strode across the parking lot. When he reached the group, he handed Evelyn and Kendall each a hard-plastic case. "Lidar guns. You hit 'em, we'll chase 'em."

"Wonderful," Kendall muttered as she turned and slid into her car. Now she could look forward to an evening of sitting stationary on the side of the interstate playing with a laser speed gun.

Thirty minutes later, she'd settled into her assigned spot on the eastbound side of Interstate 40 with half the motor group, calibrating her equipment and listening to the chatter on the radio from Evelyn and the guys stationed on a stretch on the westbound side.

"All set," she said into her radio once she had the Lidar ready to go. She rolled down her window and rested the speed gun on the door sill, glad she'd at least be able to enjoy the pleasant evening. Last month, she'd been freezing her butt off on a similar assignment.

Her car was situated just after a sweeping curve, safely well off the shoulder and in a blind spot for the approaching drivers. Before long, she'd clocked three cars at more than ten over the posted limit and called out the descriptions to the motor officers waiting a quarter of a mile up the road.

A subtle chime indicated a new text message on her cell, and, without looking at the display, she punched the button to retrieve it.

"Bored yet?" Evelyn asked.

"Yep. Gonna be a long night." She smiled to herself. She could always count on Evelyn to know when she needed a distraction. In fact, she didn't know what she would have done without Evelyn these past few months.

When Evelyn told her about talking Melanie into going to the bar last weekend, she realized that she'd already mentally staked ownership of Evelyn's friendship. She'd essentially lumped Evelyn into the pile that fell on her side as she and Melanie divided up their things. Realizing that Evelyn had contact with Melanie so recently had thrown her a bit.

Working out tonight?

Evelyn's text interrupted her thoughts and made her feel guilty for her possessiveness. She needed to respect Evelyn's obvious desire to stay friends with both of them. Should she have more right to her loyalty because they worked together? Logically, she knew the answer was no, but given the trust fellow police officers often placed in each other, the lines between personal loyalty and professional blurred.

Not tonight. I have a date.

Her days had finally begun to fall into a routine that didn't include brooding over Melanie. She'd started working out seriously again, sometimes meeting up with Jeb Riggs or Evelyn and hitting the weights after their shift. But she'd also been corresponding with several of the women from the dating Web site, looking for enough common interest to meet in real life.

Same one from last weekend?

Nope. New one.

Two in one week?

Just trying to be a player like you.

Kendall liked to tease her. She glanced down at her display as a silver sedan flew around the curve—seventy-seven miles per hour was near-suicidal rounding that bend. She keyed her radio and called out the description and what she could catch of the tag as the car cut between two others to get in the far left lane.

Ha. Just a façade. Costs less if I don't actually have to wine and dine anyone.

She read the snarky tone in Evelyn's words, but there was truth behind them. As much as she and Melanie teased her, Evelyn had clearly always wanted something permanent. Even when Evelyn acted like she didn't mind being single, Kendall could practically feel her comparing every budding relationship with what she thought they had, which was partly why she had never confessed that they were having problems.

Inside, she liked being that ideal for someone else. If she let Evelyn believe that they had it all, maybe someday she'd be able to convince Melanie as well. In the end, the only person she'd fooled into believing she was happy was herself.

❖

Saturday afternoon, Evelyn drove through the new retail area looking for a treasured parking spot. Though the multi-use neighborhood had already been open for a year, she had only been there a handful of times and now she remembered why. Clustering clothing boutiques, restaurants, a movie theater, and various other shops made good business sense, but the ensuing weekend crowds kept her from frequenting the area.

After finally nabbing a spot at the far end of a lot, she worked her way back toward the center of the neighborhood. Here, the designers had added a town-square feel, with shop fronts facing an open courtyard that featured a well-manicured lawn, stone benches, and a fountain play area for the kids. This afternoon, the couples pushing strollers and kids carrying treats from the ice-cream shop gave the streets the intended small-town atmosphere. Not bad for a suburb of a fairly large city, she had to admit. However, she knew from the crime statistics that the illusion of security was just that.

In the center of the square, she found Melanie sitting on a bench watching people walk by. After their night out last weekend, she had called Melanie every day. Her initial motivation, to remain a good friend, had evolved into a genuine desire to talk to Melanie. Their conversations exceeded her original expectation that they would exchange pleasantries and ring off, but instead they'd wandered into deeper conversations and she found she didn't want to hang up the phone.

She slid onto the bench, bumping her shoulder against Melanie's. "Hi there."

Melanie smiled. "Hey."

"Do you want to skip the movie and people watch?" She would much rather stay out here and talk to Melanie than sit silently next to her in a theater pretending to care about the action playing out on-screen.

"Yeah?"

"Sure. I can definitely wait for this one to come out on Redbox. I'd rather see it at home anyway."

"Because you have the attention span of a three-year-old when it comes to movies, and at home you can pause it for snack and bathroom breaks?"

"Exactly." She smiled.

"Too bad. Because I really want to see this one." Melanie stood, then took her hand and pulled her to her feet. As they walked toward the theater, Melanie released her.

"I'm glad you called," she said. Her fingers tingled and she slid her hand in her pocket, clenching and relaxing her fist a couple of times.

"Were you busy today?"

"No. I spent the morning cleaning the house and doing laundry, nothing exciting. This is a welcome change."

"Is this okay? I didn't know if you'd be seeing the movie with Kendall or not."

They'd all gone together to see the previous two thrillers in the series. "We haven't made any plans to."

"I wasn't sure—it's still weird how we all three fit now, isn't it?"

"We don't all three fit anymore, I suppose. But I want you both in my life. You invited me, I didn't have plans, so I accepted. Simple."

"And if Kendall asks you to see it with her?"

"If it's good enough, I might go again. Otherwise, I'll tell her I've seen it. I don't intend to keep my friendship with you from her."

"I know. It doesn't make sense, but—spending time with you feels a little like sneaking around."

Evelyn didn't offer an argument or explanation. She felt it, too. When she'd gotten Melanie's call, she'd been excited to see her, followed immediately by a bit of guilt. But when Melanie hooked her arm into the crook of her elbow, all she felt was happy.

"Maybe it's just me, I—"

"No." As they reached the doors, she guided Melanie to the side, out of the way of the other patrons going in. "It's not just you." She wasn't sure if Melanie knew what she was confessing to.

"It's Kendall, isn't it?"

"What?"

"We feel strange hanging out without Kendall."

"Um—sure." Obviously, they weren't exactly on the same page. She hadn't wished once that Kendall was with them.

"Let's just forget all this awkwardness and go enjoy the movie."

"Absolutely." She covered Melanie's hand and pressed it to her arm, absorbing the warmth of her skin.

❖

"That was by far the best of the series. The special effects were amazing," Evelyn said as they passed through the lobby of the theater.

"I agree." When they stepped outside, Melanie paused while her eyes adjusted to the sunlight. She always found it a bit disorienting to exit a darkened theater and find that it was still daylight outside.

Once in the open air, surrounded by the crowd of people leaving with them, she missed the intimate shadows of the theater. She'd sat next to Evelyn, their forearms touching on the armrest between them, captivated by the way the flickering light from the screen played across Evelyn's expressive features. As the movie rolled, she spent nearly as much time sneaking glances at Evelyn's reactions to the film as she did actually watching the screen. When Evelyn caught her looking and smiled, her stomach lurched in an entirely new and disconcerting way.

What the hell had that been all about? Yes, Evelyn was a beautiful woman, but she had never experienced such awareness of her. First, they'd had that odd moment before they went inside when she wondered if she'd missed a part of their conversation. But the serious look in Evelyn's eyes had dissolved before she could figure out what it meant. Now here she was thinking about how the amber cast of a particular scene in the film had saturated Evelyn's features in a rich glow that had warmed her from the inside.

"Well, I'm over here." Evelyn pointed down the street opposite from where Melanie had parked.

"I didn't have lunch, yet," Melanie blurted, not wanting to part. A week ago, she would have said her reluctance centered on avoiding her empty apartment, but today, she genuinely desired Evelyn's company.

"You mean other than the tub of popcorn we polished off in the movie?"

"Popcorn isn't lunch. Do you want to get something?"

"Sure." Evelyn gestured to a restaurant on the next block. "Are you in the mood for Mexican?"

"Absolutely."

The little place was packed, but as soon as Melanie caught the spicy aromas inside, she decided the wait would be worth it. When they finally placed their orders, she followed the cantina employee down the cafeteria-style line, requesting nearly every available condiment.

"Let's eat outside," Evelyn said after she'd paid for both of their meals. She protested but Evelyn refused to take money for her share.

She picked up her tray and followed Evelyn onto the patio, where they settled at one of the round tables under a brightly colored umbrella. The afternoon sun reached into the cool shade and caressed her bare arm. Perhaps that would explain the warmth crawling up her neck. It was certainly more plausible than attributing it to the sweet smile on Evelyn's face.

"Have you been busy at work?" Evelyn asked as they dug into their over-stuffed burritos.

She nodded. "During the winter we do mostly maintenance on existing accounts. But beginning a couple of weeks ago and through summer to fall, we'll be extremely busy. At least I hope so."

"You need to take the work when you can get it, I guess."

"Generally, yes. But I'm finally at the point where I can leave the heavy lifting to somebody else." Lucas was more than capable of taking the reins, and now, after several months of self-inflicted seventy-plus hour weeks, she was finally ready for a break. "In fact, I've taken this entire weekend off."

"Really? Do you have any exciting plans? Other than this, of course."

"Some reorganizing, shopping, and plenty of relaxation." Melanie couldn't help but smile at the double meaning of her words. She'd awakened this morning with the need to reclaim her home. Two hours and a trip to the furniture store later, she'd secured a modern bedroom set for the spare room and scheduled delivery for the following weekend. Tomorrow, she would pick out linens for the new bed, perhaps a thick comforter with bright geographical shapes, or maybe a dramatic black-and-white one.

"That's one way to go."

"What?" Lost in her decorating ideas, she nearly missed Evelyn's words.

"Relaxation. It's one option, but if you'd rather have a little excitement, I have another suggestion."

"I'm listening."

"I'm meeting the girls for paintball tomorrow. We're taking on a group of cocky paramedics from the fire department."

"I hate to ask, but Kendall—"

"She's working an extra job."

"Has she been doing that a lot lately?"

"Mel—"

"I know. I don't want to put you in the middle."

"Then don't," Evelyn said quickly, and sighed. "Yes. She's working a lot. Probably, partly for the same reason you have been and partly because she's got bills to pay and isn't used to being on her own."

"I'm sorry."

Evelyn remained silent for several tense seconds. Melanie met her eyes, resolutely trying to convey her sincerity. Her concern for Kendall was second nature, but she didn't want to make Evelyn uncomfortable in the process.

"If you want to know how she is, you should ask her. If you're in for paintball, we're meeting at nine." Evelyn's indifferent tone stung, as if she cared little whether she joined them or not. Before she could consider why that mattered, Evelyn changed the subject. "How is your mother?"

"I had lunch with her the other day. She's overly concerned with my love life, but otherwise, she's good."

Evelyn laughed. "She tried to fix you up with the dry cleaner, didn't she?"

"Yes."

"Damn. I thought she was saving her for me."

"I turned her down, so if you're still interested I'm sure I could arrange—"

"No, no. That's okay." Evelyn raised her hands as if warding someone off. "She's worried about you."

"Hopefully, I've convinced her that she doesn't need to be."

"She's your mother, it's her job." Evelyn covered her hand.

"Yeah, then what's your excuse?"

"My excuse?"

"For worrying."

"I care," Evelyn said without hesitation. Her fingers tightened around Melanie's.

"Well, don't worry. I've decided spinsterhood isn't totally unappealing. But I absolutely refuse to get a bunch of cats."

"Please, you're gorgeous, smart, and successful. It's against the laws of nature for you to be single."

"You think I'm gorgeous?"

"Yeah, me and every other lesbian you know."

Her laughter skidded to a halt in the back of her throat as she met Evelyn's eyes. Coupled with Evelyn's fingers now holding hers more tightly, the compliment felt incredibly personal.

"Do you really not know how beautiful you are?" Evelyn asked softly.

"I guess I just never thought about you seeing me that way." Heat sang through Melanie's body, flushing her skin with an astonishing awareness.

"Me either." In the shadow of their umbrella, Evelyn's eyes looked big, dark, and intense. Melanie knew the moment Evelyn realized that she'd revealed too much. Her gaze shifted away just as Melanie saw the fear. Then she released Melanie's hand and stuck her own under the table in her lap. "Besides just because we're friends doesn't mean I'm blind."

"Evelyn—"

"Hey, look, I'm just trying to help boost your ego a bit here. You're not going to be a spinster. When the time is right, you'll meet someone." She straightened in her chair, her posture matching her now-stilted tone.

"Yeah, maybe," Melanie said as the strange energy between them dissipated.

For the rest of the meal, their conversation didn't stray beyond the kind of safe small talk you might have with a casual friend. But she couldn't forget the soft feel of Evelyn's skin on hers. Over the years, they'd touched casually many times, and though she was aware of Evelyn's beauty, she couldn't remember having an errant thought about her. So why now did she miss the intimacy of moments ago?

❖

"Kendall?"

Kendall paused with a bag of Doritos poised over her shopping cart and turned at the voice from behind her.

"I thought that was you. I don't know if you remember me. Tiffany, Richard's cousin." She pushed her own cart down the chip aisle toward Kendall.

"Yeah, hi."

Tiffany swept her hand down her neck, drawing Kendall's eyes toward the dip in her V-neck T-shirt. "Richard told me about you and Melanie." Tiffany poked her lower lip out and scrunched her eyebrows in what she guessed was intended to be a sympathetic look. "How are you?"

"I'm okay."

"I know how tough it can be. Last year, I split up with my partner of twelve years."

"Wow. I'm sorry."

"It's okay. I'll always love her, just as I'm sure you will, too. But it's best that we're apart now."

Despite her words, Tiffany didn't sound convinced. Kendall wondered if Melanie had said something similar in the past few months. If she were being honest, she'd felt the end was inevitable long before Melanie had the guts to cut it off. "I'm sorry just the same."

"She was cheating on me. Anger carried me through most of the pain." Tiffany's voice remained calm, but her eyes reflected echoes of turmoil. Maybe Tiffany had some depth that Kendall hadn't picked up on before. "But it's gotten better." Tiffany laid a reassuring hand on Kendall's shoulder. "The saying's so clichéd, but time really does heal."

Kendall nodded and Tiffany squeezed her arm and then released her. "It was a bit rough in the beginning. But I'm recovering."

"Keeping busy?"

"Absolutely." She thought she sensed flirtation behind Tiffany's concern. "I'm working a lot but trying to have some fun, too." She threw out a line, giving Tiffany an opening if she wanted one.

"That's important. Everyone needs a little release now and then." Tiffany winked, driving a bus right through that opening. "Let me give you my number." She flipped open the purse in the top of her cart and extracted a business card. "My cell is on there. Call me, anytime."

As Tiffany walked away, Kendall admired the way her yoga pants hugged her tight ass. Depth or no depth, Tiffany might be worth a second look.

"Tiffany," she called. "Would you like to get some coffee some time?"

"Sure. When?" Tiffany smiled.

She glanced down at her groceries. "Right now?" Tiffany smiled and Kendall walked away from her cart, leaving it in the middle of the aisle.

Chapter Ten

We're going up against *them*?" Melanie stared at the five women clustered together near a water cooler inside the registration tent. Tall, broad-shouldered, and dressed completely in camouflage, they made an intimidating first impression. She doubted the pink bandana holding back her hair and matching T-shirt would inspire fear in her adversaries.

"Don't worry, they look scarier than they are. Besides, this game isn't about brawn."

One of the women lifted a black-and-silver gun with a U-shaped attachment on the top and sighted down the barrel. When she snapped her gum loudly, Melanie jumped.

"Come on, I'll introduce you." Evelyn laughed and, taking her hand, she led her to the group of women. "Hey, ladies, this is my friend, Melanie." One by one, she introduced their opponents, all paramedics or firefighters. Melanie had already met their three teammates, fellow officers, at the bar the other night.

One of the paramedics, Becca, blatantly raked her eyes over Melanie. As the tallest of the group and the only blonde, Becca stood out. "What's up? You guys bring a ringer?"

Melanie laughed. "Hardly."

"We'll see, won't we?" Becca smiled, a pleasant lifting of her full lips.

"Come on, Mel. Let's get you some gear." Evelyn grabbed her sleeve and guided her toward the equipment-rental office.

While Evelyn signed out their gear, Melanie studied the map of the play area, fifteen wooded acres with both natural and man-made hiding places, which was divided into several sectors for either private or public participation.

"We'll be in sector three, just our group. When we get out there, stay inside the purple markers or you'll wander into someone else's game."

"I don't think I'll be straying far from your side." She'd never be mistaken for adventurous, but for the chance to spend the day with Evelyn, she'd decided to venture outside her comfort zone. Now she just hoped she wasn't the first one eliminated. The occasional percussion of paintballs being fired in the woods echoed through the air. "Does it hurt?"

"Depends on where you take it." Evelyn looked up from the form in front of her and squeezed Melanie's shoulder. "Relax. A bruise is usually the worst of it. If it makes you feel any better, I promise I'll try to jump in front of the bullet for you."

She smiled. "I don't think that will be necessary. Just knowing you would do it is good enough for me."

"Sign here." Evelyn pushed the sheet of paper toward her and held out a pen.

"What exactly am I signing away here?"

"Your right to sue if you're injured."

"I thought you said a bruise was as bad as it gets. Why do I need to waive my legal rights for a bruise?"

"Actually, I said a bruise is *usually* the worst of it." She grinned as Melanie signed the form with a flourish.

"There. But if I sustain an injury, you have to take care of me."

"Done."

"I'm serious. And I'm not expecting just a ride home from the hospital here. I want the full pampering."

"Absolutely. Sponge baths and all," Evelyn said as Melanie passed the form back. The images her words evoked sent a tremor through Melanie's hand and the paper rattled. Melanie clamped down on it, hoping Evelyn hadn't noticed. But her teasing nod at the document and her next comment proved she did. "Do you want it in writing?"

Melanie smoothed out the wrinkles and handed over the form, then shoved Evelyn's shoulder. "No. What's next?"

"The fun stuff. Let's get you a gun." Evelyn's eyes sparkled with anticipation.

"For someone who carries a gun every day, you're surprisingly excited about having one today."

"I so rarely get to shoot at anyone with the other one," Evelyn said solemnly.

"I'd say that's a good thing." She didn't like to think about Evelyn in a situation dangerous enough to require her to use force.

Evelyn collected two guns and various other items from the teenager working in the equipment office and then handed half of it to her. She led Melanie to a picnic table in the corner of the registration tent where the rest of their team had already gathered.

After a stressful week at work, Evelyn had looked forward to today's match. Sergeant Stahlman had been on her ass to make more arrests. She already spent more time in court than half the officers on the shift, but he wasn't satisfied, or rather the higher-ups weren't. She didn't make the right type of arrests, he had argued. The brass wanted major drug busts, gang-bangers locked up, and guns off the street. She could bust her butt all shift answering dispatch calls, but no amount of domestic-violence collars or burglary suspects could impress those who mattered. Maybe those incidents weren't flashy, but it was all important police work as far as she was concerned.

Today, though, she could forget about all of that for a while and blow off some steam with her friends. Having Melanie along only made her day better. They'd fallen into the habit of talking on the phone each evening. She looked forward to six thirty, knowing Melanie would call her while she drove home from work. If she wasn't busy, she found a quiet spot, parked her patrol car behind a building somewhere, and stole a few minutes' conversation. If work kept her running all night, she settled for the occasional text sent hurriedly when she wasn't driving.

"Is all of this really necessary?" Melanie held out her mask and gestured toward the rest of the protective gear. She knew paintball wasn't Melanie's thing, but it was cute how she was willing to try and, once they got started, she might actually enjoy it.

"Absolutely. I wouldn't want anything happening to that pretty face." She moved closer and touched her thumb to Melanie's chin. Electricity crackled up her forearm. Her eyes locked with Melanie's, and there she found the same mix of attraction and confusion that swirled within her own body.

"Well, this isn't going to be a cute look." When Melanie smiled tightly, she let her arm drop and stepped back. She needed to figure out this new reaction she seemed to be having to Melanie, but she didn't want to make her uncomfortable in the process.

"Are we going to play or what?" Someone called from behind them.

Melanie smirked and slid the mask down over her face. Somehow, even in the camo-colored plastic and goggle-shaped eye shield, she looked good.

"You're ready," she said, tapping Melanie's shoulder.

"Ha. I may look ready, but I don't have a clue what I'm about to do."

"Let me show how this gun works. Then you just follow one of us and do what we do." She took Melanie's gun and ran through how to attach the CO_2 canister and the 200-round hopper. After she'd demonstrated disengaging the safety and firing, she handed the gun back.

"Got it," Melanie said, with more confidence in her voice than she demonstrated by the awkward way she handled the gun.

❖

Melanie crouched behind a tree, pressing her chest against the rough bark and listening intently for any unusual sound that might signify an approaching enemy. Unfortunately, so far she'd barely missed eliminating Evelyn when she accidentally fired her gun. Then later she'd nearly covered a feisty squirrel in paint when he'd rustled the leaves behind her too loudly.

Evelyn knelt behind her own tree several feet away. She gestured to their teammates on her other side, then turned and met Melanie's eyes. Despite the mask that covered most of Evelyn's face, her smile shone in her eyes. When Evelyn waved her hands in elaborate signals, Melanie had no idea what she intended to convey, but she smiled in response anyway. Evelyn raised her eyebrows as if asking for her understanding, and she shook her head. Evelyn repeated the signals, and this time she made out that she was supposed to dash toward a massive fallen tree trunk ten yards in front of them. After another set of sharp gestures, she could almost hear Evelyn saying that she would "cover" her.

She shouldered around the tree until she could see her target, and when Evelyn waved she started running. She cringed when she heard the pop of paintball fire nearby but didn't feel the expected impact. Sliding on her right hip, she bounced against the log, then pulled her gun up and swept the area for targets. After ensuring she wasn't in immediate danger, she glanced back over her shoulder at Evelyn.

Evelyn nodded then lifted her gun in a signal for Melanie to cover her. Evelyn pointed to the left and she swung her gun in that direction, scanning the trees. Though she was on alert, the flash of movement ahead surprised her. Her body humming with adrenaline, she hesitated for only a few seconds before squeezing off two rounds. Her ammo made contact with a pair of dull thuds, followed by a low groan. With only a slight rustling sound, Evelyn bumped her shoulder as she wedged against the tree.

"Good job," Evelyn whispered as Melanie's victim slumped away through the trees.

"One down," she said, grinning.

"Okay, get ready. We're going to move again." Evelyn peeked over their shelter. "There's a large boulder over there. It's a little farther away, so keep your head down and hustle."

They continued through the woods, alternating movements as they stalked their prey. Their teammates circled from the other side, and soon, they had the remaining three members of the opposition backed into a corner at the boundary of a neighboring sector. Their enemies mounted a final effort, attacking like kamikaze pilots on a suicide mission.

Melanie had to respect the fact that they went down fighting and even took out one of Evelyn's team in the process. Evelyn shot one of the other team members, and she tagged another. But while she mentally celebrated her success, two rounds splattered against her chest and one hit her upper arm. She spun around just as Evelyn fired quickly, eliminating their final enemy.

"You okay?" Evelyn grasped her shoulder.

She nodded. The initial sting of the shot had faded quickly. Though the burst of adrenaline had begun to wane, she still felt wired.

"Did you have fun?" Evelyn asked as they walked back through the trees.

"More than I thought I would." She'd begun by simply mimicking Evelyn's military-style movements but had soon found herself immersed in playing war. "That was a rush. I'm sorry if I slowed you down."

"Are you kidding? You did great. You eliminated one and distracted the other one long enough for me to get her."

Melanie laughed and swiped at the paint on her sleeve. "I'm so glad I could sacrifice myself for your victory. But what happened to jumping in front of a bullet for me?"

"I guess my reflexes were too slow for that."

As they reached the equipment tent, their other teammates approached and exchanged high-fives with Evelyn. Among the myriad of voices, she made out pieces of the conversation.

"They're already asking for a rematch."

"Oh, they want to get smoked again, huh?"

"Anytime, anyplace."

Wrapped up in watching Evelyn and her friends enjoy their victory, Melanie started when someone spoke from close behind her.

"Nice shooting out there." Becca wore splotches of Melanie's blue paint on the front of her shirt.

"Thanks. I didn't realize that was you. We all look the same in these masks. No hard feelings?"

"Of course not. A bunch of us usually go out for pizza and beer afterward. Would you like to join us?" Becca asked.

Melanie glanced at Evelyn, but she was engaged in conversation with one of the other girls. "I think I might," she said as she turned back to Becca. The casually offered invitation suggested that a group of the women would be along, but she sensed something more personal behind Becca's inquiry.

Becca's flirty smile confirmed her interest and Melanie smiled back hesitantly. It had been so damn long since she'd done this. For so many years, she'd stayed ensconced in her comfortable cocoon of coupledom, and now, whether she liked it or not, she had to emerge and date again. And Becca, with her wide smile, smooth tanned skin, and clear blue eyes, could be as good a candidate as any.

Evelyn's burst of laughter drew her attention. A few feet away, Evelyn clowned around with her friends, and Melanie enjoyed watching her unnoticed. Evelyn's paintball mask had pulled several strands of her dark hair from her ponytail, and the gentle breeze feathered them against her face. She brushed at them impatiently, finally catching them and shoving them behind her ear.

Evelyn caught her eyes, smiled, and waved her over. After getting the name and address of the restaurant from Becca, she moved to Evelyn's side. Evelyn held out her hands, her wide palms facing up, her long, slender fingers slightly bent. If she put her hands in Evelyn's would her skin be warm or cool? What would Evelyn think of the calluses that roughened her palms? *When did I start thinking so much about Evelyn's hands?*

"Melanie," Evelyn said. While she'd been daydreaming, Evelyn had apparently expected a response to something.

"Yeah?"

"You don't get to keep that stuff." Evelyn pointed at the mask and gun she still held.

"Oh, yeah, here." She shoved the equipment into Evelyn's waiting hands.

While Evelyn returned their gear, Melanie listened as the other women talked about work. The police officers complained about the workload, teasing the paramedics about sleeping away their days in the fire-station bunks. The paramedics countered that they had longer work shifts and dealt with more abuse from patients than the police.

"Nobody fights the girl with the gun," one of them insisted, "but they think they can talk to us any way they want to."

"Yeah, and the families are worse. They all think that being able to use WebMD is equivalent to medical training. Everyone is ready to call their attorney if we don't do what they think we should."

"Well, their taxes do pay our salary, you know," one of the police officers said, sarcasm heavy in her voice, and they all nodded in agreement, clearly having heard some version of this statement.

"Okay, ladies, let's not go down that path," Evelyn said as she rejoined them. "At least not until I've had a couple of beers." As the group headed for the parking lot, Evelyn spoke to Melanie. "The others are going out for pizza. Do you want to?"

"Yes. Becca already asked me."

"Oh." Evelyn glanced at Becca, her eyes darkening in an emotion Melanie didn't recognize.

"Is it okay if I go? Do you mind me tagging along?"

"Of course not. That's great."

She watched for a moment longer, trying to discern the change in Evelyn's mood, but she'd closed off any hint on the surface.

CHAPTER ELEVEN

Evelyn held the door open and waited until the rest of her friends entered before she followed them inside. They trailed through the tables dotting the front of the dining room and into an alcove to the left of the bar. By the time they all filed in, their server had pushed together two tables and the group began to settle in.

Becca slipped into the chair next to Melanie, and when she leaned closer to speak quietly to Melanie, jealousy churned in Evelyn's stomach. She jerked her eyes away and dropped into a seat diagonal from them.

Alisha, one of the other paramedics, sat down next to her and touched her shoulder. "Nice shooting today."

"Thanks."

"Yeah, I think I still have some of your paint behind my ear." She brushed back her straight, ebony hair. "Would you check for me?"

She smiled at Alisha's obvious ploy but didn't want to embarrass her, so she leaned in as expected and examined the pale skin of Alisha's neck.

"All clear," she said, inhaling Alisha's flowery scent before she sat back.

"Thank you." Alisha brushed her fingers over her forearm.

"No problem." Alisha's caress didn't elicit the tingle she'd experienced earlier when she touched Melanie.

Across the table, Melanie smiled at Becca and her stomach clenched. What was she feeling? Even as the question flashed through her brain, she recoiled against the answer. She could *not* be attracted to Melanie Cook. She had a gorgeous, interested woman sitting right next to her, so she had no business looking at Melanie. Besides, Melanie should be dating someone like Becca, who was smart, sexy, and, most importantly, not Kendall's best friend. But she couldn't keep her eyes from Melanie, and she apparently was so deluded that she imagined Melanie was looking at her, too.

When their eyes met for the third time in what seemed like a matter of minutes, she didn't think she'd imagined it. Could they really be sitting here sneaking glances at each other, despite getting attention from two perfectly nice, safe women?

Perhaps she felt protective of Melanie. She'd invited her along with this group and now felt obligated to watch out for her. She might be able to convince herself that was true, but just then Becca winked at Melanie and covered her hand on the table. She curled her fingers, letting her nails bite into her palm. She could talk in circles for as long as she wanted, but the fact was, she wanted to be the one holding Melanie's hand. And despite how this new development freaked her out, her damp palms and the nervous flutter in her stomach told her it was true. But that didn't mean she had to act on it, did it?

Vowing to keep things platonic, she forced herself to concentrate instead on having a pleasant evening with the other women at their table. She ordered another beer and listened to Alisha's story about the debacle of her brother's wedding the weekend before. Over the next round, she and one of the other officers swapped tales of their days in the academy so many years ago.

By the time they settled their checks two hours later, she tallied five beers and two shots of tequila on her tab. When she stood to pull on her coat, the force of those drinks rocked her. She should have paced herself a bit better. She'd have to leave her car and call a cab.

"You okay?" Melanie asked, seeming to suddenly appear beside her.

"Yeah," she mumbled. When she tried to move around the chairs pushed haphazardly away from their table, she stumbled, then quickly righted herself. Melanie placed a steadying hand on the inside of her elbow.

"I'll take you home."

"'S okay. Taxi." Her head swam and forming a sentence took too much effort.

"You took care of me when I was drunk—"

"Not drunk."

"So let me repay you." Melanie ignored her protest and steered her through the front door.

Becca touched Melanie's shoulder and jealousy punched Evelyn in the gut. She imagined grabbing Becca's hand and twisting her offending fingers. "Do you want to drive Evelyn's car and I'll follow you and bring you back to your truck?"

"No, thanks, Becca. She can retrieve her car tomorrow."

"At least let me help you get her into your truck." Becca tried to grasp Evelyn's other arm, but she jerked it free.

"I can walk just fine." She pulled free from both of them and sauntered over to Melanie's truck. "And stop talking about me like I can't hear you." When she heard the locks click, she opened the door and flung herself up into the passenger seat. Melanie lingered outside with Becca, and she closed the door quickly so she wouldn't have to hear their good-byes.

In the few minutes until Melanie got in the truck, she began to sober up. The edges remained blurred, but she regained her grasp on details and then quickly wished she hadn't. She'd like to be inebriated enough that she wouldn't notice the lean muscles in Melanie's forearm as she grasped the wheel or wonder if the worn denim covering her thighs felt as soft as it looked.

"Get a grip," she mumbled, realizing too late that she'd spoken aloud.

"What?" Melanie asked.

"Nothing."She slumped against the door, hoping Melanie would dismiss her words as drunken rambling.

She wanted to ask if Melanie was interested in Becca but didn't want to hear the answer. Though she was the one who'd been telling Melanie she would someday be ready again, she didn't want to know if Melanie had turned that corner. So instead, they rode in silence until they reached her neighborhood and parked in a spot in front of her condo.

"Thanks for the ride."

"No problem. And thank you for today. I had fun." Melanie turned toward her.

"Me, too." She wanted to escape the truck, but at the same time she longed to spend more time with Melanie. She searched for something to prolong their conversation and ended up nervously blurting, "I'm so glad we've been hanging out."

"Honestly, I didn't know if we would stay friends after the breakup."

"Why not?" She had a pretty good idea what the answer would be, but she really didn't want to talk about Kendall.

"I wasn't sure we had enough in common other than Kendall. But these past couple of weeks, it's been like getting to know you all over again—or in a different way."

"Yeah." *What a dope. "Yeah." Is that the most intelligent thing you can say right now?*

"I've really enjoyed spending time with you."

The genuine warmth in Melanie's words brought a flush to Evelyn's face. "Me, too."

"When I decided to end my relationship, I had mentally prepared to miss her, but I wasn't ready to let you go." The low timbre of Melanie's voice vibrated in the still cab of the truck, making the few feet between them not nearly enough space.

"Your voice has never done that before," she said, unable to stop the words before they slipped out. Why did she keep saying things in her outside voice?

"Done what?"

Turned me on so completely. Those words she somehow kept locked down. She stared at Melanie, her mind racing for some explanation for what she was feeling. "Uh—never mind."

"Ev?"

Jesus, one syllable. The shortening of her name wasn't new, but she'd never heard it caressed in quite that way.

"It's nothing."

Melanie slid closer and brushed her hand over Evelyn's shoulder. When Evelyn trembled, Melanie tugged a bit of her sleeve between her thumb and forefinger. "It's obviously something."

"I—I'm just tipsy."

"You said you weren't drunk."

She wasn't.

"You know you can talk to me about anything, don't you?"

She nodded. But she didn't mean it. The openness in Melanie's clear green eyes asked for a confession that she couldn't give. Guilt kept her from pouring out her growing feelings.

So instead she indulged in a moment more of gazing at Melanie's face and trying not to think about how soft her full lips looked. When Melanie shifted, a smear of bright-yellow paint peeked out from the neckline of her T-shirt.

"You have some paint—" She halted when she touched Melanie, just above her collarbone.

Melanie froze, too. She clutched Evelyn's shirt sleeve tighter, pulling the fabric against Evelyn's arm.

Her skin tingled where Evelyn touched her. Evelyn's molten-chocolate eyes were locked on her mouth, and her heart raced with anticipation and nerves as she realized Evelyn's intention. "Ev?"

"Yes?"

"Are you going to kiss me?"

"What? Shit." Evelyn pulled back, but the few added inches weren't enough space to clear the fog in Melanie's head. "I—ah, yeah. I—almost—"

Melanie closed her eyes and drew a steadying breath. She needed to think, to be rational, to remember how much this would hurt Kendall. The arousal building within her matched Evelyn's hot gaze. She wanted so badly to kiss Evelyn. Would her lips be soft and tender? Or firm and demanding? But Kendall's feelings, the chance that they might screw up their friendship, and the scent of alcohol on Evelyn's breath convinced her that she needed to find some self-control.

She was an affectionate person by nature. Over the years, she and Evelyn had shared numerous touches and embraces. But they had always been platonic; nothing had ever felt as intimate as this moment. "This is not a good idea." It was downright dangerous. She shoved a hand through her hair.

"You're right. But there's no need to beat ourselves up, either. It's just a kiss and we didn't even do it."

"There's nothing simple about you and me sharing a kiss." She sighed. She appreciated Evelyn's attempt to downplay the situation. But she couldn't reduce the swirl of emotions inside her right now so easily. "I'm tired of everything being so complicated."

"Maybe you and I are just emotional after everything that's changed lately. Let's not make what *almost* happened a bigger deal than it needs to be."

The knot in her chest eased. She'd almost made a mistake, and now Evelyn seemed to be giving her an out. But the echo of disappointment in the wake of her relief was unexpected.

"I mean, even if we had, we're such good friends, it would probably be like kissing a sibling or something," Evelyn said, her words still slightly slurred.

Melanie nodded slowly, though she knew better. Evelyn might be able to blame intoxication for her actions right now, but she had no such excuse. Considering the mental images haunting her lately, she could no longer pretend she had only benign feelings for Evelyn.

"Should we try it?"

"What?" Panic shot through her. *No! Don't kiss her!* The screaming in her head was clear. Touching Evelyn would surely destroy her tenuous control.

"Let's get it out of the way—prove to ourselves this is only situational so we can move past it."

Did Evelyn really believe they could kiss each other chastely and then forget about it? Perhaps she wasn't experiencing the same attraction that Melanie was. If that was the case, maybe Evelyn's rejection *would* help her let go of this infatuation. Melanie shifted closer, her gaze focused on Evelyn's lips. She rested her hand on Evelyn's thigh. She would have thought touching Evelyn so intimately might be awkward, but feeling the firm flex of her denim-encased muscles only intensified her desire. She could imagine stroking the soft line of Evelyn's jaw before taking her face in her hands and pulling her closer. She stopped herself before she conjured the feel of Evelyn's lips moving against hers.

"God, I hope you're not serious." She couldn't initiate the kiss, but she didn't have the strength to stop it if Evelyn did.

"No. Not entirely." Evelyn pulled her lower lip between her teeth, and she suppressed a moan. How the hell could she suddenly be finding Melanie so damn sexy?

She sighed and opened her door. She needed to get out of this truck before she did something stupid. She slid to the ground, then circled and opened Evelyn's door.

"Let's get you inside," she said, aware that they'd been in the same situation the previous weekend, but now their roles were reversed.

As Evelyn dropped to the ground, she stumbled a little, caught her arm around Melanie's shoulder, and righted herself. Melanie steadied her briefly, then stepped back to close the door. Evelyn would have to get herself to the front door, because if she had to walk more than a few steps with Evelyn pressed to her side, she just might throw her down right here on the sidewalk outside her condo.

❖

Evelyn patrolled the same neighborhood for the fourth time in an hour. She couldn't remember the last time work had been this slow on a Monday afternoon. They had three newly graduated rookies on their shift, so the training officers had been grabbing all of the incoming calls in order to get a variety of incidents. She'd been trolling the usual areas looking for a traffic stop that might lead to something interesting. Today, when she needed a little distraction, she couldn't even find an expired tag or a busted taillight.

The musical peal of her cell phone gave her a moment's hope for diversion, but when she saw Melanie's picture on the caller ID, she felt an odd mix of anticipation and dread. She wanted to talk to Melanie—craved it—but was embarrassed by her behavior last night. She'd apparently been just drunk enough to lower her inhibitions but not quite enough to eradicate the details. She'd woken up this morning with a low-grade headache and the trickling memories of the way she'd acted the night before.

Still she couldn't deny herself the pleasure of Melanie's voice, so she answered the phone.

"Hey, I'm just calling to check on you."

"I've mostly recovered." When the light turned green, she continued through it and pulled into the driveway of the elementary school on the corner. She circled to the back and parked in the shadow of the building.

"Are you busy?" Melanie asked.

"Nope. Everyone must be on their best behavior tonight."

They talked about the minutiae of their respective days until they both fell silent. She searched for something else to say—anything except what she knew she should.

"So, did I really suggest we kiss just to get it out of the way?" she finally blurted.

"Yes."

She groaned, squeezed her eyes shut, and pinched the bridge of her nose. "I'm so sorry."

"Don't be."

"Can we just blame it on the tequila?"

"I don't see why not."

"Wonderful."

"But wouldn't it be better if we just talked about it?" Melanie asked.

"I don't think that's going to help." Damn Melanie's openness. The last thing Evelyn wanted to do was rehash what had to be the weakest come-on she'd ever perpetrated.

"You said yourself you weren't wasted. So what was behind that comment?"

"Any chance you'll let this go?"she asked.

"Please, Ev?"

She couldn't take the naked vulnerability in Melanie's plea. She sighed. Maybe she needed to do this now; over the phone might be easier than in person anyway. Her limbs felt weak and her heart hammered. She took a deep breath and forged ahead. "Okay. Recently, I've been thinking—well, I've been thinking about you—a lot—in ways that I shouldn't." *God, that was smooth.* Melanie was quiet for so long that Evelyn rushed to fill the awkward silence. "I know it's not a good idea, and I've mostly got a handle on it. Oh, hell, I shouldn't have said anything."

"Evelyn—"

"Think we could blame the tequila again?"

Melanie laughed, and the familiar soft chuckle began to ease her tension. This was Melanie. No matter how uncomfortable this conversation, they could get through it. "A day later? Yes, I'm sure a few shots of tequila could be culpable."

"Thanks."

"But, Evelyn?"

"Yeah?"

"I didn't drink any tequila."

Was she saying she felt the same way? Stunned, Evelyn couldn't formulate a response. What now? They still couldn't act on these feelings. Could they? Kendall would hate them both. She was certain of that. Sure, Kendall said she was cool with Evelyn and Melanie remaining friends, because she believed ultimately that Evelyn's loyalty still lay with her. But dating Melanie would most certainly cross a line.

As if summoned by her guilt, Kendall called her on the radio, which started her heart racing again.

"Was that Kendall?" Melanie asked.

"Uh-huh. Hang on." She picked up her microphone and answered.

"What's your twenty?" Kendall's voice crackled over the air asking for her location.

"Seventh and Ramsey." She gave the intersection closest to the school.

"Is she on her way?" Melanie's question did little to soothe her contrition.

"Yes." She didn't know what else to say. Suddenly she found herself in an impossible situation. She'd pursued a number of women that she wasn't even that interested in, looking for the connection she thought Kendall and Melanie had. Now, her apparent illusions about that relationship had been blown apart and she was—

God, was she falling for Melanie?

"I'm sorry," Melanie said softly.

"For what?"

"For putting you in what must be an uncomfortable position." She scoffed. "You didn't do this."

"You work with Kendall. Add talking to me every day, and it can't be easy. Should we get some distance? Maybe I shouldn't call you for a while."

"Is that what you want?" The idea sent a shaft of panic through her chest. When Melanie didn't answer for an excruciatingly long minute, Evelyn wished she knew what she was thinking. Did the idea of separation hurt Melanie as much as it did Evelyn? Or was she trying to decide how to let her down easy?

"No," Melanie finally said, sounding as if she admitted it reluctantly. "But I don't want to cause problems between you and Kendall."

"Mel—" If she had any idea what to say, she wouldn't have the chance now anyway. Kendall's patrol car turned the corner of the building and headed toward her. "Kendall's here."

"Okay. Let's take a break for a while—see if that eases some of the tension."

"I don't want—"

"I think it's the right thing to do." Melanie sounded sad and not at all convincing. "Have a good week, Ev." Before she could argue further, Melanie had disconnected.

Kendall stopped next to her car, facing the opposite way, and rolled down her window. Evelyn punched the button to lower hers as well.

"What a boring day," Kendall said.

"No kidding."

"Do you want to hit the gym after work?"

"Absolutely." Maybe a good, hard workout would clear her mind. "How was your weekend?"

"Good, actually. I meant to call you but I got busy. I wanted to talk to you about something."

Evelyn waited, stifling the urge to defend her time spent with Melanie. Had one of the girls from paintball talked to Kendall? She hadn't said or done anything inappropriate toward Melanie in front of them.

"I've sort of been seeing someone—nothing serious. But more than a couple of dates."

"Yeah?" Her panic eased.

"I didn't want to tell you because of who it is."

"As long as you're happy and don't let anyone treat you badly, I'm happy for you."

"Even if it's Tiffany?"

She laughed, but Kendall didn't join in. "Oh, you're serious."

Kendall nodded.

"How did that happen?"

"I ran into her at the grocery store and we went out for coffee."

"Wow. This is unexpected. If I remember correctly, you called her a ditz."

"Well, yeah, when I thought she'd rejected you."

"So now, you're into her?"

"Yeah, maybe, I don't know. We're hanging out."

"Hanging out?" It was a phrase she had used when she wanted to sleep with someone she'd been dating but wasn't sure if she was serious about her yet. Kendall's averted gaze confirmed that she meant exactly that. "Wow."

"It had to happen eventually, right? I mean, Melanie's not changing her mind. I have to move on."

"Yeah, I guess so."

"Anyway, that's partly why I told you. I wanted you to know, of course. But I also know you're still friends with Melanie."

She nodded, uncomfortable with the direction of this conversation.

"Tiffany and I are having dinner with some mutual friends of mine and Melanie's next weekend. So, there's a chance she'll hear about it. I thought maybe if you told her first it would—"

"No."

"Evelyn—"

"I don't want to be in the middle of this."

"You'd rather she be blindsided in front of our friends?"

"Why don't you tell her?"

"We haven't spoken in months. I don't want this to be the first thing I say to her after so long."

"Damn. Okay, I'll tell her."

"Soon?"

"Next time I talk to her." She hedged, thinking about Melanie's request that they take some time apart. The dinner wasn't until the weekend. Maybe in a few days she could use this message as an excuse to call Melanie.

CHAPTER TWELVE

W hat's up, Boss? I've never seen you this distracted."
Melanie threw her pencil onto her desk and watched
it roll across the unfinished layout for her next project. Lucas
caught it as it fell off the edge.

"Just dragging a little this week." She'd wasted an entire
morning at the office pretending to work on her newest account.
Usually, she had no problem losing herself in her work, no matter
what was going on in her life. The past few days, she'd had trouble
summoning enough creative energy to accomplish much. So she
plodded on, doing busy work and promising she would complete
the drawings later. Since she had a meeting with the client in the
morning, *later* had arrived. "I'm not feeling this design at all."

"Want me to take a crack at it?" He rubbed his chin, his fingers
rasping against his stubble.

She pushed the grid paper across the desk. She'd already
sketched out the dimensions they had to work with and taken
detailed notes on the clients' specific desires. He scanned the notes,
then pulled the plans closer and bent over them.

She leaned back in her chair, comforted by the rhythmic scratch
of his pencil against the paper. He worked quickly, sometimes in
long, smooth strokes and other times making short, staccato lines.

"Do you want to tell me what's going on?" he asked as he
continued working.

"Nothing."

"It's something. And the fact that you don't want to talk about it tells me it's personal, not professional."

She didn't respond, but her silence would confirm that he was right.

"Okay. But I'm here if you need a sounding board."

She rubbed the back of her neck. "Damn it, Luc. I never let my personal life get in the way of work."

He shook his head, never looking up from his work. "Not even after all the shit with Kendall. It has to be a woman, right?"

"Why would you say that?"

"Because women and money are the only things that get me that twisted up. And we're not so different." He lifted his head and met her eyes, his gaze conveying understanding with no judgment.

She focused on his half-finished drawing and looked closer, impressed once again with his skills. She liked to see his excitement when she gave him a project to design. When he stood in the middle of a finished project surveying the results of his idea, his dark eyes shone with pride. She remembered those feelings from early in her career. Over the years, after countless clients, the intensity had faded, but the satisfaction of what she'd built remained.

"What would you say to someone who hypothetically developed feelings for a close friend?"

"I'd say I'm flattered, but I'm seeing someone."

"Very funny."

He smiled. "Who's the friend?"

"That shouldn't matter if it's hypothetical."

"It does." He rested the tip of his pencil against his cheek. "Is it Steve?"

She didn't bother answering, certain he didn't think she had a crush on the kid just out of high school that she'd hired a few weeks ago.

"A close friend, you said. It shouldn't be hard to figure out, since you don't have many." He stared at her, narrowing his eyes. Then, when he worked it out, his eyes flared and he lifted his brows. "No way? Evelyn?"

She bit her lip.

"Oh, Melanie. That is not a good idea."

"I know. Damn it, I know."

"When did this happen?"

"I'm not really sure. We've been hanging out. But I just thought I needed a friend. Now I'm having all these inappropriate thoughts."

"At least you know they're inappropriate. You can't date Kendall's best friend."

"Why does she automatically get custody of our friends?"

"We're talking about more than custody here."

She launched herself out of her chair and across the office to the window. The parking lot of the strip mall next door didn't offer much of a view, but she wasn't interested in the scenery.

"Does she feel the same way?"

"I think so. Yes."

"Melanie, this will end badly."

She sighed. "I know. If we pursue this, she'll lose Kendall. I can't make her choose between us."

"Not to mention that if this goes bad, you screw up your friendship with her. So then you both lose Kendall *and* each other."

She couldn't risk everything for the chance it might work out. She was fresh out of a long-term relationship. Evelyn was desperately trying to stay loyal to opposing forces. What made her think the two of them were in any shape to begin a serious situation? She didn't want anything too deep so soon after Kendall, and if she met someone new she intended to take things slow. But she wasn't the type that could have a casual fling with a friend. She was too emotionally involved already.

"What do you think?" He gestured to the paper in front of him. "It's still rough, but once we clean it up a little, I think the clients will like it."

"It's great. I think they'll love it." She pulled another piece of paper in front of her. "Let's work up a couple of variations for them to look at. They strike me as the type of couple who likes the control of making choices."

"No problem." He leaned forward, resting on his forearms, and watched her sketch. "Decorative brick instead of stone on the wall. A three-piece furniture arrangement could replace the outdoor sectional. We could offer a scaled-back version of the outdoor kitchen as an option."

"All good ideas. But don't think I don't know that you're making sure your first design is the best."

"Hey, if the client thinks my design is the most desirable, what can I do?"

"The customer is always right." She emphasized that message with her employees, even when it meant they had to stifle their opinions and smile at a difficult customer. But every one of her employees knew that she wouldn't let them be mistreated. As long as they stayed professional and reported any problems to her, she would take care of them. She'd built her business based, at least in part, on this balance of customer service and employee satisfaction, and the loyalty she'd earned on both sides kept her company growing and strong.

❖

"Did you talk to Melanie yet?" Kendall asked as she lay back on the weight bench. Guilting Evelyn into delivering her bad news had been wrong. But she just couldn't visualize having that conversation with Melanie so soon after their breakup.

"Not yet." Evelyn stood at the head of the bench, her hands hovering over the bar as Kendall lifted it off the stand.

"When do you think you might?" She lowered the weighted bar until it nearly touched her chest, then pressed it back up.

"I don't know. I haven't heard from her this week."

"Okay." She pushed the bar up a few more times and then traded places with Evelyn.

They continued working out in silence, moving on to the bicep curls.

"I'm meeting Tiffany after work for drinks. Do you want to join us?" She issued the invitation without thinking, belatedly realizing that the three of them out for drinks might be awkward.

"I can't. I'm working an extra job."

"Tonight?"

"Yeah. One of those national morning shows is taping a concert series downtown tomorrow morning. They had to start setting up the stages in order to go live early in the morning. Riggs and I are babysitting the equipment overnight."

"You're working all night, after a full shift this evening? When will you sleep?"

Evelyn waved her free hand, still curling her barbell. "I'll be fine."

"You didn't tell me this when I asked you to the gym before work. You could be napping now."

"It's just one night."

She shook her head. "But what's the point of working yourself to exhaustion? I know you don't need the money that bad."

"Working to distraction," Evelyn mumbled.

"What?"

"Nothing."

She set down her weights and turned to face Evelyn. "What are you trying to distract yourself from?" Given the way Evelyn avoided eye contact, she clearly wished Kendall would drop the subject.

But she already felt like she'd neglected her friendship with Evelyn lately. After the breakup, she'd been so wrapped up in her own drama that she had selfishly taken whatever help Evelyn had offered. Then when she started dating again, she thought maybe she should include Evelyn in some of her plans, see if any of her dates had a friend to double with. But she hadn't been single in so long, she hadn't wanted Evelyn to see how horribly inept she was at first dates.

"Are we gabbing or are we working out?" Evelyn turned away. She set her preferred weight level on the leg press and contorted herself into the machine. "You probably don't remember this, but us single girls have to stay in shape, you know?"

Kendall thought she detected an edge of bitterness in Evelyn's voice. Could she be upset because she was seeing someone again?

Evelyn didn't have a problem getting dates when she wanted them, so why would Kendall's social life bother her? Maybe this was about Melanie. If Evelyn had been harboring the hope that they might get back together, she could view Tiffany as a threat to that future.

She'd told Evelyn that this thing with Tiffany wasn't serious, but maybe she didn't believe her. Kendall enjoyed Tiffany's company. Since that day at the grocery store, they'd been out a number of times—dinner, the movies, and to the symphony. Tiffany had season tickets, and while it wasn't Kendall's thing, she'd still had a pleasant evening. They'd kissed and even engaged in some serious groping on her couch one night, but their physical relationship hadn't progressed further. If she accepted Tiffany's recent invitation for a weekend out of town, though, that would most likely change.

Only a few weeks ago, she had a hard time kissing a woman without thinking about Melanie. However, even during the few hot-and-heavy moments with Tiffany, she had been firmly present and the thought of taking the next physical step excited her.

"Seriously, are you going to stand in the middle of the room all day, or are you going to spot me on these squats?" Evelyn called.

"Sorry. I got it." Smiling, she crossed to the weight stand and pulled a twenty-five-pound weight to match the one Evelyn carried to the squat machine. "You know, if you need to talk to me about something, you can."

"I know." But obviously she wasn't going to today.

She nodded, accepting that Evelyn had never been one to pour her heart out anyway. Melanie had always drawn things out of her. So as much as it pained her, she hoped that if something was troubling Evelyn, she might talk to Melanie about it.

Evelyn rubbed her eyes, wishing she could simply close them. She rested her elbow on the window sill beside her and propped her head up with her hand. The rhythmic patter of the rain against the roof of her car had nearly lulled her to sleep. The downpour that began only an hour after she and Riggs had started this security detail had waned to a steady shower that had continued for the past several hours.

The metal silhouette of the stage and lighting structures rose and stretched eerily against the moonlit sky, taking on a strange vitality. As the early morning hours arrived, she fully expected to see it come to life, pulling up from the ground and testing the joints of its skeletal arms like the tin man.

"Great, I'm starting to hallucinate," she muttered. For the first part of the shift, she'd tried to occupy herself by playing games and reading e-books on her phone. When she'd taken this assignment, she'd expected the boredom and the urge to text Melanie during this huge block of downtime. But after she'd fought that desire for the first couple of hours, it became too late to contact her anyway.

Now, only two hours remained until daybreak. Then an hour after that, several more officers scheduled to work during the taping would relieve them.

After tonight, she had to pull one more regular shift, and then she was off for the weekend. And, other than an obligatory visit to her parents, she hoped for a relaxing two days. Working like a maniac this week hadn't driven thoughts of Melanie from her head. If anything, the exhaustion made them even more distracting. By the time she crawled into bed at whatever hour in her crazy schedule she could, she was so addled that she seemed unable to stop from dreaming about Melanie as well. So she'd changed tactics and planned a leisurely weekend, hoping that being rested might help her be stronger than her currently taxed system did.

Her phone chirped, signaling a text message. She grabbed it from the cup holder and unlocked the screen to see Riggs's text.

Still awake?

Across the parking lot, she could see the shape of his figure in the glow of what she assumed was his iPad. He'd admitted earlier that he'd downloaded a series of vampire movies to keep him awake tonight. She would much rather have been parked next to him, so at least they could keep each other alert. But because the concert site wasn't protected by a fence, the client had instructed them to watch from either side of the property. Given the size and bulk of most of the equipment, she was certain they would have time to catch anyone before they could make off with it.

She typed back.

Still here. How's your movie marathon?

I can't imagine why my daughter likes this shit.

She laughed.

Because the guys in it are hot.

Shut up.

He hated acknowledging that his little princess had become a teenager.

At least it passed the time. I'm bored crazy over here.

Think about the paycheck.

No kidding.

If she'd accomplished nothing else this week, she'd padded her savings account quite nicely.

With two kids, one only a few years from college, Riggs worked as hard as he did for the money—for his family. She didn't have anyone to work for. She'd always assumed she would someday meet the woman who would make all the late hours, directing traffic in the rain, and putting her life at risk daily mean something more. She had even entertained thoughts about having kids, or maybe fostering or adopting. But so far, those ideas were just dreams for the future.

In her twenties, she hadn't stressed about whether that future would come. Now in her thirties, she'd begun to feel twinges of yearning for what her friends and co-workers were building. When one of the guys complained about his wife and envied her freedom, she played along, acting like she really was the luckier one. Of course, as they say, the grass was always greener.

❖

"I miss my friend," Melanie said as soon as Evelyn opened her front door.

"Me, too."

"Can we try?"

Evelyn ignored the pang of hope in her heart. Her mind tortured her with a rapid-fire slide-show tease of them trying all sorts of sexy things with each other. But Melanie meant could they try to get back to the comfortable friendship.

She stepped aside and waited for Melanie to enter. "Come in, but you'll have to go to my bedroom with me." Heat rushed to her face as she realized what she'd said. She rushed to explain. "I'm having dinner with my parents and I'm not ready yet." She shoved a hand through her wet hair.

"I'm sorry. I can go if you're busy."

"No, I'm glad you came. Make yourself comfortable," she said as she continued through to the master bathroom. She left the door open, but if Melanie responded, she didn't hear her over the roar of the blow dryer close to her ear.

When she flipped off the appliance and turned toward the bedroom, she wished she hadn't. Melanie—stretched out on the bed, her head on Evelyn's pillow—folded her arm behind her and cradled her head in her palm. *She looks good in my bed.* She admonished herself for the lusty thought. Melanie had come here today seeking her friend, and she needed to be just that—a friend.

"Long week?" She hoped Melanie didn't notice the way her voice cracked.

"You have no idea." Melanie smiled, that same familiar smile that never used to make her stomach flip like this.

"I might." She looked away and rubbed her favorite hair glue between her fingertips, then arranged her hair. A light coat of hair spray finished the look—one her father wouldn't approve of. He liked her hair slicked back and tightly bound—professional and sophisticated, he called it. But she wore it back every day at work. On her off days, she often preferred it free.

"Kendall asked me to tell you something. I agreed because I hoped you'd rather hear it from me than someone else." She decided that jumping into Kendall's news might diffuse some of the awkward tension while they both avoided talking about that big elephant.

"That doesn't sound good."

"Well, that depends on how you approach it. Kendall's kind of seeing someone. Honestly, I don't think it's serious, but she's introducing her to some of your mutual friends this weekend."

"Anyone I know?"

"Well, she said mutual friends, so I assumed you knew them."

"I meant the girlfriend."

"I know. Does it matter?"

"No. But tell me anyway," Melanie said.

"It's Tiffany."

"Tiffany? Seriously? That's my replacement?"

"She's not trying to replace you."

"But *Tiffany*? She called her a ditz."

"That's what I said."

"I did not see that coming." Melanie drew her brows together and pressed her mouth into a tight line.

She crossed to sit on the edge of the bed. She'd expected her news to bruise Melanie's pride, maybe hurt her feeling, but she hadn't considered that it might cause her to have second thoughts.

"I don't think it's serious." She wanted to take Melanie's hand, but instead she pressed her palms against her thighs. "Are you—having second thoughts about the breakup?"

Melanie's eyes, filled with confusion, flew to hers. "No."

"Because I think Kendall would still get back together with you."

Melanie shook her head. "It's not that. I want her to be happy. I just didn't expect she would pick someone like Tiffany."

"You expected it would be someone more like you?"

Melanie chuckled. "I guess not. If we were each looking for someone just like each other, we should have just stayed together, huh? I'd expect the next person I date to be totally different from Kendall."

She nodded. "That makes sense." Afraid she couldn't conceal the disappointment in her expression, she turned away and returned to the bathroom. She pretended to be preoccupied with checking her reflection in the mirror. Melanie had said more than once that she thought Kendall and Evelyn were just alike. But less than a week ago, Melanie seemed to be struggling with their relationship in much the same way as she was.

"Evelyn."

"Yeah?" She didn't look at her.

"We can get past the awkwardness and stay friends, right?"

"Yeah." She wanted to believe they could. If Melanie wanted that, she'd try like hell to suppress everything that got in the way. "Come to dinner at my parents' house with me," she suggested. An evening with her father tended to make her shut her emotions down. Maybe she could interact more rationally with Melanie under those circumstances.

"I don't know."

"Come on. My mom loves you. You can take the focus off me."

Melanie sat up and brushed her hands over her deep-green T-shirt with her company logo on the left breast. Evelyn didn't allow her eyes to linger on Melanie's chest, since she'd just taken a vow of platonic friendship.

"I'm not dressed for dinner." When she watched Melanie's legs flex beneath her khaki shorts as she slid off the bed, she told herself she was only assessing Melanie's clothing.

"You look fine. It's nothing formal."

"That's why you're obsessing about your appearance."

She checked her reflection in the mirror one more time, then misted on a subtle scent. "I'm sure there's some psychological explanation for that, having to do with fortifying myself before facing my father. But you don't have that issue."

Melanie laughed. "I know you're joking—"

"Sort of."

"But you should be proud of what you've accomplished. I'm sure your parents are."

"Lord, I don't want to get that deep right now." She couldn't get emotional about her complicated family dynamic just before going to dinner. She glanced at her watch. "It's time. Are you with me?"

"Sure. Why not?"

"Great. I should warn you. Mom was asking about you and Kendall so I told her about the split. She'll probably shower you with sympathy."

"And you waited until I'd agreed to come tell me this."

"Yes. Let's go or we'll be late."

"I'll follow you. Then I'll be free to leave if the tension becomes unbearable."

CHAPTER THIRTEEN

Melanie, it's so good to see you. How are you doing, sweetie?" Margaret Fisher's face filled with sympathy, from the watery kindness in her blue eyes to the compassionate downturn of her mouth.

"I'm good, Mrs. Fisher."

"Please, call me Margaret, dear. Now come in, both of you. No need to stand on the stoop." She moved aside and touched each of their shoulders as they entered.

The first time Melanie had been to the Fisher home, Evelyn had given her a tour of the large Colonial-style house that she'd grown up in. Among the ornate furnishings, Evelyn had pointed out the antique trunk she used to push close to her bed in order to throw a blanket across and make a secret cave. She'd recalled the time, as a teenager, that she climbed out her second-story bedroom window onto the porch roof and shimmied down the post to the railing.

Despite the marked differences in the sites of their upbringing, Evelyn's memories didn't seem all that different from hers. Her stories all took place inside a double-wide trailer situated on a half acre of land in a small town thirty minutes from Nashville. Evelyn had grown up in a big, meticulously decorated house. But, as Evelyn pointed out where she played as a child, the happiness shining in her eyes let Melanie know she saw this place as home.

Today, Margaret Fisher welcomed them both in with a wide smile and a look of love for her daughter. The savory aromas of comfort foods filled the air. She could practically taste the roast beef, rich gravy, and yeasty rolls. She imagined there would also be a heaping bowl of mashed potatoes and a vegetable casserole or two.

"Something smells wonderful."

"Why thank you, dear. Evelyn doesn't come around often enough, so when she does, I try to feed her well." Margaret led them into the kitchen where the island was already covered with plates and bowls laden with food.

"I eat plenty." Evelyn poked out her stomach and rubbed her hand over it. "Too much, sometimes."

"Please, you're in better shape than anyone I know." She pushed Evelyn's shoulder playfully and felt the flex of her upper-arm muscles. She'd bet the abdominals Evelyn purposely bloated were just as taut, as well.

"Your father got caught up in court, but he should be home any minute."

She sensed the tension in Evelyn's posture, but other than a slight tightening at the corner of her jaw, Evelyn's expression didn't change. She crossed the kitchen and picked up several small squares of polished stone in variegated shades of brown and tan from the counter.

"Mom, what are these?"

"Samples. I've finally talked your father into letting me redo the kitchen. I'm trying to decide which granite will go best with the new cabinets.

"Wow, all new cabinets?"

"Aside from the appliances, this kitchen hasn't been overhauled since you were a child. I'm working with a designer who is helping me make better use of the space."

"Better use of the space? Yeah, that sounds like designer-speak." Evelyn smiled as she leafed through several sketches and floor plans. "Actually, Mel, it sounds like something you'd say."

"Very funny," she said.

"Just don't let them take you for a ride, Mom. Those creative types charge way too much for a few drawings."

"What? Most of my clients couldn't draw a stick figure. They couldn't come up with anything close to my brilliance if their life depended on it." She protested then looked at Evelyn's mother and blushed. "I don't mean you, Mrs. Fisher."

"No, dear, you're right." She nodded solemnly. "Stick figures have always given me problems."

Melanie laughed and some of the heat drained from her face. "Would you girls set the table while I bring the food in?"

"Certainly, but I can help with the food, too," she said. She picked up a bowl of potatoes and followed Evelyn into the dining room. A table, covered with an ivory tablecloth and surrounded by six elegant chairs, dominated the center of the room. She carefully set her bowl down in the center.

She joined Evelyn at the matching sideboard along the far wall. Evelyn counted out four sets of highly polished silverware, setting each piece down next to a stack of silver-rimmed plates.

"This is nice." She touched the ornate pattern on the end of a fork. She preferred a simpler, classic design, but these were obviously of good quality and well-cared for.

"She'll want to use the good stuff."

"Of course. Your attendance is a special occasion," Melanie said.

"Don't let her brainwash you, too. I visit plenty."

"She's your mother. You couldn't be here enough for her." Melanie laughed and returned to the kitchen for another dish of food. As they carried way too much food for four people into the living room, she deflected questions from Margaret about how she was coping with the breakup.

"I feel badly that I hurt Kendall, but I made my decision based on the hope that both of us can be happy." Uncomfortable with Margaret's sympathy she tried to tactfully dismiss her concern.

She was saved from further questioning when Evelyn's father came home. As he entered the kitchen, Margaret immediately shifted her attention to him.

"We're ready to sit down to dinner, dear," she said as she took his coat and briefcase and placed them in the closet in the hall just outside the dining room.

"Sorry I'm late." He smoothed a hand over his hair, though she couldn't see a strand out of place.

"It's quite all right."

"Good evening, Melanie. I'm glad you could join us," he said. He loosened his tie and then rolled up his shirtsleeves, revealing a thick, silver wristwatch.

"Thank you, sir."

"How's business?" One of her best crews maintained the landscaping at Evelyn's parents' home.

"Very good."

"Wonderful. It's quite impressive, the way you've brought the company along over the years."

"I have some good people working for me and that helps tremendously."

"Certainly. But like anything else, ultimately, your commitment is what makes it work."

She nodded, but she sensed he might be talking about more than business and wondered what either Evelyn or Margaret might have told him about her relationship. Did he think she hadn't worked hard enough? He couldn't possibly know enough about her situation to justify judgment. Feeling defensive, she forced herself to take a deep breath. His words and tone had left open the possibility that he was simply talking about business, and she decided to believe that was so.

Margaret called them into the dining room and they settled around the table, Charles and Margaret at either end and she and Evelyn seated on the sides, across from each other. At Margaret's urging, they joined hands and said grace before passing the serving dishes.

She and Evelyn filled their plates under Margaret's watchful eye. She tried to balance taking enough food to satisfy Margaret with how much she actually thought she could eat. Luckily, she stayed active enough at work to keep her metabolism up or she would need several miles on the treadmill to counteract this meal.

"Everything is delicious," she said after tasting a few scrumptious bites.

"Thank you, dear. Have as much as you'd like. When we're through, I'll fix you girls a couple of plates to take home."

She met Evelyn's eyes, reading the apology in them. She smiled, trying to let Evelyn know she was having a good time. When the tension remained in Evelyn's expression, Melanie winked at her. The corner of Evelyn's mouth lifted in a half smile, and then she looked down at her plate.

"Evelyn, the firm has a position open that I thought you might be interested in. With your background—"

"I have a job."

"Hear me out. One of our investigators has left. It pays quite well, certainly more than a government salary."

"No, thank you."

She didn't need to hear the finality in Evelyn's tone to know that the subject wasn't open for discussion. Evelyn had complained about similar offers over the years. She didn't hold the investigators who dug up dirt to help defend criminals in any higher esteem than the attorneys themselves.

"You don't want to be a beat cop for the rest of your life, do you?"

Evelyn clamped her mouth shut on what was surely a defensive response. Her shoulders lifted as she took a fortifying breath. "I like what I do. But if the right opportunity comes along, I'm willing to make a change. A position at your firm is not the opportunity I'm looking for."

Charles looked like he wanted to argue, but before he had a chance, Evelyn changed the subject.

"Mom, how's the new pastor at church working out?"

"Very well. He's intelligent and enthusiastic. But he's young, so some of the older ladies are resisting his charms."

"His charms, huh? So, he's too good-looking and the old biddies don't trust him?"

"Exactly. But he jumped right in and is already organizing a new outreach for the less fortunate."

"The homeless," Evelyn said, meeting Melanie's eyes. "She doesn't like that term so she calls them less fortunate instead."

"Well, not having a home is certainly unfortunate," she said, her overly agreeable tone meant to convey her amusement to Evelyn.

They spent the remainder of the meal talking about Margaret's church activities, including an invitation for Melanie to join them for Sunday services anytime she wanted to. She gave the appropriate responses, involving herself enough to be polite. But mostly she found herself watching Evelyn interact with her parents, trying to read the minute changes in her expression or figure out the meaning behind the nuances in her voice. She'd learned a lot about Evelyn by the time Margaret served the made-from-scratch lemon-meringue pie.

Margaret and Evelyn fell into reminiscing about Evelyn's childhood, as families sometimes do when a new audience is available. She'd heard some of the stories before and some were new. Margaret talked about Evelyn's circle of friends and their exploits, most of which involved mild rebellion and the usual high-school drama.

She boasted about Evelyn's athletic prowess, recalling her feats on the soccer field and softball diamond while in high school. Melanie snuck glances at Charles during the tales and wasn't surprised to find pride shining in his eyes as well.

"She was extremely competitive," Margaret said.

"I know the type," Melanie replied. She'd been practically married to one.

"No," Charles said, drawing three sets of eyes. "Dedicated."

"That's what I said," Margaret said.

"She wasn't simply competitive. She was dedicated to her team and their success." His serious expression indicated that he drew a clear distinction between the two.

As their only child, Evelyn had obviously been the center of their world. Melanie got the impression that Evelyn's relationship with her father became more complicated only after she graduated from high school. Despite their professional differences, Evelyn and her father loved each other, and her mother tried to balance delicately in the middle.

❖

"Dinner was delicious, Margaret." Melanie folded her napkin and placed it on the table next to her plate.

"Thank you. Evelyn, you should bring Melanie by again soon. I'll make meatloaf."

"My mother's meatloaf is world-famous. She won't even tell *me* the secret ingredient."

"Maybe on my deathbed."

"Mom!" Evelyn refused to think about losing her parents. Though in their late fifties, they were in good health. But their parents, her grandparents, had all passed away while relatively young.

"If I tell you, you might make it yourself and you won't need to come over anymore."

Melanie laughed. "Not likely."

She glared, but Melanie just smiled in response. So, her culinary skills might be a little lacking. She passed two Subways, a KFC, and her favorite Chinese take-out place on the way home from work anyway. Besides, she used to eat at Kendall and Melanie's at least one night a week, and Melanie was an amazing cook. She made a mental note to talk to Melanie about starting that tradition again.

"I'll just have to hope she meets a nice young woman who will cook for her, then."

Her mother had come a long way since she'd come out to her after high school. Their relationship had been strained for quite some time. But now, like Melanie's mother, her own simply transferred her criteria for a son-in-law onto a hypothetical daughter-in-law. "She has to cook now, too? This list is getting long. I don't know where to find this superwoman." She met Melanie's eyes and smiled.

"Since you brought it up, have you been seeing anyone new?" Margaret asked.

Her amusement from a moment ago shifted into something heavier, and Melanie's gaze seemed as muddled as she felt inside. She didn't want to see anyone new; she wanted the woman sitting across from her now—the one woman she shouldn't desire. "Uh—no, Mom, I'm not."

"I've heard that Internet dating is the popular thing these days. But girls, please be careful if you try that. I saw a very disturbing story on *20/20* and—well, it can be dangerous."

"I'm not meeting people on the Internet." In truth, she wasn't meeting anyone at all. If she didn't count Tiffany, and she didn't, she couldn't remember the last time she'd met someone new. She'd tried dating a district attorney but found that having the job in common wasn't always a plus, at least not if it was the only thing they had in common. The prosecutor was hot, but all she wanted to talk about was the scumbags she put in jail all day long. Evelyn loved her job, but she didn't want to come home and wallow in the darkest parts of it. She wanted her relationship to be a bright light, a shelter from the worst of humanity that she saw every day.

"I'm only asking you to be careful." Her mother made a similar request nearly every time she visited, sometimes in reference to her job and sometimes her safety in general. Once she'd even cautioned her about the hidden dangers of BPA in plastic food-storage containers. Evelyn welcomed the warnings, which had started when she entered the police academy, as evidence of her mother's love and concern for her.

"I'm always careful." She heard the disappointment in her own voice. Melanie had asked for her friend back and she tried like hell to honor the request, but in truth, the more time they spent together, the more Evelyn wanted to give her, to share with her. She could see them here again, making sexy eyes across the table, each anticipating what they would do to each other when they got home. Her face grew hot and, trying to cover up the blush she knew spread up her neck and over her cheeks, she fumbled to her feet. "I'll clear the table."

"Evelyn, may I have a word with you?" Her father stood as well. His request was firm and not the least bit questioning.

"I, uh—" She stopped, holding her plate limply.

"Go ahead, dear. I'll get these." Her mother took the plate from her, leaving her no choice except to follow her father into his office.

When they stepped inside she caught the familiar faint odor of his favorite cigar. She didn't have to look at the mahogany bar in the corner of the room to know there would be a crystal decanter of his favorite scotch. Her father was an old-fashioned man, so much so that she swore he secretly referred to the room as his study. The brown leather sofa and deep-green wallpaper hadn't changed since they'd first moved into the house when she was a child, and a part of her found that sameness comforting.

As he crossed to pour himself an after-dinner drink, she sat on the sofa. "What's up?"

"Your mother told me about Melanie and Kendall."

She nodded, not sure where he was going with this.

"You should tread lightly."

"Tread lightly?"

"Yes. Kendall is a loyal friend and you wouldn't want to jeopardize that relationship." He stared into his glass as he casually swirled his drink. When she didn't respond right away he met her eyes. She clenched her teeth. She'd seen that sharp look before, at the moment when he knew he had the upper hand with a witness. "Don't worry. I don't think either Melanie or your mother suspects anything."

"There's nothing to suspect." She didn't let on that Melanie was more aware of the situation than he thought, preferring to let him focus singularly on her. To most people her expression wouldn't betray the lie. She'd mastered that particular skill quite well during her years as a police officer. But her father's ability to read faces was exceptional, so much so that his prey generally didn't realize they'd been found out until they'd revealed a valuable nugget. Knowing this about her father made Melanie's ability to conceal her emotions even more impressive.

A small smile twitched at the corner of his lips. "I've watched that face since you were a little girl, Evie. I know when you're hiding something."

She couldn't remember the last time he'd used that endearment, and a pang of nostalgia broke through her guard. "It's under control." She resisted the urge to call him "Daddy," as Southern daughters were prone to do.

"Make sure it stays that way."

She hadn't let him tell her what to do since she'd entered the police academy against his wishes, and she resented the authority in his tone. But she withheld the defensive argument that pushed against the back of her teeth.

"I didn't try to sway you when you 'came out' to us." The exaggerated air quotes annoyed her.

"I guess telling you I didn't want to go to law school at the same time served a purpose then." He'd found that piece of information much more upsetting than news of her sexual orientation. But then again he'd never really had to face her sexuality. She didn't talk to her father about who she dated, and she'd never brought anyone home to meet her parents.

"Getting involved with Melanie would be a bad idea."

"I know."

"So be careful."

She nodded. "Like I told Mom, I'm always careful."

She ignored his doubtful expression and strode out of the office, trying to exude more confidence than she felt.

CHAPTER FOURTEEN

Thanks for today," Evelyn said as she walked Melanie to her front door.

Melanie unlocked the door and entered, leaving it open as an invitation for Evelyn to follow. Though spending too much time with Evelyn was dangerous, she sensed she might need to talk about the visit with her parents.

"Did I distract him sufficiently?" she asked over her shoulder as she passed through the living room and into the kitchen. From the foyer, she heard the front door close and waited to see if Evelyn had left.

"Maybe too well," Evelyn said as she paused at the entrance to the kitchen and rested her shoulder against the archway.

"What was the secret conference in the office all about?" She opened a bottle of her favorite Riesling and pulled two glasses off the rack under the cabinet.

"Actually, it was about you." When Evelyn reached for the glass she offered and their fingers touched, Evelyn's smooth nails tickled her sensitive fingertips. She simultaneously fought her urge to pull her hand away and her desire to tangle her fingers around Evelyn's. In the end she released the glass slowly, relishing the warm brush of skin on skin.

"Me?"

"Yep." Evelyn took a sip of the wine, but her eyes never left Melanie's face. "He warned me not to act on my very obvious attraction to you," she said quickly, as if forcing the words out, then assessing her reaction.

"Really?" She kept her voice casual, but Evelyn's statement sent arousal vibrating through her like the taut string of a crossbow.

"Yeah."

"How did he—"

"He observes people for a living. And he's particularly good at reading me."

"I wouldn't like knowing someone could see through me like that." She led Evelyn back into the living room and they settled on the couch with their wine.

"Try growing up with him."

"How was it, really—growing up? Your relationship with him now has always been clear. But I get the impression things were different when you were younger."

Evelyn sighed and set her glass on the coffee table. "I remember sitting in that office and watching him work. I have no idea why I wasn't bored to death, but I could spend hours in there. I loved listening to him practice his closing statements, the passionate way he wove the stories. My mother hated him letting me in there."

"Considering the kind of people he might represent, I imagine she was worried about the effect of the harsh tales of their crimes."

"Alleged crimes," Evelyn said sarcastically.

"Of course."

"In the beginning I was too young to understand what he was saying anyway. Then when I was a little older, I became conflicted by my admiration of his quick mind, coupled with disdain at how he could twist logic to suit any argument without regard to what I believed his values to be."

"He's a brilliant attorney, which is what often causes the problems for the two of you."

"How so?"

"You respect his talent and intelligence, but you don't like his vocation. And he wants so badly for you to be like him, but he can't see that you don't have to walk in his footsteps to do that. You're already as quick and as bright as he is, but you use your talents differently."

"Yeah, for good instead of evil."

She smiled. "Something like that."

"He may be arrogant, but in this case, I'm more annoyed because I know he's right." Evelyn shifted forward and rested her elbows on her knees. "I keep telling myself that thinking about you the way I have been crosses a line in my loyalty to Kendall. But ignoring the way I feel hasn't helped make it go away. I've been trying like hell to figure out a way to think of you as just a friend." Agony laced Evelyn's voice and brought an ache to her heart. Everything about her posture and tone suggested that she felt alone.

Melanie touched Evelyn's shoulder and she flinched, but she didn't move her hand. Instead, she rubbed Evelyn's back in a slow circle. She needed to let Evelyn know that she wasn't the only one struggling with this attraction. "I can't stop thinking about you."

Evelyn's head dropped, hanging in front of her, and she shook it slowly. "Don't tell me that."

"Why?"

"I'm trying to stay sane and I can't—"

She leaned closer, sliding her arm around Evelyn. She lifted her chin with gentle fingers and forced her to meet her eyes. "You can't what?"

Evelyn bit her lip as if she could trap the truth behind such a tenuous seal. "I can't be around you without wanting you. Hell, I want you even when I'm nowhere near you."

Should she play it cool—act like she could be unemotional and platonic? She searched Evelyn's expression, trying to discern what she needed. If she were detached, would this be easier on Evelyn? In the end, the velvet need in Evelyn's eyes decimated her. She didn't want to release Evelyn. She wanted to shut out that rational voice and give in to the insane urge to kiss one of her closest friends—consequences be damned.

"Mel," Evelyn whispered, her voice rough with arousal and her eyes communicating so much more desire than words ever could. Did she read the same struggle in Melanie's expression? "One of us needs to be strong enough to stop this."

"I'm sorry, that's not me," she said. Her stomach twisted in anxious anticipation, but arousal trumped fear. She tilted her head and brushed her lips against Evelyn's. Her nerves melted under the warmth of Evelyn's mouth. She slipped her hand against the back of Evelyn's neck, under her hair, and traced her tongue over her lower lip.

They clung together, each holding on as if afraid the other would suddenly come to her senses and pull away.

Evelyn opened to her, meeting each stroke of her tongue, pouring all the passion she'd caged into this kiss. Finally not holding back, she caressed Melanie's wine-flavored lips, tasting the sting of sour apple and tart grapes. She twisted, urging Melanie back into the couch. As she rose over her, Melanie's thigh slipped between hers. She pressed down instinctively, craving the firm pressure against the fly of her jeans. When she rotated her hips, Melanie shoved one hand under her shirt and ran her nails over her back.

Evelyn eased back, needing to breathe. She angled to one side, bracing herself on one elbow and kept her forehead pressed to Melanie's temple.

"God, Mel." She couldn't have anticipated how deeply the taste of Melanie's lips would rock her. *I am in very big trouble here.* Hell, she'd practically humped Melanie's thigh just now and had thoroughly enjoyed it.

"Yeah," Melanie whispered. "That was nothing like kissing a sibling."

She couldn't pull her eyes from Melanie's face, so close to hers. Melanie's pupils were dilated, her irises little more than a verdant ring around their dark centers. They had been friends for years and she had never felt this spark, no, this inferno of sexual attraction. If she'd been asked, she would have guessed a kiss between them would be a little awkward, uncomfortable, even. But, for her at least, nothing had ever felt more natural or genuine.

"What now?" she asked, as she touched the spot on Melanie's neck where her pulse beat visibly under her skin.

"We'll talk about it. But first, I want to do that again." Melanie pulled her back in, covering her mouth more aggressively.

❖

"Stay," Melanie murmured, throwing her arm across Evelyn's chest. She'd be content to lie here on her couch kissing Evelyn all night. But if the high of arousal waned even slightly they would both probably realize how uncomfortably situated they were. Evelyn reclined against the arm of the sofa and Melanie sprawled across her, resting her head on Evelyn's shoulder. While they'd kissed, their legs had tangled together in a desperate effort to get closer to one another, to create teasing, agonizing friction between them.

"I shouldn't." Evelyn didn't move.

"Nothing more has to happen." She snuggled closer.

After a long pause, Evelyn said quietly, "I can't be your rebound."

She tilted her head back, but Evelyn was staring at the ceiling, and from this angle Melanie could only see her chin. "That's not what this is."

"You haven't dated anyone since Kendall."

That was true, but she and Kendall had been emotionally separated for so long that her mind felt clear. She'd made her decision with clarity and wasn't looking for a fling to convince her it was right. "You're not a rebound."

"Then what am I?"

She sighed. "A friend." Yeah, it was a lame answer. But she couldn't define what was going on between them. Evelyn was one of her best friends—her closest friend, given her current relationship with Kendall. She'd never wanted to jeopardize that, but now that she'd kissed her, she had definitely changed their relationship. So she either took the chance of pursuing it or figured out how to be just friends with the woman whose kiss had liquefied her insides.

"You kiss all of your friends like that?"

She smiled. "Okay. You're more than a friend."

"I never would have imagined we would be in this position."

"What position would you like us to be in?"

"All of sudden, I'm not having any trouble imagining you in any number of positions." Evelyn groaned. "How is it possible that just saying that can feel strange and turn me on at the same time?"

"I know what you mean." Her stomach flipped as she too conjured up pictures of exploring the attraction between them. But thinking this way about a woman she'd previously only thought of as a friend still felt foreign.

Evelyn eased away from her and scooted to the other end of the couch. "I can't be rational about this while I'm touching you." She rubbed her fingertips against her forehead and muttered, "Am I really considering doing this to Kendall?"

"You don't have to."

Evelyn looked up, her expression changing as if she hadn't realized she'd spoken aloud. "Just ignore it." She nodded slowly. "I've tried that and failed miserably at pretending I only have friendly feelings for you. And I don't see it getting any easier."

"Let's take Kendall out of it for a minute. If we didn't have our guilt to think about, what would you be saying about this situation?"

"There's still our friendship to consider."

"You don't think we could be mature enough to retain it if things didn't work out?"

Evelyn shook her head. "I don't know. I think that's just something people say. But do they really do it?"

"Eventually. Depending on the breakup, it may take some time and work." She leaned forward and rested her hand on

Evelyn's knee. She wanted to respect her desire for distance while they talked, but now that they'd crossed a line, she found it even more difficult to be near her and not touch her. "If we are going to start something here, I don't want to make the decision thinking about how it might end."

"So we're back to Kendall? She'll be pissed."

"No doubt. I'll be straight with you, Ev. She and I don't have a relationship right now. So if I'm only considering my stakes in this, it's easier for me to be selfish and say I want you and I don't care what she thinks. But I also know what her friendship has meant to you and yours to her, and it's hard for me to be the one that comes between you."

"I don't want to hurt her either. And I don't want to lose her. But this…" Evelyn covered her hand and heat arched from Melanie's fingertips and up her arm. "God, I can't explain it, you know?"

"I do." Had this energy been lying dormant between them, needing only the right circumstances to come to life—needing both of them to be in the right place? "We could take it slow."

"We could." Evelyn's warm eyes, full of hope and hazy with arousal, met hers. She bent her head and kissed her temple.

Melanie angled back, capturing her lips. Evelyn's tongue slid against hers and the spark inside her flared into a dancing flame. Evelyn moved from her mouth to her neck, first kissing, then lightly sucking the sensitive skin there. Evelyn rose, supporting herself on her arms as she covered her body. She gave herself over to the blaze, basking in the lick of heat against her skin wherever Evelyn's mouth touched her.

Immersed in the exquisite feel of combing her fingers through Evelyn's silky hair, she allowed herself to tremble on the edge of losing control. She tested herself, sliding her palms under Evelyn's shirt and over the curve of her sides. Dizzy with the sensation of Evelyn's satin skin, she traced her fingertips up and into the dips between each of Evelyn's ribs.

"Melanie." Evelyn warned her.

"I know,"she murmured against her mouth. "Just a minute more, please." She smoothed her hands to Evelyn's back and pulled her down more tightly against her.

"God, Mel." Evelyn groaned as their hips ground together.

She smiled. "I just wanted to make sure I wasn't the only one feeling this way."

"If you mean horny and seconds away from forgetting about the shred of honor I'm clinging to," Evelyn kissed her and rotated her hips slowly, "yes, we're both there."

When Evelyn eased back, Melanie sat up. Evelyn moved quickly to the other end of the sofa, putting some much-needed distance between them.

Evelyn pulled in a full breath, then said, "I don't think we should sleep together until Kendall knows about us."

"I don't know how well you think you know me, but I'm not that easy. I don't have sex on the first date."

"Was this a date? And I took you to my parents' house for dinner. I really know how to show a girl a good time, huh?"

Melanie laughed.

"It shouldn't make any difference, but—"

"But it feels like less of a betrayal if we don't have sex," Melanie said.

"Well, yes." She had no idea how she would tell Kendall. But she naively clung to the hope that their friendship would survive.

"And you're still worried I'm going to change my mind about pursuing this."

"A little." These new feelings about Melanie were all wrapped up in their history together. She'd known Melanie for five years and cared so much about her already. But now, the old boundaries of their friendship were dissolving. Things with Melanie already felt so much more intimate than if she were getting to know someone new.

"I told you, you're not a rebound."

"Okay. But a lot has changed in the past few months, for both of us. There's no reason to hurt her until we know what this is, right?"

"Okay. So—no sex until then." Melanie rested her fingers against the side of her neck, and the feather-light touch sent a tingle along her skin.

"Yeah. That shouldn't be too hard."

"Well, we've known each other this long and never had sex, so what's a little bit longer?" Melanie smiled.

"Right. But I can't stay here tonight." She stood and Melanie followed her to the door. They shared a lingering kiss, and when Melanie released her, she longed to stay after all. She could feel Melanie's eyes on her as she walked away, but she forced herself to keep going.

The next time she slept in the same bed with Melanie, she wouldn't have to resist touching her. She'd finally found someone who made her want to lose control and she'd just taken a vow of celibacy. Easy enough.

CHAPTER FIFTEEN

Evelyn nodded at the security guard as she passed through the metal detector at the entrance to the courthouse. She ignored the beeping alert of the machine and headed for the elevator. As the car rose, her stomach knotted more with each passing floor. She'd been dreading this case for weeks.

Eight months ago, she and Kendall had responded to a domestic-violence call. A man had brutally raped his estranged wife, then stabbed her six times. The 9-1-1 call came in from the couple's eight-year-old daughter, who watched the whole thing through the slats in a closet door. Since that date, she had listened to the chilling phone call several times. The suspect could be heard ranting in the background, yelling at his fallen wife as if she could still hear him. Before the police arrived, he aimed a .22 caliber pistol at his own head and pulled the trigger. After a quick triage, the medics had left his deceased wife on the bedroom floor, scooped up the fatally wounded suspect, and rushed him to the hospital. Doctors saved his miserable life, and officers spent weeks guarding his hospital bed until he was well enough to be taken into custody and transported.

She later learned that the gun belonged to the wife, who had purchased it for her protection after she'd kicked her husband out. He'd forced his way into the house that night, and when she went for the gun, he took it from her.

When questioned by police, he said that he raped and stabbed her to teach her a lesson. He hadn't intended for her to die. He also admitted during questioning that he knew his daughter was in the apartment. He said maybe she wouldn't make the same mistakes that her mother had made. He later recanted the entire confession, saying the police had coerced him—a common, though trite, excuse.

Everything about this case made her sick to her stomach. Frankly, she'd been surprised to get a subpoena for it. She'd assumed he would take some type of plea.

The hallway leading to the courtroom was filled with people. The case had received a lot of attention, and several television stations were already setting up for remote broadcasts. The defendant's family clustered in one corner to the right of the courtroom door. Some of them had to remain outside since they would be called to testify later. Along the other side of the hallway, the witnesses for the prosecution sat on a row of benches against the wall. She recognized a couple of the officers and the crime-scene tech.

Off to the side, District Attorney Sarah Wales talked quietly to the lead detective on the case. They'd all been part of a pretrial conference last week so there would be no surprises in the prosecutor's line of questioning. But with Evelyn's father behind the defense table, everyone was a bit nervous about what trick he might try to pull out on his client's behalf.

"Long time," she said when Sarah looked up as she approached. The detective moved away to join the rest of the officers on the benches.

"Too long." She winked and Evelyn felt the familiar flip of her stomach. Even incredibly straight women had this effect on her.

"While you've been out lounging about on maternity leave, I've been here at least once a week helping your colleagues lock up the bad guys,"she joked.

"Yeah, that's what I was doing. Eating chocolate and getting massages while my infant daughter cared for herself."

"I thought so." She grinned. "Congrats, by the way."

"Thanks."

"You're dying to whip out a picture, aren't you?" She barely had the words out before Sarah had her phone in her hand, swiping her finger across the screen. When she turned the phone around, Evelyn gave the obligatory "awww." The baby was gorgeous. With her mother's ivory skin and a downy cap of matching red-gold hair, she was undoubtedly Sarah's child. She'd been dressed in a cute little pink-and-white polka-dot outfit, and the photographer had managed to coax out a smile.

"She's beautiful."

"I know," Sarah said, her eyes shining with motherly love. "It seems she's got my quick temper, though."

She laughed. "Good luck with that."

"Thanks." Sarah put her phone away, then shifted her case notes into her other arm. "I hope we'll get you on the stand today, but it might not be until tomorrow or the next day. I have a feeling getting a jury may be a chore. Once we get started, you guys can go down to the DA lounge and I'll send someone for you."

She didn't look forward to a day watching television in the lounge with the other guys. "I thought he would plead."

"I heard your father advised him to. But he refused."

Though she and her father purposely avoided talking about his cases, she wasn't surprised to hear he'd advised his client to plead. Between the 9-1-1 call and his self-inflicted wound, Evelyn couldn't imagine any defense that didn't involve mental illness. Even without his confession, the evidence recovered from the scene should be sufficient to obtain a conviction. Charles W. Fisher might be the most successful criminal-defense attorney in town, but even he couldn't pull out a not-guilty verdict on this one.

"Are we going to be down here all day?" A young officer shifted in his chair. He hooked his hand inside the top of his Kevlar vest and pulled it down. The damn things had a tendency to ride up.

"Probably. It's a media circus up there. Wales will want to get everything right." Evelyn slouched on a small sofa perpendicular to him. A detective occupied the only other chair in the small room. They all faced a plasma television on a nondescript cabinet. The hosts of the morning talk show on the screen were artificially perky—the man had too much hair product and the woman's voice was just plain annoying.

"It's all politics, kid. This nut job is either going to jail or a psychiatric hospital, but either way, he'll never see freedom again. This trial is about the lawyers." The veteran detective pulled his gaze from the screen and glanced across the room at the officer. "Wales wants to move up in the DA office and Fisher," now he looked at Evelyn with no apology in his expression, "well, he likes to win."

She held his gaze but didn't respond. This detective wasn't the first to voice his opinion of her father, and she'd learned early on not to address such talk. Even though she felt able to be objective, her words were usually taken as those of a blindly loyal daughter.

"I need a smoke." The detective stood, banging his shins on the coffee table as he tried to get to the door.

"Me, too." The young officer followed, tossing an unnecessary apologetic glance at her.

She was still glaring at the doorway when Kendall appeared in it.

"Hey. What did I do?"

"It's not you."

"Good." Kendall dropped onto the sofa beside her and tapped two fingers against her knee. "I think we're in for a long day. I heard they're having trouble picking a jury."

"How do you get away with showing up late? Last time I did that, Sarge knew before I could even get off the stand."

"The girls in Case Prep like me."

She shook her head. "Of course they do. You still got it, huh? Tell me what you say to them."

"Sorry, babe. But now that we're both single, you're the competition." Kendall grinned. Ironically, Kendall had been trying to set her up for years, and now that she was actually excited about a new relationship, she couldn't share it with Kendall.

"Single? What happened to Tiffany?"

"Over."

She looked at Kendall in disbelief. "You made me tell Melanie."

"Yeah, sorry. Things were going pretty good. Then last night she tells me she's getting back together with her ex."

"I'm sorry."

Kendall shrugged. "Apparently, they've been on again, off again for years, but they always go back to each other."

"Didn't you do any background on her before you tried to fix me up with her?"

"Please, I've hooked you up with every respectable woman I know. These days I only need to hear *lesbian* before I get the digits for you."

"I thought your standards for me had been dropping. I just didn't realize how bad it had gotten. You're officially fired. No more setups." She shoved against Kendall's shoulder. "So, other than your active social life, how are you?"

"I'm good." Kendall answered quickly, then seemed to consider her answer further. "Yeah, I'm okay. If you had asked me six months ago, I couldn't have guessed Melanie and I would be where we are. I miss our life, Evelyn."

She hadn't said she missed Melanie or that she still loved her. Evelyn's guilt kept her silent. She couldn't grill Kendall about what she truly meant without feeling like she did so for her own gain.

Kendall leaned forward, resting her elbows on her knees. "I hate being single. Sometimes, when I fixed you up, I thought how it must be exciting to meet new people. But going home alone just sucks."

"It's not that bad." Was she a hypocrite? She already looked forward to the next time she'd see Melanie. But she had plenty of years of being single herself to draw from. "Take the time to be comfortable with yourself. Do something you've always wanted to do."

"Like mountain biking?" Kendall said, laughing.

"Maybe not. But something just for you."

"Yeah, you're right. I can do anything I want to without checking in with anyone or considering what someone else wants." Sarcasm dripped from Kendall's words. "Please, don't talk to me about personal growth right now, okay?"

She nodded and pushed back farther into the sofa. Guilt gnawing at her stomach, she couldn't think of a thing to say that wouldn't make her feel worse. So they watched the stupid talk show in silence.

❖

Evelyn didn't wait for the light to change before she crossed the street. She strolled along the side of city hall toward the parking garage. She'd been released from court just in time to check in for her shift. If she had even thirty minutes more, she would have asked Melanie to meet up with her. Instead, she'd settle for a phone call.

As much as she wished for more, hearing Melanie answer, her voice soft and wonderfully intimate, made her day better.

"Hey, I only have a few minutes between court and my regular shift, but I wanted to hear your voice," she said. Despite a lingering shadow from spending the day with Kendall, she couldn't stop the smile pulling across her face.

"It's good to talk to you. I might be able to get away from the site around lunchtime tomorrow. Will you be free?"

"Probably not. I think I'll be in court." She would be incredibly busy this week, but perhaps a little space would be good for them. She had to figure out if there was a way to remain loyal to Kendall while still exploring whatever was happening with Melanie.

"Okay."

Evelyn didn't want to be the one to put that disappointed tone in Melanie's voice. "If something changes, can I call you?"

"Sure."

"I'm sorry. I want to see you, but by the time I get off tonight I won't be worth a damn."

"I need to be at the site for an early delivery, so I'll probably be asleep by the time you get done anyway. How's the trial going?"

"Slowly. As expected. I should get on the stand tomorrow, but I'll have to be available on the off chance the defense wants to recall me later this week."

"Do you think he will?" Melanie's choice of pronoun forced her to remember that they were talking about her father.

"I can't imagine why. But I wouldn't put anything past him."

They talked for a few more minutes about their hectic schedules for the coming week. When Melanie invited her for a late dinner after work Friday night, she couldn't refuse. Between now and then she'd have to get a better grasp on her intentions. She didn't want to lose Kendall's friendship. But the idea of forcing herself to ignore her feelings for Melanie left her feeling sad and lonely.

Melanie offered to come to her house and cook dinner for her, saying that she could have it finished and ready when she got home from work. She understood the hesitance in Melanie's tone as she voiced the offer. They already had keys to each other's homes, in case of emergency, but the new facet to their relationship added more intimacy to Melanie letting herself in and waiting for her to come home. She agreed to dinner, letting Melanie know how much she appreciated the gesture. And, despite her uncertainty about the future, she hung up feeling optimistic and hoping the next couple of days passed quickly.

❖

"Hello," Evelyn called as she walked through her own front door late Friday night.

"In the kitchen."

Had Melanie not replied, she could have simply followed the delicious aroma that tantalized her as soon as she entered the house.

She paused at the threshold of the kitchen, taking in the domestic scene before her. Melanie had dug out the only apron she owned—the one with THE COOK IS SMOKIN' printed across the front. Underneath, she wore a soft peach T-shirt, and her navy athletic shorts peeked out under the hem of the apron. Evelyn allowed herself a moment to admire the graceful curves of her high cheekbones and to imagine pressing her lips to the hollow just beneath the elegant line of her jaw. Melanie looked amazing in her kitchen.

"Don't just stand there. Go put on something more comfortable than that uniform and get back in here. I'm starving and dinner is almost ready."

"I'm getting pretty hungry myself," she said. In the quickly charging air between them, the words sounded more suggestive than she'd intended. But a rush of arousal followed her statement, and she would have forgotten about dinner in a second if Melanie made the smallest move.

Melanie only smiled and gestured toward the hallway leading to the bedroom.

"Do I have time for a shower?"

"A quick one."

She winked. "I'll just wash the important parts," she said over her shoulder as she walked away.

By the time Evelyn returned to the kitchen, her hair still wet and shiny, Melanie had set two places at the oval table centered in the dinette area on the other side of the kitchen island. She'd left the homemade flatbread pizzas to cool on the countertop and poured them each a tall glass of sweet tea.

Evelyn leaned against the island and rubbed her right eye with her fist. When she lowered her hand, Melanie moved close to her and smoothed a finger over her adorably disheveled eyebrow.

"You look tired." Melanie drew her into her arms and rested her hands on Evelyn's hips, enjoying the way Evelyn leaned into her. "Do you want to do this another time?"

Evelyn shook her head. "Just a long week. I'm okay."

"Clearly you're not. Is it work?"

Evelyn drew her eyebrows together and remained silent so long that she debated prodding her again.

"This trial wore me out. I spent almost two whole days waiting to get on the stand, then worked my regular shift. I didn't know I could get so tired from sitting around all day."

"Sometimes inactivity can be as tiring as—"

"That's not it."

"Aside from the long hours, what was going on inside the courtroom that stressed you out?"

"This guy—the defendant—what he did to his wife was evil. And his kid saw the whole thing. The crime-scene photos alone would make any sane person sick."

She didn't ask for specifics. She didn't want to hear them and Evelyn wouldn't want to give them.

"Knowing that my dad was in there defending that monster…"

"I don't know how he reconciles it either. But it's his job."

"I know. It's nothing new. We haven't been on the same page professionally in a long time. But in my mind, he's always been a good man. He provided for his family, taught me right from wrong. He's the exact opposite of this guy. So why was it so easy for him to defend him?"

"Do you know that it's easy for him? Have you and he ever talked about it."

"We have a hard time getting past how disappointed he is that I'm not just like him." Evelyn shook her head and slipped away from her. "I thought you were starving. This pizza smells amazing. Let's eat." She took a pizza cutter from a nearby drawer.

"Why do you want so much for him to see things your way now?" Melanie asked as she took the plate Evelyn handed her.

"Why does my relationship with him matter so much to you?" Evelyn countered just as casually, though her voice carried a bit of an edge.

She shrugged and followed Evelyn to the table. "Maybe we're getting to that age, but I've seen some of my friends lose a parent without warning."

Evelyn shook her head and tried to move away, but Melanie put their plates on the table and wrapped an arm around her shoulders. "You can't guilt me into—"

"I'm not. Not really." She pulled out a chair and waited until Evelyn sat, and then she dropped into the one next to her. "My dad was sick for a long time before he passed. If only one good thing came out of that, it's that I got a chance to connect with him in a way that I never had before." Her throat grew tight with the effort of containing her sudden tears. "I'm not saying overlook everything. But maybe don't hold on to old pain. He's your father. You clearly love each other. Tell him how you feel. Honest communication now could keep you from having regrets someday. And, you never know, you just might build a relationship you can treasure in the present as much as you do the one you had in the past."

Evelyn squeezed her hand. "Thank you. I'll think about what you've said."

CHAPTER SIXTEEN

"Dinner was great, thank you," Evelyn said as they stood next to each other at the sink. Melanie washed a plate and handed it to Evelyn, who dried it. Evelyn took a half step to the side so that their shoulders would touch. Melanie's warmth, even through their shirtsleeves, inspired a giddy feeling that still surprised her. Melanie excited her and made everything feel new, even though they'd been friends for years.

"I'm sorry you've had a rough week." Melanie took the towel from her. "I'll finish this. You go get comfortable and relax on the couch. I'll join you in a minute."

"I don't mind helping." She reached for the towel, but Melanie held it at arm's length, using her body to block her while she playfully tried to wrestle it back. When Evelyn's cell phone rang from the other room, they both stopped. "Saved by the bell."

"I totally had you," Melanie said, taking a step away. "Grab that if you want to."

She retrieved her phone from the living room and hesitated when she saw Kendall's name on the display. She answered the phone because she didn't want to start ducking Kendall's calls.

"Hey, I looked for you after work but you disappeared quickly," Kendall said.

"Yeah, sorry. I couldn't wait for the weekend, I guess." After a week of pulling what amounted to double shifts, she'd waited just long enough for the next shift to relieve them before she took off.

"I hear you. That trial was brutal, huh?"

"I'm just glad it's over." The week had ended in the expected guilty verdict. Even her father's smoothly worded questions hadn't been enough to cast doubt in the minds of the jurors in this case.

She felt Melanie's presence behind her, smelled the clean scent of her perfume seconds before Melanie rested her hands on her shoulders. When Melanie massaged her tense muscles, she barely kept herself from groaning.

"Let's unwind. Meet me downtown," Kendall suggested.

"Ah, I don't think so." Melanie bent and pressed her mouth to her neck, making it hard for her to concentrate on Kendall's words.

"Come on, you said you'd be my wingman when I needed you. So, I need you tonight. And I think we could both use a little distraction."

"Now isn't a good time."

Melanie paused and gave her a questioning look.

"Not a good time? I'm trying to save you from yourself, Evelyn." Kendall's voice took on a light teasing tone that usually meant she was about to deliver a line of BS. "I'm rescuing you from the misery of spending Friday night alone watching crappy television. I've let you be a hermit for too many years, my friend. But we're going to fix that."

"Can't we fix it tomorrow night?" she asked. *Damn. I'm not alone. I feel better than I have all week and I can't even tell you that.*

"You're seriously not coming out with me?"

"Sorry. Next time. Okay?"

"I guess. Have a good night." Kendall didn't wait for her to respond before she hung up. She set her phone on the table, stood, and took Melanie into her arms.

"That was Kendall."

"What was she trying to talk you into?"

"She's going to a bar and wanted me to be her wingman."

"Wingman? What about Tiffany?"

Evelyn shook her head.

Melanie nodded. "I probably could have called that one. That girl wasn't right for either one of you."

She threw up her hands. "Then why did you let Kendall set her up with me?"

"Please. I decided a long time ago to stay out of that situation. Kendall was determined to find you a woman, and I don't think I could have stopped her. Besides, you didn't exactly put your foot down and say no."

"I know. And what's worse is at some point I stopped really trying to find my own dates. A part of me hoped Kendall would get it right and save me some work."

"You should go."

"What?"

"Go meet her."

"Are you trying to ditch me?"

"Of course not."

"Then what's up? I was enjoying where this evening was headed."

"You were looking forward to making out until we could barely stand not going any further, then forcing ourselves to stop, thus ending the evening almost painfully turned on?"

"When you put it that way—absolutely." Evelyn raised her eyebrows, but Melanie's expression said she wasn't budging, so she tried one more tactic. "She'll expect me to hit on women with her."

Melanie laughed. "Are you trying to make me jealous?"

"Did it work?"

"Maybe."

"Am I supposed to go out with her and fake it, when I really just want to be here with you?" She traced her fingers along Melanie's forearm. "My feelings about us haven't changed. We should just tell her and get it over with."

"We will, soon. But for tonight, go hang out with her. Flirt with whoever you want—" she raised an eyebrow but Melanie shook her finger at her, "but no touching." She pulled Evelyn close and kissed her. "I'll be around all day tomorrow, cleaning the house, if you want to hang out."

"I will definitely call you. Maybe we could have a post-date breakfast."

Melanie smiled. "Okay, smart-ass. Go get dressed. But don't look too hot."

"I'm not sure I can help it," she said as she walked down the hall toward her bedroom.

❖

"I thought I said not too hot." Melanie rested her hands on Evelyn's hips, hooking her fingers inside the belt loops on Evelyn's faded jeans. Her white button-down shirt practically glowed against her olive skin, and when she moved, the loose waves of her dark hair cast the fruity scent of her shampoo into the air.

"This old thing? You've seen me in it a dozen times."

"True. But I've never seen you in it and subsequently imagined you out of it before tonight." She traced her finger into the deep vee of Evelyn's neckline. "You should close one more button up here."

"But I always wear it like this."

She fastened the button in question, then smoothed her hands over the front of Evelyn's shirt. "That's much better. Now you're ready."

Evelyn smiled. She picked up her keys and shoved her phone in her pocket. "Don't wait up," she said with an exaggerated wink.

Melanie walked her to the door and stepped outside with her. She grabbed Evelyn's belt, pulled her close, and gave her a kiss she could remember while she hit on girls with Kendall. When they broke apart, both breathless, she said, "You have to go, before I take you back inside."

"That sounds like a better plan." Evelyn laughed, then pulled her in for another kiss. Seduced by the play of Evelyn's tongue against hers, she lost track of everything around her until the familiar sound of Kendall's voice forced her back to reality.

"Okay, I came over here to drag your ass—"

They jerked apart. For a second, Evelyn's eyes were still soft with arousal and her lips were bruised from the kiss. When regret replaced the warmth in Evelyn's gaze, Melanie had to close her eyes.

"Are you fucking kidding me?" Kendall said, her voice rising with every word.

She took a deep breath before turning to face Kendall. Accusation flashed violently in Kendall's glare.

Melanie stepped between Evelyn and Kendall, wanting to shield Evelyn from her anger. She didn't regret anything that had happened up to this point—she never could—but she wished this moment had been different for both Evelyn and Kendall.

"Kendall—"

"No," Kendall barked, surging forward until she was in Melanie's face. "You don't get to talk. I don't want to hear a *damn* thing you have to say."

Evelyn touched Melanie's elbow as if she meant to draw her away, but Kendall cut her eyes sharply toward her and Evelyn dropped her hand.

She tried again. "Please, don't—"

"Don't what, Melanie? Don't get mad because I just found my *best* friend making out with my ex?" She stepped back, her eyes darting between Evelyn and Melanie, finally landing on Evelyn and narrowing. "How long did you wait after we broke up before you went after her?"

"It's not like that," Evelyn said. Her voice held no plea for understanding, only resignation.

"I get it, Ev. She's hot." Kendall looked Melanie up and down in a way that dismissed their years together and reduced her to a piece of meat. "Have you wanted her all these years? When I talked about our sex life, were you wishing it was you?"

"Damn it, Kendall," Melanie shouted. Evelyn's face burned bright red and she looked as if Kendall had slapped her.

Kendall glared at her, then shook her head, turned, and walked away. Evelyn stared after her with a heartbroken expression.

Acutely aware that their scene had played out in front of Evelyn's condo for all of her neighbors to witness, Melanie put her arm around Evelyn and attempted to urge her back into the house, but Evelyn drew away. "Ev, let's go inside."

Evelyn nodded, but she still seemed hazy. She took Evelyn's hand and pulled her toward the door. Her skin was clammy and her fingers trembled in Melanie's. Once inside, Melanie led her to the couch and they sat down.

"Do you want something to drink?"

"No."

"Ev, about what Kendall said—"

Evelyn waved a hand, and when she met her eyes she seemed more focused. "She was wrong. I never had an inappropriate thought about you once while you two were together."

"I wanted to be sure you didn't doubt that. I'm sure she knows that, too. She's just shocked and angry."

"I can't say I blame her. This was probably the last thing she expected."

"Well, it wasn't in my five-year plan either."

"I didn't want her to find out this way." Evelyn shoved her hand through her hair. "I spent the entire week on this case with her wishing I could figure out how to tell her, keep her friendship, and not lose you."

She hadn't seen Evelyn all week, but they'd talked on the phone often. And each time, she'd gotten the impression that Evelyn was holding something back. At first she assumed it had to do with the case, but she soon realized there was more to it. Evelyn had been distant and not as responsive as usual. After the case and her father, Kendall was her next guess.

"Did you come up with anything?"

"Only that it wasn't possible. Looks like I was right."

"I'm sorry, Evelyn."

"It's not your fault."

"It's at least as much my fault as yours. I shouldn't have let this happen."

"I'd like to think you couldn't help yourself," Evelyn said.

"Well, it definitely would have been difficult to resist. But I'm not sure I tried hard enough."

"I owed her more than this." Evelyn's voice cracked.

Melanie touched Evelyn's hand, encouraged when she didn't immediately pull away. "We didn't do this to hurt her."

"I know. But that's what happened, isn't it?" Evelyn slipped her hand free and stood. "I'm sorry. I'm tired. Do you mind if we cut the rest of our evening short?"

"Are you okay?"

"Yes. I—I need to think."

"Of course." Melanie stood as well, the distance in Evelyn's eyes turning her body cold. Should she push Evelyn to talk or give her time? In the past, when dealing with her "friend" she'd have pushed, but since their relationship had changed, it seemed the rules had as well. Evelyn had all but dismissed her, clearly asking for space. With anyone else she had only begun to date, she would grant that—possibly even taking this bump in the road as a sign they weren't meant to be. But letting Evelyn go just wasn't that simple.

Evelyn nodded and walked to the door, obviously expecting her to follow.

"Will you call me?" Perhaps she sounded pathetic, but she wanted to know where they stood. Historically, Evelyn didn't stay in a relationship that proved to be too much work. Would she so easily throw aside what they might have been building in order to restore her friendship with Kendall? A selfish part of her wanted to believe she couldn't—that Evelyn felt this new connection between them as deeply as she did.

Evelyn turned and pulled her into her arms, holding her tight. She cupped her hand against the back of Melanie's head and inhaled deeply, then released her. "I'll call you."

"Good. Because whatever you decide about us, I don't want to lose your friendship."

"Hey," Evelyn drew back, her eyes soft with emotion, "don't start your contingency plan yet. I haven't given this up. I just need a little time."

"Okay. Fair enough. You know where to find me."

Evelyn pressed her lips to hers gently and Melanie told herself it wasn't a good-bye kiss.

❖

"Can I get you anything else?"

"No, thanks." Kendall dismissed the waitress without looking at her. She absently stirred artificial sweetener into her fresh cup of coffee.

"Would you like me to take your plate?"

"Sure." She leaned back and waited while the woman removed the platter loaded with scrambled eggs, turkey bacon, and wheat toast. She'd been pushing the food around for the last thirty minutes, unable to summon her appetite.

Ever since she'd rounded the corner at Evelyn's condo and seen Evelyn and Melanie together, she'd felt like someone punched her in the stomach. She had gone to the bar without Evelyn and had a horrible time. And the fact that this morning she felt compelled to sit in this booth, the same one where she and Evelyn held their ritual breakfasts, angered her even more. She'd never felt more betrayed, and the fact that *Evelyn* had twisted the knife in her gut made her physically ill.

She'd known the moment that she'd seen them together that this was not their first embrace. Something had been going on behind her back, and now she felt like an even bigger fool. Evelyn had put her hands on Melanie as if it were her right, all the while acting as if she were still Kendall's loyal friend. That was unforgivable.

CHAPTER SEVENTEEN

Monday afternoon, Evelyn entered the precinct with a ball of nerves rolling around in her belly. She stopped to check the subpoena book, quickly visited the restroom, and logged on to a computer to get her e-mail. And when she couldn't procrastinate any longer, she plodded into the roll-call room. Kendall sat at a table by herself, while most of the other guys still milled around, socializing as they waited for their lieutenant and sergeants to brief them before they headed out on the streets.

She took a deep breath and ambled toward Kendall. She returned the greeting of several of the guys but didn't let them deter her from her goal.

She waited until she stood beside Kendall to speak. "Can I talk to you?"

When Kendall glanced up, Evelyn recoiled from the icy detachment in her eyes. "No."

"Kendall, I just want to tell you that we—"

Kendall surged to her feet, her face only inches away. In her periphery, Evelyn caught several heads turning in their direction. When Kendall spoke, her voice was low and dangerous, her words forced through a rigid jaw. "I don't want to hear anything you have to say. Especially not here."

She gave a terse nod and stepped back. Embarrassing them both in front of their peers wouldn't accomplish anything. She'd have to hope Kendall came around or she could find an opportunity to get her alone. She had purposely not tried to contact Kendall for the remainder of the weekend in order to give her time to cool down. But obviously not enough time had passed.

She crossed the room and took a seat at a table by the door. Riggs sat down beside her, looking as if he wanted to say something. But she was spared when the lieutenant took his place at the front of the room. As soon as they were dismissed, she slipped out the door, hurried to her car, and drove out of the parking lot.

For the next seven-and-a-half hours, she buried herself in work, volunteering for every call as soon as she finished the last. She ran from one end of the sector to the other, until even the dispatcher, a regular on their channel, sent her an instant message on her laptop asking what was up with her tonight. She brushed off the inquiry with a joke about dealing with citizens. While she knew officers who carried on personal conversations over the computer, she didn't. Anything she put in the computer became government property and could be retrieved by ITS.

She had only an hour left in her shift when she got dispatched on a robbery at a convenience store in her sector. No other officers nearby were available, and she heard the dispatcher calling for someone to check in and back her up. After a moment of radio silence, Kendall keyed up and said she would be in route. A bubble of hope formed in her heart, though her head said that Kendall was a good cop and would do her job no matter the personal issues. Kendall's willingness to back her up didn't indicate an inch of forgiveness.

"Mr. McCandless, you have to calm down."

"Calm down—I've just been robbed. My coworker was shot."

"I know but—" Kendall didn't even get a full sentence in.

"The man put a gun in my face and my life flashed before my eyes. I've only been the manager a month. They made me transfer from Green Hills to take this store and a man puts a gun in my face, then shoots the man standing next to me." He spoke rapidly, not even taking time to breathe between sentences. By the end of the tirade, his strained voice faded on a gasp. He wrung his slender hands together then wiped them on his pants legs. Beads of perspiration trickled out of his hairline and down the side of his face. He swiped at them, plastering his thin, brown hair to his forehead.

"I know it's a lot." A robbery and a shooting would stress even the most experienced convenience-store manager. McCandless obviously wasn't a seasoned employee. "But your clerk is on the way to the hospital and the paramedics said he's going to be fine. You're not hurt. Why don't you sit down for a minute?" Kendall glanced around the small break room, then gestured to a table and chairs nearby.

She had arrived just behind Evelyn, who had her hands full dealing with the injured clerk and the hysterical manager. One of the paramedics gave her a look when McCandless got in his way one too many times, so she had ushered the upset man into the back room, separating him from the scene and her from Evelyn.

He pulled out a chair, startling himself when the metal feet scraped loudly across the floor. She sat in the one opposite him and took a small notebook out of the breast pocket of her shirt.

"Now, can you tell me what the guy looked like?"

"Guys. There were two. One black and one white."

"Did they both have guns?"

"Yes."

"Which one shot the clerk?"

"The white guy. I don't know his name, but I've seen him in here before. The other guy freaked out when he fired the gun, said they weren't supposed to shoot anyone." He answered her questions quickly and clearly, more calm now that he had something to focus on.

"And what did the white guy do?"

"He told him to shut up, and they grabbed the money and ran out."

"Did they leave in a car?"

He nodded. "A tan Oldsmobile."

"You're sure it was an Oldsmobile."

"Absolutely. It was an Alero. I recognized it because my mother used to have one just like it."

"Good. Did anything else stand out about the car—tinted windows, rims, bumper stickers, damage anywhere on it?"

"Not that I recall."

"Okay. Excuse me for one second." She turned away and transmitted the vehicle description over the radio for other officers in the area.

She managed to draw out some details about the suspects' clothing and personal appearance and put them out as well. When she'd gotten everything she could from McCandless, she asked him to call whomever he needed to in order to get the security-camera videos pulled. She also gave him a card and told him not to go anywhere in case the detective had more questions. He flipped a cell phone from a holster on his belt and was on the phone with his district manager before she got out of the room.

She stepped outside as the ambulance pulled out of the parking lot with the victim. During the robbery, two customers had been inside the store and one man was at the gas pumps. Now they had been separated and were being questioned by other officers.

"What do you have?" Sergeant Stahlman called as he strode across the parking lot.

She filled him in on the manager's account of the incident. By the time she'd finished, Evelyn had joined them and added what little she'd been able to get from the injured clerk. "I have to update the captain so he can brief the media." He nodded to their captain, who had just parked his unmarked car in the front of the parking lot. "I need one of you to complete the report and gather supplements from the other officers and the other to head over to the hospital to meet the detective."

"It's my zone. I'll do the report," Evelyn said.

"I've got the hospital. I'll do my supplement while I'm there and take it by the station when I'm done." Kendall addressed Sergeant Stahlman, purposely not looking at Evelyn. Instinct screamed at her to make eye contact, share a nod or a smile, but she steadfastly squelched the impulse.

Stahlman nodded, pantomimed smoothing his hair back from his forehead as if preening for the media, then headed across the lot toward the captain's car.

"Kendall," Evelyn said, taking a step toward her.

She started to turn away without responding, but she didn't get far. Jennifer Prince pulled her patrol car up close, stopping only a couple of feet from where she stood.

"Hello, ladies," she said as she climbed out of the car.

"What are you doing on this side of the river, Princess?" Evelyn asked.

"Sarge sent us to patrol the neighborhood for your suspect."

Kendall nodded. "The manager said he's seen him in the store before, so it's possible he lives over here."

"Okay. I'll be in the area. Call me if you get anything else on him." She pulled open her car door, then said, "A bunch of us are going out for drinks later. You two should come along."

When Evelyn glanced at her, she knew she was trying to gauge her willingness to socialize in the same crowd.

"Maybe next time," she said. Without waiting for Jennifer to respond, she skirted Jennifer's car. A night out with the girls actually sounded like fun, but only if Evelyn wasn't there.

As she walked away she heard Jennifer ask, "Wow. What's her problem?"

"Me." Evelyn sighed.

"What? Why?"

She was out of range so she didn't catch the rest of Evelyn's response. Evelyn would probably go out with Jennifer and the others. Maybe she'd have a few drinks and spill the whole story. By tomorrow, not only would Evelyn and Melanie be laughing at her behind her back, but so would all their friends.

❖

Evelyn paused in the doorway of the bar, already wishing she hadn't come. She'd only done it to prove to herself that she could go one more day without seeing Melanie. They had texted on and off all weekend, but she had purposely stayed away, testing herself, and Melanie hadn't pushed. Since she might have torpedoed her friendship with Kendall, she wanted to know that these new feelings for Melanie were real. Tonight, instead of going out drinking, she only wanted to go to Melanie.

But Jennifer had already seen her and waved her over to a table across the bar. And a man trying to enter the bar bumped into her then shoved her farther inside. He pushed past her without a word.

"Excuse me. No, I'm sorry, totally my fault," she mumbled as she forced herself forward.

The place had been open just over a year and she had been here only a handful of times. The small area had been designed as the counterpart to the clubs down the street with their thumping music, fog machines, and laser lighting. The jukebox in the corner only played if someone pumped quarters into it and didn't have any club mixes on it. The square tables in the center of the room didn't leave enough space for a dance floor anyway.

But the bar was popular among the lesbians who weren't interested in watching a drag show or bumping and grinding on the dance floor. The bright décor supplemented the absence of auditory stimulation. Vividly colored paintings studded the warm reddish-orange walls, and strings of white LED lights followed the lines of the dark exposed beams along the ceiling.

Every stool at the bar was occupied, and women squeezed into the spaces between and lined up three deep, awaiting the attentions of the two bartenders scrambling to keep up with drink orders.

"Hey, girl," Jennifer called as she approached. "Have a seat." She pulled out the chair next to her and Evelyn dropped into it. "Can I buy you a drink?"

"No, thanks. I'm good." Alcohol was not in her plan for the night. She wanted a clear head, not a place to drown her thoughts.

"Are you sure?" The waitress brought over a tray of shots and lined four of them up on the table in front of them.

"Tell me these aren't all for you."

Jennifer laughed. "Of course not. The other girls are at the bar. So, before they get back, tell me what's going on between you and Miss Kendall. Why were you all tense and twitchy around each other?"

She grimaced. Was she really contemplating whether to confide in her one-time one-night stand about her feelings for her friend who used to date her other friend? When had her life become a soap opera?

"Come on. It stays between us."

Maybe sharing with someone would help. At one time, she would have hashed her problems out with Kendall or Melanie. Until she got her head around what direction she was headed, neither was an option. Kendall wouldn't speak to her. And she couldn't talk to Melanie about her feelings for Melanie until she knew exactly what she was feeling for Melanie. Hell, her thoughts were even confusing her.

"Absolutely between us, okay? I don't want to be the gossip of the department."

"I swear." Jennifer held her hand up as she made the vow.

She nodded and started slowly, telling a circuitous story. But once she began she couldn't stop talking and eventually poured out the whole tale, ending with Kendall's discovery of them kissing and subsequent refusal to talk to her.

"Wow." Jennifer had leaned forward during her narrative, and now she settled back into the booth. "And Kendall didn't beat the shit out of you?"

She let her head drop forward as Jennifer's words illuminated her guilt. "I'm an ass, aren't I?"

"A little bit, yeah. Did you think there was any way she would be okay with this?"

"No, I guess not. I kept telling myself not to do it, Jenn. I knew she'd hate me. But—I've just never felt like this before. I don't even know how to explain it."

"Okay, but it's a rule, Evelyn. You don't date your friend's ex. Especially not a long-term one who only recently dumped her."

"I didn't mean for this to happen."

"You took a risk, followed your heart, I guess I get that. But it might have cost you."

"It almost certainly did."

"Is she worth it?"

"What?"

"Melanie. What's between the two of you?"

"It's so strange. I've always thought she was amazing and gorgeous, and who wouldn't be half in love with her. But she was in a relationship with my best friend—happily, I thought. After Kendall—well, after Kendall started dating again and I began spending time alone with Melanie, things changed. And now, it's new—but it's familiar, you know."

"Cut the bullshit and just tell me, Evelyn. Are you serious about her?"

She didn't need to think. The rush of emotions that followed Jennifer's question provided her answer. "Yeah. I am."

"Then I hope it works out for you."

"That's it?"

"Did you think I was going to say something else?"

"I thought you might tell me how to fix things with Kendall."

Jennifer grunted a humorless laugh. "Good luck with that."

She shook her head and rubbed her fingertips over her forehead. "Shit."

"You two had a secret behind her back. She feels like a fool, and for good reason, I think."

She nodded. Kendall felt betrayed, she got that. But how could she explain or apologize if Kendall wouldn't listen to her? The only option was to wait until Kendall was ready to talk.

"What are you going to do about Melanie?" Jennifer asked.

She shrugged. Would Kendall be more likely to come around if she and Melanie weren't together? And even if she would, could she do it—stop spending time with Melanie? Just the thought made her chest ache. Maybe she'd screwed everything up with Kendall, but would throwing away the connection she'd built with Melanie right that wrong? Her heart said no. None of the women she'd dated made her feel even half of what she felt when she was with Melanie—when she held her and kissed her.

She needed to see her. She'd convinced herself she could think more clearly if she stayed away. But her head swam with images and memories of Melanie. She wanted to be with her, to talk out this situation with her.

She stood and put a hand on Jennifer's shoulder. "I have to go. Thanks for listening."

"You just got here," Jennifer said, grabbing her hand.

"I need to be somewhere else."

"I guess your decision is made."

She nodded. "I think it is."

As she walked out of the bar, she texted Melanie and asked if she could see her soon. Her phone beeped with a response before she reached her car. When Melanie asked her to come over, she smiled, hoping that meant Melanie wanted to see her just as badly.

CHAPTER EIGHTEEN

Melanie opened the door before Evelyn had a chance to ring the bell. She leaned against it and smiled, and Evelyn's doubts began to melt under the warmth spreading through her. Melanie wore a T-shirt and old blue sweats, and her disheveled hair indicated she must have fallen asleep and just woken up when she texted.

"I wasn't thinking—you have to work in the morning. If it's too late, I can just go home."

"Come here." Melanie took her hand and pulled her inside.

"I missed you." When Melanie loosened her hand as if about to let go, she held on and Melanie wrapped her fingers back around Evelyn's.

"Me, too," Melanie said softly. "How was work?" Her question was purposely general, but she surely meant how had things gone with Kendall.

"She won't talk to me."

"Do you think we should stop seeing each other?"

"No. Would I be a better friend if I said yes? Maybe. But," she urged Melanie closer and rested her hands on her hips, "I can't believe that making all three of us miserable is the best solution."

Melanie rested her forehead against hers. "I don't want to be the reason you two can't be friends." The sadness in Melanie's tone sent a streak of panic through her chest.

"Please, don't tell me that you've decided we shouldn't be together."

"Ev—"

"No, Mel, no." She didn't want to hear that she'd lost Melanie, too.

"Maybe if we weren't together, maybe Kendall would—"

"She wouldn't."

"It's worth a shot, Ev. She already hates me. You can tell her I came on to you."

She pressed two fingers to Melanie's mouth. "I'm not going to do that."

"She might forgive you."

"I'm happy, Mel. For the first time in my life I know what other people feel. When I'm not with you, you're all I can think about." She laid her hand against the side of Melanie's face, stroking the hollow below her cheekbone. "I understand why Kendall's hurt and I know it's my fault—"

"Our fault."

"Okay, our fault. And I miss her, I do. But this—your friendship matters, too." Flooded with emotions, she swallowed the words that would convey just how much she felt for Melanie.

"Evelyn."

"No." She covered Melanie's mouth with hers. What began as a means to silence Melanie quickly deepened. Melanie threaded her fingers behind her neck and pulled her closer, slanting their mouths together. Melanie's hands found their way to her hair, holding her, and she traced the shell of her ears with her thumbs.

She shoved her hand under Melanie's shirt, desperate for skin, and when she found it, on Melanie's soft belly, she couldn't contain the sigh that whispered against Melanie's lips.

Melanie kissed her jaw, then moved to her neck, biting gently. Sharp points of arousal followed each scrape of teeth against her skin.

"Melanie?"

"Yes?"

"Kendall knows about us now." She eased her hand back and grasped the hem of Melanie's shirt.

"Yes."

"Does that mean the ban on sex has been lifted?" She pushed the shirt up, pausing after she'd exposed several inches of Melanie's stomach. She'd never been so nervous at the thought of escalating a physical relationship.

"I suppose it does." Melanie placed a hand over hers. "But don't you think we should talk about this a bit more first?"

"No, I don't." She walked them to the couch and urged Melanie back. "I'm tired of thinking and talking." Moving on top of her, she added, "I've wanted to touch you for so long. Please, let me."

Melanie met her eyes, arousal burning as hotly there as in her own body. Melanie guided her hand farther under her shirt and up her torso until her palm covered the lacy cup of Melanie's bra. She snuck her fingers inside and caressed a hardening nipple, then paused.

"What's wrong?" Melanie gasped.

"Nothing." She smiled, Melanie's breathless tone had her trembling with the effort of holding back. "I'm just waiting for my brain to catch up. Right now all I can think is, 'You're touching Melanie's breast.'"

"Yeah? Do you think it will catch up soon?"

"Maybe. Why?"

Melanie grabbed her wrist and pushed both of their hands beneath the waistband of her boxers. "You might have to outrun it, because I really need you to touch me right now."

When her fingers grazed soft hair, then slipped into moist flesh, Evelyn groaned. "You're not wearing panties."

"You're stating the obvious." Melanie lifted her hips, causing her fingers to probe deeper. Melanie closed her eyes and a small smile lifted one side of her mouth. Entranced by Melanie's sigh of pleasure, she stroked her slowly, giving a little more pressure with each pass over her clitoris.

Melanie pulled Evelyn's shirt up until it tangled around her shoulders. "Take this off."

Evelyn sat up and yanked it over her head.

"Your bra, too," Melanie said breathlessly. God, Evelyn was gorgeous. She drank in the sight of Evelyn's tight abs, strong shoulders, and lean, muscled arms. She'd seen Evelyn in a swimsuit before, knew she had a great body, but she'd never looked at her in this light.

She hooked her hands around the waistband of Evelyn's jeans, her fingers making Evelyn's skin jump. Testing, she raked them lightly over her belly and she twitched in response. Evelyn reached behind her and unhooked her bra, revealing small, perfect breasts. Melanie traced two fingers around the swell of her chest, circling toward her nipple, which puckered in anticipation of the touch she didn't yet deliver. "Beautiful."

Evelyn stretched over her, putting her hand back in Melanie's boxers. When Evelyn cupped her and slipped a finger inside, Melanie moaned. She wrapped her leg around Evelyn's hip and pressed up, seeking more. Evelyn ground her hips between her legs, trapping her hand between them, creating the pressure she wanted.

Evelyn buried her face in her neck as she thrust against her. Melanie hugged her shoulders, loving the feeling of being pinned beneath her, and planted her feet into the sofa cushion, scrambling for leverage to bring them even closer together.

When Evelyn sat up, kneeling between her legs, she tried to rise with her. But Evelyn placed a hand in the center of her chest and held her in place.

"I want to slow down," Evelyn said, her eyes liquid with need.

"Later. We have all night." Right now, she didn't care if their first time together was a quick, half-dressed romp on the sofa.

"Exactly. We have all night. So what's the rush?" When Evelyn worked her boxers over her hips and down her legs, her hands trembled and Melanie could tell her control wasn't as strong as she tried to make it appear. Challenged, she cupped Evelyn's small breast. She rubbed her thumb lightly across her nipple and it tightened. Evelyn bit her lower lip, her eyes dark with desire, and heavy arousal throbbed between Melanie's legs.

She grasped Evelyn's hips and tugged her back down. As Evelyn sprawled across her, she slipped her leg between Evelyn's.

"No rush. Take your time," she growled in Evelyn's ear as she bent her leg and pushed her thigh snugly against her center. "But you don't mind if I amuse myself while I'm waiting, do you?" She smiled, slipped her hand between them, and toyed with Evelyn's nipple. Evelyn shivered. "Sensitive, huh? Now there's something I didn't know about you."

"Yeah. It's funny the things that don't come up in five years of friendship."

Intrigued, she braced her hands on Evelyn's shoulders and pushed her up. She rose and took one of Evelyn's nipples into her mouth, sucking gently and flicking it with her tongue.

"Oh, God, hold on, Mel." Evelyn arched her back, but with Melanie's legs tangled in hers, she was unable to get away.

Melanie switched her attention to Evelyn's other breast. Evelyn moaned and cradled her head to her chest. Intoxicated with the power of controlling Evelyn from beneath her, she wrapped her arms around Evelyn's torso, her palms flat against her strong back. Evelyn's hips moved against hers and she braced herself against the sofa. Evelyn's motions teased the pleasure building between her legs, and even when she wrapped her legs around Evelyn's hips and pulled her closer, she didn't get quite enough pressure.

She released Evelyn's nipple, unwound her arms, and lay back. "I need you." She moaned, distantly aware that she'd probably never had the control at all.

Evelyn scooted down the sofa, pausing to kiss the hollow of her hip and her stomach just below her navel. Melanie trembled. Evelyn looked up, her gaze heavy with arousal, then lowered her head and dragged her tongue along her clit. Melanie barely had time to register the singe of bliss before Evelyn returned with even more fervor, sucking her fully into her mouth. Numb pleasure started at Melanie's fingertips and toes and traveled to her center, seizing her muscles with each stroke of Evelyn's tongue and the pull of her mouth.

Sensation overwhelmed her. The contrast of Evelyn's warm mouth and the cool leather against her bare ass heightened her experience. Far too quickly, she was in danger of tipping over the precipice.

"Oh, don't stop," she gasped, clutching Evelyn's shoulder. She craved the impending release yet wished she could prolong the ecstasy that assailed her. When Evelyn pressed two fingers inside, the last shred of her will slipped away and she gave herself up to the crashing orgasm.

She arched and cried out, her muscles rigid, her hand firm against the back of Evelyn's head. Evelyn continued to thrust slowly and gentled her tongue, lapping through the contractions that pulsed in her flesh.

Melanie sighed and flung her arm over her forehead as she sagged into the sofa. Evelyn laid her head on her thigh and stretched her arm up, resting her hand in the center of her chest. When Melanie took a deep breath, her chest rose then fell into a slight concave, and the swell of her breasts embraced Evelyn's fingers.

Evelyn turned her cheek into Melanie's leg and kissed the soft skin of her inner thigh. "That was amazing."

"I think that's my line." She lay quietly for a moment longer, enjoying the aftershocks. When the sharp points had smoothed into a languid flutter, she said, "I did learn another thing I didn't know about you."

"What's that?"

"Jennifer Prince was right. You are a stud in bed."

Evelyn smiled. "Yeah?"

"Mmm-hmm, but we didn't actually make it to the bed, did we?"

"Not yet."

❖

Evelyn opened her eyes slowly, first registering warmth against her back, then the solid feel of an arm around her waist and legs pressed firmly along her butt and thighs. She rolled over and Melanie stirred only long enough to snuggle closer to her side. Evelyn smiled and kissed her forehead. Last night hadn't been a dream, and waking next to a very naked Melanie Cook didn't feel strange at all. In fact, she felt as if she'd been waiting for this day for most of her life.

The way things currently stood with Kendall cast the only shadow on her morning. She'd always thought that when she finally found someone who made her feel this way, she would share her happiness with Kendall and Melanie. She'd imagined the four of them going out to dinner or taking vacations together. And of course, the love of her life, still faceless in her mind, would get along great with her friends.

Reality had definitely thrown her a curve. That faceless love now had Melanie's beautiful features—the same delicately arched brows that she currently traced with her finger, the strong chin with the slightest indentation, and the full lips that last night had brought exquisite pleasure as they puckered around her nipple. Had she just so easily cast Melanie as the love of her life?

Even the touch of panic at that thought couldn't erase the memory of last night. She squeezed her thighs together as she recalled the hours they'd spent touching each other. She glanced at the clock. They had plenty of time, if she woke Melanie right now, for another round. But they'd gone to sleep only a few hours ago as it was, and since Melanie had to be at work so much earlier than she did, she should probably let her sleep.

Melanie moved in her sleep and her hand brushed down Evelyn's chest and came to rest low on her stomach, her fingers teasing the crease where her hip and thigh met. Her skin tingled under Melanie's hand and set off a fuse that crackled the few inches to her clit. She shifted her hips and Melanie stirred and opened her eyes.

"Hey, good morning," Melanie rasped.

"Yes, it is." She stroked Melanie's hair back and tucked it behind her ear. "You should sleep for a bit longer."

Melanie nodded groggily and closed her eyes. She burrowed her face into Evelyn's neck and kissed her softly.

"Mmm, I don't think you can do that." She pressed her cheek to Melanie's forehead.

"Why not?"

"Because I kept you up all night and your alarm is going off in forty-five minutes. You should sleep until then." She sat up and moved to the edge of the bed. God, it would be so easy to get lost in making love to Melanie again. But she could stave off logic for only so long. Now, she needed to get her head around what had happened. Wherever they went from here, she could not let Melanie get hurt.

"Where are you going?"

"For a run."

"Damn. I forgot how much of a morning person you are," Melanie said

"Do you want to go?"

"Hell, no. Lucas and I are building a retaining wall today. I'll get my exercise lugging around stones and bags of mortar. Do you have to?"

"I can't lie here much longer without touching you."

"So touch me." Melanie caressed her thigh. She met Evelyn's eyes as she slid her hand slowly upward. "We can be quick."

Evelyn bent and kissed Melanie's forehead. "Take a power nap. I'll be back in an hour."

"If you time it right, you might catch me in the shower and we'll see," Melanie said with a wink. She grabbed Evelyn's arm and pulled her down for a proper kiss. When she released her, Evelyn fought the desire to crawl back into bed with her. "I'll make you breakfast when you get back."

"I could get used to that." The words were out before she could stop them. She searched Melanie's face for a reaction, but if Melanie inferred anything meaningful from the statement she didn't show it.

"My workout clothes are in the second drawer," Melanie said.

Evelyn went to the dresser and found a pair of navy athletic shorts, a sports bra, and a gray T-shirt. As she smoothed the T-shirt down, she laughed. In black letters, RUNNING SUCKS was printed across the front.

"My favorite shirt." Melanie's words were muffled by the pillow as she turned over.

"Cute. I'll see you soon."

She stopped at her car on her way out and picked up her Bluetooth headphones. She selected the GPS workout tracker on her phone and her favorite playlist, and she then jogged down the walk to the street. By the time she'd covered two blocks she had settled into her pace in almost perfect rhythm with the music.

"Oh, man, you're an idiot," she muttered to herself as P!nk's edgy voice and the image of Melanie naked filled her head. "Sleep be damned, you should have stayed in bed."

Instead, she ran. She wound her way through Melanie's neighborhood, trying to lose herself in the unfamiliar scenery. But each block looked remarkably the same as the next, so she let her mind wander back to last night.

She had forever changed her friendship with Melanie, not that it wasn't already altered, but sleeping together—well, that was a whole new level of intimacy. She'd had casual sex with a friend before, Jennifer Prince being one example, but last night was different. Touching and being touched by Melanie went beyond sex, beyond anything she'd felt before. If she were feeling this with anyone else, she might want to pull back and slow down. But Melanie—well, she couldn't even think about distancing herself from Melanie.

The soreness in her thighs as she ran brought back memories of the night before. So instead of dwelling on how complicated the situation was, she decided to entertain herself with visions of making love with Melanie. By her fourth mile, her head was filled with the flex of muscles in Melanie's arms as she braced herself over Evelyn and thrust inside her—her fingers driving Evelyn to orgasm. She completed her fifth mile in record time, pushing to get back to Melanie.

By the time she returned to Melanie's apartment, she was both worn out and amped up from her fantasy-fueled mile at near top speed. As she headed for the bedroom, she smiled when she heard the shower running.

She stripped off her clothes and left them in a trail leading into the steam-filled bathroom. She opened the shower door and pushed Melanie against the wall. Her lips cut off Melanie's cry as her back hit the cool tile wall. She kissed her deeply, pouring out the arousal she'd nurtured while she ran.

"Good run?" Melanie asked when she released her.

"Great run," she answered as she stepped beneath the stream of hot water. She cranked the dial to the right, preferring the temperature a bit cooler against her heated skin.

"So, now you think you're just going to hijack my shower?"

"Actually, I believe I was invited."

Melanie stepped close behind her, then reached around and twisted the knob. "I like it hot." She pressed the length of her soapy body against Evelyn's back. Melanie's hands roamed over her breasts, and when she rolled her nipple between her thumb and forefinger a jolt of pleasure shot to Evelyn's groin.

When Melanie began to slide her hand down her belly, Evelyn caught it and held it in place. "You'll be late for work."

Melanie pressed her lips to the back of her neck. "I don't care. "I think my boss will understand."

"Well, then by all means…" She released her hand.

Molded against her, Melanie reached down and parted her, then stroked her more firmly. Evelyn braced her hands against the shower wall to compensate for her suddenly unsteady legs. Her clit swelled and she squeezed her muscles tight, enjoying the pressure of Melanie's fingers but also craving them inside her.

"Mel," she said hoarsely, loud enough to be heard over the shower spray.

"Yes, babe?" She phrased it as a question, but her self-satisfied tone indicated she knew that Evelyn was trying hard not to beg for her touch.

She grabbed Melanie's wrist and tried to push it down farther, silently indicating what she wanted.

"Oh, no, honey. If I'm going to be late for work, you're going to make it worth it. Tell me what you want." Melanie punctuated her demand with a quick pinch of Evelyn's nipple.

"You know what I want."

"Yes. But I want you to ask for it." Melanie placed her hand between Evelyn's shoulder blades and pushed, increasing the angle of her back. Then she bent and trailed kisses between the rivulets of water running down her back, her warm lips against cool skin making Evelyn shiver. Melanie reached between her legs from behind and cupped her, inching her finger into the slick folds and rubbing the underside of her knuckle against her clit.

"Mel, please." She gasped, pulling in a deep breath of steamy air.

Melanie remained silent. She continued her motion, the pace and pressure slightly less than she needed to progress her arousal. Her other hand worked Evelyn's nipple, alternately stroking and tugging at the hard tip.

"Ah—okay, please. Please, I want you inside me." Her plea tumbled out quickly, running the words together. Melanie held off until once more she uttered, "Please."

When she glided inside, Evelyn sighed and clamped greedily around Melanie's fingers. Melanie pulled back, paused long enough for her to miss her—to need her filling her again, then she thrust in. Evelyn shoved against the shower wall, pushing back into Melanie's hand. As she tightened and released around Melanie's fingers, she increased her pace. Melanie wrapped her other arm around Evelyn's hips, reached under her, and stroked her clit, matching the speed of her thrusts.

As Evelyn shuddered and trembled toward release, Melanie laid her head against the back of her shoulder and whispered encouragement. Evelyn's thighs tensed as she seized around Melanie's fingers. She rested her forehead against the wall and somehow managed to keep her feet under her during the waves of pleasure undulating through her.

When she sank to her knees, Melanie went with her and kissed her tenderly.

"You know we can't linger down here, right? We'll drown." Melanie joked.

"Wow, no basking in the afterglow for me, huh?" She swiped at heavy strands of hair that the shower spray was pushing in her face.

"If you wanted to bask, you shouldn't have molested me in the shower."

"Really? I think you're confused about who molested whom." She ran a hand over her face and shoved her hair aside again. "But you might be right. Once the sex is done, the shower floor isn't so hot anymore."

CHAPTER NINETEEN

Melanie pulled her truck up behind one of her company vans, grabbed her messenger bag from the front seat, and slid out of the truck. After glancing at the dark clouds overhead, she hurried past the van and around to the back of the house. She hoped the forecasted showers would hold off until afternoon so they could do the bulk of today's work.

Lucas had already set up a mobile office of sorts under the umbrella of a wrought-iron patio table. He and the rest of their crew gathered around the blueprints spread out on the table. She hung back, confident that he had the briefing under control.

After the group had received their tasks for the morning and dispersed, she approached the table.

"Coffee?" Lucas asked, lifting a cup out of a cardboard drink carrier.

"Yes, please."

"Creamer?"

She grabbed the cup and took as big a gulp as she could, considering how hot it still was. He held up the miniature cup of flavored creamer, with a curious look. "Thanks." She took the creamer and dumped it in the rest of her coffee. "Sorry I'm late." She'd texted him as she left the house to let him know he should start without her.

"No problem." He didn't seem to try very hard to stop the grin from spreading across his face. "Traffic bad?"

"No, actually. There was a—uh, problem with my shower."

"A problem? If you need a plumber, I know a guy."

"A guy? No, I handled it."

"Glad to know you got it handled." Suspicion laced his tone.

"Yep." Her face flushed hot as she thought about Evelyn's hands on her.

"I guess I don't need to ask how things are going with Evelyn."

"I know. You don't approve." She downed the rest of her coffee and picked up a shovel. "I'll start working on the line of shrubs on the east side of the lot."

"You don't need my approval." He followed her, keeping his voice low enough that the other guys wouldn't overhear them. "Are you happy?"

"Yes, I am." She didn't have to think about it. She was happy, for the first time in quite a while. She'd let herself get swept away in her feelings, perhaps not questioning them because she trusted Evelyn. And last night—well, last night and this morning—had been incredible. Any concerns about sex between them being awkward had dissipated when Evelyn touched her. They had retained the playfulness of their previous friendship, while adding a new level of flirtation and arousal.

She only wished Evelyn hadn't lost Kendall's friendship. Maybe in time Kendall would come around. The three of them had such a deep history that she held on to a bit of hope that they might all be friends again someday. She'd seen it happen in the lesbian community before. But she wasn't sure if Kendall's pride would ever let her get there.

Evelyn power-walked through the parking lot at the station, trying to keep the wind from ripping away her umbrella. The rain had started on her drive in, and the weather app on her phone predicted it would continue all evening.

She stepped into the lobby and paused long enough to close her umbrella and glance at her watch. She'd made it to work with a couple of minutes to spare. Considering how early she'd originally gotten up this morning, her rush now was almost comical. After Melanie left for work, she'd lain back down in Melanie's bed, intending to linger for only a minute. She'd closed her eyes and her memories of the previous night had drifted into sex-filled dreams.

Three hours later, she'd woken with just over an hour until it was time to be at the station. She'd hurried home and jumped into her own shower, trying desperately not to get distracted by imagining what she would do to Melanie there. She threw on a uniform, clumsily gathered her equipment, and ran out to the car.

Now she slipped into the roll-call room and took an empty seat at the back. The lieutenant had just stepped behind the podium and cleared his throat. He met her eyes then flicked his gaze to the clock over her head and back to the officers in front of him. She followed his example and scanned the group, then realized that Kendall was not among them.

Her name was among those read out to get subpoenas from the book after the briefing.

After they were dismissed, she approached Sergeant Stahlman. "Where's Kendall?"

"I thought you might be able to tell me," he said as he handed over several pieces of paper summoning her to court in the coming weeks.

"I haven't seen her." She bent and signed the book, indicating her receipt of the paperwork.

"You two are friends, aren't you? She put in a request to go to West Precinct. Found a guy over there that wanted a trade. He starts with us tomorrow."

She shook her head, trying to make sense of what he said. "What? How could that even happen so fast? Doesn't it take a while to get something like that done?"

He shrugged. "Usually, but apparently this guy out at West, his father is a city councilman. I guess he has friends in the right places. All I know is this came down through the ranks. But hey, it worked out for Kendall, huh? I didn't know she wanted to move."

"Me either."

"Well, if you talk to her, tell her no hard feelings. I hope she likes it over there."

She nodded but knew she wouldn't be talking to Kendall. If she had any hope of reconciliation, it had dissolved with Kendall's transfer.

❖

Evelyn knocked softly, and when Melanie didn't answer the door, she used her key and let herself in. She found Melanie in the living room, snuggled beneath a blanket on the couch. The flickering television cast the only light on her, but the sound had been muted.

Melanie looked so peaceful that she didn't want to disturb her. She was debating whether to leave quietly and go home when Melanie opened her eyes.

"Hey," she said, yawning as she sat up. The blanket fell around her waist.

Evelyn hugged her, then sat beside her. Melanie's nipples created a distracting, dark shadow under her white tank top. She wanted to lean over and suck them right through the thin cotton.

"Are you aware that you're grinning at my breasts?"

"Um, yeah. Is that a problem?"

Melanie smiled. "Not really. They like it."

She flicked her eyebrows up suggestively and touched one of the hardening bumps. "I can tell."

Melanie swatted her hand away. "How was your day?"

She shrugged. "Dark and rainy. I spent half my shift working wrecks and the other half stuck in traffic trying to get to alarm calls." High wind and power surges often caused a large number of false alarms at residences and businesses during storms. "Kendall wasn't at work today."

"Is she sick?"

She shook her head. "She changed precincts to get away from me."

"Already. I didn't know government could move that fast."

"I know. Apparently she pulled some strings. I underestimated her desire to avoid me."

"I'm so sorry, Ev."

"Please stop apologizing. I went into this with my eyes open."

"It's hard not to apologize when I know you're beating yourself up about this. I was afraid you'd have regrets."

She took her hand. "Not regrets. Not really. I—what I feel—" Why was she trying to avoid saying what she truly felt? She searched for a way to justify what she'd done, to explain why she'd ultimately been disloyal to Kendall. Then the answer was simple: only one thing was stronger than her bond to Kendall. She was in love with Melanie. She sat back and took a deep breath. How long had she been in love? Did Melanie feel the same way? And should she tell her?

Melanie yawned. "Can we finish this conversation in bed? I'm beat."

"Oh, honey, you didn't have to wait up for me. I could have gone home." Melanie had been up since early that morning and they hadn't slept much the night before. Her confession of her feelings could wait. Maybe she'd try to orchestrate a more romantic moment.

"I wanted to see you."

"All right, let's go tuck you in."

❖

"We've got K-9 coming. Let's establish a perimeter and hold it."

For the next couple of minutes, officers keyed up on the radio giving their locations, laying out the shape of their perimeter. Evelyn visualized their locations, and when she came to a stop at a nearby intersection, she gave the streets out as well.

She had responded to the call for help in locating a suspect in a stabbing. As the first officers arrived on the scene, they determined that the seriously injured victim was an Asian gang member and the suspect most likely belonged to a rival group. The victim gave a good description of the man who had fled on foot, and enough officers had been close that they now believed they had him contained in this neighborhood. Both K-9 officers had been helping out in another sector and weren't close to them yet.

She scanned the area around her slowly, searching the concealing twilight for motion. Her radio was eerily quiet. Did her fellow officers feel as frozen and impatient as she did, waiting for their quarry to reveal himself? Her muscles tensed with the effort of priming for flight at a moment's notice. By the time he made a move she would already be seconds behind. Despite her readiness, she was actually surprised to see movement from a line of shrubs behind the apartment complex across the street. She was too far away to make out his features, but he wore a dark T-shirt and jeans, the same clothing description reported by the victim.

"Where is the dog?" she muttered as she watched the guy creep around the edge of the building. He hadn't looked in her direction yet, but he clearly tried to stay close to the wall, in the shadows. She keyed her radio. "Fifteen, I think I've got the suspect over here."

Her sergeant called the K-9 officer, who responded that he was still five minutes away. If she didn't take this guy into custody, they might lose him. She opened her door and slipped out, crouching next to her car. The dog probably wouldn't make it in time, but a couple of her fellow officers were already on their way.

She pulled her gun and, holding it at her side, she circled the car and moved to her left, using the cover of a neighboring building. She needed to get much closer before making her presence known. When she was close enough to have a chance in a foot race if he decided to run, she raised her gun and called out, "Police! Show me your hands!"

He tensed and froze. He turned, making a half-hearted show of lifting his hands to chest level in front of him. When he twisted one side of his mouth in a cruel sneer, she could practically hear him saying, *All alone, huh? Think you can take me?*

His eyes darted around as if gauging the odds of successful flight. The apartments he'd tried to use for shelter before blocked him in on both sides. His only choice was to come at her or turn and run away from her, but by the time he turned she'd be several steps closer and building momentum.

"Fifteen, I have him at gunpoint on the east side of the K building." She immediately heard several sirens start up nearby. They'd been headed to her silently so they wouldn't alert the suspect of their location, but now the cavalry was coming full force. In the time it took her to speak into her shoulder mic, he must have made his decision. As her finger released the button, he dashed forward. She yelled, "Stop!"

But he didn't. She registered his hand moving toward his back pocket and the flash of the streetlight reflecting off something metallic. The loud report of her gun as it bucked in her hand nearly drowned out her next shouted order.

She staggered back a couple of steps as he crumpled to the ground in front of her. Tires squealed and, seconds later, Riggs and another officer pushed past her. Riggs trained his gun on the inert suspect while the other officer rolled him onto his back. A slick of wetness spread across the front of his shirt. Riggs nudged aside an open switchblade with his boot.

"Shots fired. Send us a forty-seven." He barked the order for an ambulance into his radio.

Excited voices peppered the air in response, but she could barely make sense of the words. She stared at the suspect's face. His features, which had looked so mean before, now seemed almost peaceful. Stringy dark hair fell across his forehead, almost obscuring his eyes, and splotches of acne marred his cheeks and chin. He probably wasn't more than eighteen.

"Fisher." Sergeant Stahlman stepped in front of her, blocking her view as the paramedics arrived and surrounded the boy. She had no doubt that's how she would think of him—a boy. "Fisher, look at me," he said, and she shifted her eyes to his face. "Let me have your gun." He gently touched her hand.

She still clutched her gun in the hand that now hung limply at her side and didn't even feel like a part of her body. Stahlman eased the weapon from her hand, ejected the clip, and cleared the slide. He would give her gun and her spent casings, which had been marked and left where they landed on the ground, to the crime-scene officer.

"Fisher, we need to do a walk-through of the scene. Then we'll get you out of here and away from the media. You'll go downtown with the homicide detective. They'll do a drug test and a bunch of paperwork. Jeb will drive you."

"My car—"

"We'll get one of the rookies to drive it to the station. When you're done, someone will take you home." He met her eyes, as if trying to gauge how much of this conversation she would retain later. "Homicide will tell you all of this again, but you're off work for a few days. I'll call you tomorrow and check in."

She nodded.

"They'll need a statement. Do you want a union attorney?"

"No." Her mind latched onto the words. "I have an attorney."

"Do you want me to make the call for you?"

"I'll do it." She dialed the number from memory. When she heard the voice on the other end, she nearly choked on her relief and could only manage a weak, "Dad, I need you."

CHAPTER TWENTY

Thirty minutes later, Evelyn sat alone in the homicide office. Two clusters of cubicles took up the center of the room, and several older, mismatched metal desks lined the outside. She'd been in this office only a couple of weeks ago while transporting a suspect from a crime scene. She'd brought him here, waited while homicide talked to him, then took him down to be booked. But this time the adrenaline rushing through her had nothing to do with questioning a suspect.

The detective had left her in a chair next to his desk, one of the metal ones closest to the door. After she declined his offer of coffee or a soda, he left to get himself a cup. He'd scrubbed his hand over his face, most likely already thinking about the late night ahead filling out paperwork and updating the chain of command. A police shooting went all the way up to the chief of police and the mayor. The media vans had already arrived before she left the scene, and their presence would send the requests for information trickling down.

Her picture, probably the one they took when she graduated from the academy, would flash on the screen. *Breaking news. This just in.* By the morning broadcast, the entire city would have seen her face. Well, not her face as it looked now, but that of a young kid, clad in a navy dress uniform, buttoned all the way up with a tie tight around her neck. She'd been an eager recruit, soaking in everything they taught her, dying to show her father she could make a bigger, better difference than he did.

But tonight, she wasn't sure what she'd accomplished. As hard as she tried to remind herself that he'd stabbed a man, when the boy's face floated into her head she couldn't shake the feeling of despair. She wished she could go back to being that optimistic kid she'd once been.

Across the room, the door opened and Charles W. Fisher entered. He wore khakis and a plaid button-down shirt, but he walked as if dressed in a power suit. His gaze landed on her and his expression softened for just a second before he tightened his jaw and strode across the room.

She lurched to her feet, fighting the urge to stumble into his arms like a child. She shoved her shoulders back and focused on the badge pinned to her chest and the gun belt around her waist. So what if her holster was currently empty? She was a police officer and would conduct herself as such.

"Mr. Fisher, can I get you some coffee?" the detective offered.

"No, thank you."

"Okay. Please have a seat and we'll get you out of here as quickly as we can." He took the chair behind his desk, then pulled a tape recorder from the drawer and pressed the record button. "Let's start with your account of what happened."

She settled back into her seat and her father pulled a chair over next to her. As he sat, he put a hand on her shoulder and she drew a deep breath, as if she could pull his reassurance in as well.

She closed her eyes, replaying those moments in her head. Finally speaking aloud, she described the events as if narrating a documentary. As she reached the point where the suspect rushed her, ignoring her order to stop, she tried to slow things down, grasping for details she'd only registered peripherally at the time.

The detective prompted her. "Did you see the knife?"

"I think so." She immediately wished she could somehow take back that statement. She took a slow, even breath and prepared for damage control.

"You think so?" The detective's face conveyed what she already knew—she'd better come up with a better answer.

His hand in his back pocket. The flash of silver. Had she heard the snick of the blade opening or had her mind manufactured the memory based on the facts she now knew? She replayed it again— the flash of silver—silver that crystallized into the shape of a knife blade popping out of the handle.

"I saw it," she said with more conviction.

The detective stared at her, but she kept her face expressionless. If he hoped to use his interrogation skills on her, he was wasting his time. She'd grown up under the watchful eye of Charles W. Fisher; nothing fazed her. Her father's presence beside her now calmed her. For the first time in a very long time, she was glad he was in the profession he was.

"How many shots did you fire?"

"Two." That's all she'd needed. *Shoot to stop the threat.* That's what the policy said. The boy had dropped as soon as she'd fired.

"Then what?"

She took a deep breath and forced herself back into the stoic recitation of facts. "Officer Jeb Riggs arrived on scene, and he and another officer…" She tried but couldn't bring the other officer's face into focus. "I'm sorry, I don't know who it was. They secured the suspect and his weapon and called for an ambulance. Sergeant Stahlman took my gun. I came here shortly after that."

She thought they must be done, but the detective continued to ask questions, sometimes having her repeat details she'd already given. She answered honestly but succinctly, providing only the information relevant to his questions. She wasn't here for therapy but merely to provide an account of the events. The sooner she did and the paperwork got done, the sooner she could return to work.

When they'd finished, the detective finally looked at her like a fellow officer for the first time all night. "Thanks, Fisher. I'm sure someone from OPA will be in touch with you." The various reports and supplements from tonight would be handed over to the office of professional accountability for review. Someone there would ultimately clear her to return to work. "They'll want you to meet with a counselor sometime in the next few days, but you know how that goes. It's a formality."

She nodded. She'd have one more person to convince that she was fine with the events that had precipitated her use of deadly force. Logically, she was. She'd followed policy and done what any good officer would in her place. But each time she imagined his face, her stomach threatened an embarrassing revolt. And her mind played tricks, making her memory of him seem more angelic every time.

❖

"I'll drive you home," her father said as they walked to his SUV parked at a meter in front of police headquarters.

Evelyn shook her head. "Not home."

"Where to then?"

"Melanie's." She opened the passenger door and slumped into the seat. He didn't say anything, but his expression relayed his disapproval. She started to suppress her reaction, then remembered Melanie's advice about open communication. "Kendall knows and she hates me."

He still didn't speak, and when she looked over at him, he stared straight ahead as he navigated out of downtown.

"No gloating?" she asked.

"Would it do any good?"

"Just because I didn't take your advice doesn't mean I didn't hear you." She squeezed her eyes shut. She wouldn't find a quick fix to her lingering feelings about tonight's events, but somehow she knew that holding Melanie would help. That had to count for something, right? "My head knows you were right to tell me to stay away. But my heart didn't listen. Do you know how that feels?"

"I do." He glanced at her, his eyes soft with concern—not the practiced kind he used in court, but real caring.

"What happened to us, Dad?" Maybe it was tonight, or maybe it was Melanie, but something made her want—no, need to know how they had gone so drastically astray from the father and daughter of her youth. "I know you were disappointed when I went into the academy, but I always thought we'd get over that eventually. And maybe someday, you'd be proud of me."

"I am proud of you, Evie. Don't you know that?"

"You've never said it."

"I assumed you knew. I'm your father. I've always been proud of you."

"You hated that I became a police officer."

"I admit I always hoped you would take over the firm sooner or later. When you were a kid, I missed a lot because of my long hours. But I told myself I was building something for your future. You would sit in my office and listen to me practice my arguments, such a smart, rapt audience. I assumed that when you were old enough—but you didn't want any part of it. That hurt a little. But I always wished I hadn't traded away those hours of your childhood. Those years passed so fast."

Stunned into silence, she tried to absorb his words. He regretted missing out when she was a child. He almost sounded as if he were more disappointed in himself than in her. "I have a ton of happy memories involving you from my childhood. You taught me the value of hard work, of using logic to work through a problem, and the power of words to change a situation. Just because I'm not using those lessons in the way you had hoped I might, they're still valuable to me now."

"I worry about you." His hands tightened on the wheel. "I know you're smart and well-trained and I shouldn't worry because you can take care of yourself. But I know, firsthand, what kind of criminals are out there. They don't have your sense of honor, and if you corner them, they don't fight fair. Some of my clients—let's just say I pray you don't come up against them someday."

"And you think getting me a job in your firm will make me safer?"

He smiled wistfully. "At least then I could watch over you."

A thickness settled in the back of her throat. "I appreciate that you want to, Dad, but I don't need you to. You raised me to take care of myself. You and Mom made me strong enough to do that and so much more. Though I may forget it sometimes, I do the job I do so I can help others." She paused, letting the reminder to herself sink in. Now more than ever, the responsibility of her job hit home. "So, I hope you understand why I can't work for you."

"I do."

He pulled into a spot in front of Melanie's apartment and she looked up at Melanie's living-room window. The closed drapes softened the glow coming from inside, and she couldn't wait to get there. She'd been allowed a few minutes to make a call before her interview and had contacted Melanie to warn her about anything she might see on the news. After she'd assured her that she was safe, Melanie told her to call her back when she was done, no matter how late it was. But right now she wouldn't be satisfied with a phone conversation. She needed something more physical.

She reached for the door handle, but he stopped her with a hand on her arm. "Evie, about Melanie—"

"Dad, I don't—"

"I'll ask your mother to set another place at dinner next Sunday."

She stared at him, shocked by the blessing he'd just given. "I'll ask her."

"We'll see you then."

"Thanks, Dad." She leaned across the console and threw her arms around his shoulders. He squeezed back and, when she eased away, tears stung her eyes.

"Don't worry about what happened today. The investigation is a formality. If you have doubts about any part of the process, don't say anything to anyone without talking to me first. But in my opinion, you'll be back out there in a few days."

She nodded, wishing her resolution of today's events could be as simple as police procedure. She headed up the walk to

Melanie's building, knowing that her first step to healing began inside that apartment.

❖

Melanie opened the door seconds after Evelyn rang the bell. She glanced past Evelyn at the SUV leaving the parking lot, then stepped aside and waited for her to enter. For the past several hours she'd alternated between pacing and finding busywork to occupy her time. As a result her apartment was cleaner than it had been in weeks. "Was that your father?"

"Yes. I'll tell you about it later."

"I saw the news broadcast. Are you okay?"

Evelyn nodded and then stopped as tears filled her eyes. "No."

"Oh, baby, come here." Heart aching, she caught Evelyn's hand and pulled her into her arms.

Evelyn buried her face in Melanie's neck. Their embrace broke the dam, and a series of sobs and gasping breaths cascaded into her hair. She held Evelyn tighter, murmuring encouragement and rubbing Evelyn's back.

When Evelyn's crying eased, Melanie gently urged her into the bedroom. Her need to take care of Evelyn mingled with the sadness and confusion shining in Evelyn's eyes. Tonight, she could forget about the fear that had swamped her as she stared in horror at the television. Tonight, she would take care of Evelyn.

"Let's get this off you. It's digging into my hip." She unsnapped the various loops that secured Evelyn's gun belt to the leather belt underneath, then unbuckled it and lowered it to the floor next to the bed. She opened her uniform shirt, slipped it off her shoulders, and let it fall to the floor as well. The badge still pinned to the front thumped heavily on the hardwood. She ripped back the Velcro straps that secured Evelyn's Kevlar vest and removed it as well.

Evelyn stood motionless while she continued to strip her down to her panties and white T-shirt. With each layer, Evelyn's pain became more evident in the tears gathering in her eyes and the sadness painting her features. But she proceeded slowly, stroking her hands over Evelyn between each article, hoping her tender touch eased the sting of the haunting images.

When Evelyn was naked, she guided her into bed. She hastily pulled off her own clothes and climbed in next to her. She touched Evelyn's cheek, forcing back the suffocating fear that had been her companion since she heard about the shooting. Evelyn was safe. She tried to ignore the voice in her head that tacked "for now" onto the end of that sentence.

No. Evelyn was here and physically, at least, she was unscathed. That's what she needed to focus on. She folded back the covers and examined Evelyn's body, reassuring herself that nothing had touched her.

She traced Evelyn's jaw and down her neck, then followed the curve of her collarbone. Evelyn's shoulder was round and tight beneath her hand, and a groove separated it from her defined bicep. Evelyn's strength had impressed her, made her feel cherished, and totally turned her on. But now she could only worry—that all of this brawn wouldn't be enough to protect Evelyn. She placed her palm on Evelyn's chest, spreading her fingers to span her ribs.

She would not be rushed, even when Evelyn urgently whispered her desires. She caressed Evelyn slowly, converting her fear into attention. Evelyn moaned when she massaged her calves and rubbed her feet. As she worked her way back up Evelyn's legs, she lightened her touch and teased her inner thighs.

"Yes, a little higher," Evelyn said, and the muscles in her thighs visibly tightened in anticipation.

Melanie grasped her hip and rolled her over. She stretched out next to her and trailed her fingers along her spine. When she reached her lower back, Evelyn shivered. She moved over her, bracing on her arms and resting her hips against Evelyn's buttocks. Evelyn lifted her hips. She pressed harder, reveling in Evelyn's firm ass against her sensitive flesh. She thrust again and again, until her own wetness cooled on her inner thigh.

She lifted herself away from Evelyn and moved aside. "Turn over," she whispered.

Evelyn rolled over and reached for her. Melanie nestled into her and sighed. Arousal still hummed through her body—a need to please and be pleased—but for a moment she was content to be enveloped in Evelyn's arms.

Evelyn rubbed her back in long, easy passes up and down the length of her. She smiled against Evelyn's neck, then maneuvered her hand between them. She slipped her finger easily inside Evelyn with a minimum of movement. She stroked her slowly at first, and Evelyn held onto her.

At Evelyn's urging, she thrust deeper, keeping her pace controlled. Evelyn pressed her mouth close to her ear and chanted her pleasure, letting her know when she was close, when she needed just a little more. The muscles in her arm burned with each stroke, but she didn't relent, needing Evelyn's release even more than her own pleasure. Her heart filled when Evelyn clung to her even more tightly.

"Oh, God, yes," Evelyn rasped as her body tensed and she arched her back.

Melanie held on. Tears filled her throat. She buried her face in Evelyn's hair and breathed in her scent, trying to infuse herself with it—to imprint this moment into her mind.

Evelyn trembled and sighed. She rolled to her back, keeping Melanie close to her side. Minutes later, Evelyn slid the hand resting on Melanie's back down to her butt.

"Not yet," she said. "You just enjoy yours for a while."

Evelyn made a small sound of contentment, squeezed her ass, and returned her hand to the curve of her back.

She closed her eyes.

"Mel?"

"Yeah?"

"What was that? I mean, something was different, wasn't it?"

Melanie slowly opened her eyes, but she didn't answer right away. She traced Evelyn's bicep and down her forearm.

"So strong," she whispered as Evelyn's muscles tensed under her hand.

Evelyn rubbed her fingertip against her cheek, collecting the residue of a renegade tear. "What's wrong?"

"They put your picture on the news."

"That's what they do when something like this happens."

She sat up, one quick motion that ripped her away from Evelyn. She bowed her back as she wrapped her arms around her drawn-up knees. "Damn it, I didn't want to date another cop."

"I hope at this point I'm not just another cop." Evelyn's hurt feelings bled through in her voice.

"That makes it even worse."

"Are you worried about tonight? Because you know this type of thing almost never happens. Most officers go their entire careers without firing their gun."

"But it does happen. And it can get so much worse. It's not just a shooting. Remember that officer that got hit by the drunk driver while working a wreck last year?" In a follow-up story, one of the television news programs reported months later that he was still undergoing physical therapy and needed six fake teeth to replace the ones that had been smashed when his face hit the pavement.

"Hey, nothing's going to happen to me."

"Don't say that. You can't be certain. All you're doing is dismissing my very real concerns."

"I know this scared you. It scared me a little, too. But this is what we're trained for." Evelyn reached for her, certain she could reassure her.

Melanie shook her head. "I've lived with this fear for the past seven years. I can't do it anymore. I can't wait for something bad to happen."

Evelyn's heart broke at the resignation in Melanie's voice. Just now, when they'd made love, she'd felt more connected than she'd ever been with another person, more connected than she even thought possible. But maybe Melanie hadn't felt the same thing. "What do you want me to say? I'm starting out at a deficit because you're carrying over your problems from your relationship with Kendall."

"They're the same with you." Melanie rolled her eyes. "I let myself jump into this and convinced myself it could be different with you."

"It can be. It *is* different. We're different."

"But you're still a cop. I don't want to be the wife sitting at home alone every evening worrying anymore. I don't want to live for the weekends so I can spend some time with you."

"Okay, now it feels like we're talking about two different concerns." Evelyn canted her head to the side, trying to read Melanie's expression. "Are you upset that I might get hurt? Or are we talking about my working evening shift?"

"I—uh, a little of both, I guess."

"Well, that doesn't have to be an issue—"

"But it is. I've been in this position before. Our schedules suck. I work days, you're on evenings. Right now, we're wooing each other, and it's one thing to exhaust myself staying up late with you and settling for stolen phone calls when what I really want is to be with you. But I don't want to still be here years from now."

"That's not fair. I'm not Kendall."

"But I will always be Kendall's ex. I can't change that. And I shouldn't forget the lessons I learned from my relationship with her. I shouldn't make the same mistakes again."

The impact of Melanie's words was so sharp, she wouldn't have been surprised to learn she'd actually been struck. Melanie thought getting involved with her was a mistake. "You've said before that you didn't want to date another cop. But I guess I convinced myself you didn't really mean it."

"Evelyn—"

"I foolishly let myself believe you finally saw me as an individual, instead of just some carbon copy of Kendall."

She surged out of bed and scrabbled on the floor for her clothes. She tugged on her panties and her T-shirt, skipping her bra.

"Where are you going?"

"Home. I've had a very long day and I don't want to argue right now."

"You don't have to go." Melanie sat up and the sheet slid off her shoulder. Her damn nipples drew Evelyn's attention like a magnet. She jerked her eyes away and focused on getting dressed.

"What should I do, Mel?" She hated the way her voice broke on Melanie's name. "Should I stay? Maybe we could fuck again." She purposely used the word that least described what their encounter had been for her. "And then in the morning you can tell me again how you don't want to date me. Where does that leave us, Melanie?"

"I don't know. I'm just—"

"Just what?" she snapped as she pulled on her uniform pants and gathered the rest of her clothes in her arms.

Melanie stared at her as she turned and left the room. She was halfway down the hall when she thought she heard Melanie finish her sentence.

"Just scared."

She didn't turn around, because she'd made her exit and didn't know how to go back. She'd never been here before, so blindly in love with someone that she wanted to beg for whatever Melanie was willing to give her. But Melanie couldn't even distinguish her from Kendall. So obviously her feelings weren't returned. Maybe she *was* just a rebound.

CHAPTER TWENTY-ONE

A bead of sweat crept from under Melanie's ball cap and ran down the side of her face. She swiped at it, but since her hands were covered in dirt, she probably only made a streak of mud across her cheekbone. She didn't feel like expending the energy to pull the bandana from her pocket and scrub at it, though. She picked up her Thermos and took a long drink of cool water. Then she knelt and submerged her hands back into the soil she'd just dumped in the narrow flower bed that skirted the outside of a gazebo.

For the past two days, she'd traveled to several of the company's job sites and worked for a day with each crew. She liked to check in with them anyway, so she took the opportunity to get her hands into a variety of projects. This week especially, she appreciated the distraction of physical labor. She had ventured back to the office one day to work on some overdue paperwork, but she only ended up staring into space and thinking about Evelyn. They hadn't spoken since Wednesday night when Evelyn walked out on her.

This afternoon, she was back with her regular crew. She'd donated this landscaping project to the recently rehabbed community center as part of her company's commitment to local charity. Since the center resided in Evelyn's patrol area, as the day wore on she caught herself searching the street for police cars more often than she wanted to admit.

Her anger with Evelyn had almost completely waned, and now she just wanted to see her and talk things out. She had to admit that she'd started the argument. After seeing the news reports and then waiting the seemingly endless hours for Evelyn to get home, she had been swamped with emotions and hadn't handled the situation well.

Maybe generalizing that she didn't want to date a cop wasn't the best way to open a dialogue about her fears and their scheduling conflicts. But she hadn't expected Evelyn to just leave. She'd thought they would argue, try to find a compromise, then, if she was being honest, have their first round of make-up sex.

The next morning when she'd tried to call, Evelyn hadn't answered. She'd left a nervous meandering message, rambling about calling to check on her after her difficult day and if Evelyn wanted to talk she could call her back. She hung up feeling as if she'd sounded more like a concerned acquaintance than a—well, a girlfriend. And, she realized just then, that she very much wanted to be Evelyn's girlfriend.

When she didn't hear back, she sent an exploratory text asking Evelyn to call her. This time Evelyn did reply, saying only that she was spending a couple of days at her parents' house while she was off work.

Melanie stood and brushed her hands against the legs of her jeans, not caring about the smears of dark soil left behind. She arched, stretching her back, then rolled her shoulders a couple of times.

Her heart lifted when she saw a patrol car round the corner. She stopped herself from running out into the street, but she knew she was visible where she stood and didn't move. As the car pulled up to the curb, disappointment flooded her. The driver was not Evelyn. Still, it would be rude not to at least say hello, so she walked closer to the street.

Jennifer Prince rolled down the window. "Melanie?"

"Hi, Jennifer. How are you?"

"I'm good. You?"

"I'm okay."

They both nodded in awkward silence while she debated whether she should bring up Evelyn. She didn't know Jennifer very well and wasn't totally comfortable talking about her. But since Evelyn hadn't returned her call, she couldn't pass up a chance for information. "Have you talked to Evelyn?"

Jennifer nodded. "I spoke with her yesterday."

"How is she doing?"

"You broke her heart, you know."

"I meant, how is she handling the aftermath of the shooting?"

"I know." Jennifer seemed to be considering if she wanted to speak candidly. "She's a pro. She did the mandatory counseling session. But I think hanging out with her dad has helped more than anything."

She nodded, recalling that Evelyn hadn't had the chance to tell her about her apparent breakthrough with her father. "Did she say something about us?"

"She didn't have to. It was what she wouldn't say. She's never been super open emotionally, but she's even more closed off than ever."

"If you see her, will you tell her I'm thinking about her?"

"I'd rather not."

"Jennifer—"

"If you want to be with her, you should tell her. If you don't, leave her alone, Melanie. You've messed with her head enough."

"I didn't—"

"You did. She sacrificed her loyalty to Kendall to be with you. And you threw that back in her face. Now she doesn't have either of you at a time when she probably needs you both the most." Jennifer's eyes flashed, and she understood that Jennifer had shifted into protective mode.

Once more, she was faced with the bond of that brotherhood. Only this time, instead of resenting it, she appreciated it. She hoped that Evelyn drew support from it—that her fellow officers were checking in on her. Sure, she wished she were the one to offer that solace, but Evelyn's peace was the most important thing.

"For the record, I think you should be with her."

"You do?" She hadn't expected Jennifer to support their relationship.

Jennifer nodded. "I've never seen her happier than with you."

"Thanks."

As Jennifer pulled away from the curb, she wandered back to the front of the community center. She found Lucas installing landscaping timbers with one of the other guys and let him know she had to take off for the rest of the day. By the time she slid behind the wheel of her truck, she'd already sent her first difficult text of the afternoon. She started the engine, listening intently for her phone to chirp in response.

❖

Kendall parked her patrol car in front of her new favorite coffee shop. After she changed sectors she'd had to find someplace to eat where she could trust the cooks and waitresses. She'd heard officers talk about witnessing food-service employees spitting in their food and worse. Of course, she tried not to get too obsessive about it, but since she ate dinner out at least four times a week, she liked to have a reliable restaurant.

She twisted to her laptop and checked herself out of service for her dinner break, though she didn't know if she'd be here long enough for a meal. Stalling, she flipped down the vanity mirror and checked her hair, then her teeth. After a fortifying breath, she pushed open the door and climbed out.

Inside, she scanned the room and continued to a booth in the front, by the window overlooking the side of the lot she'd parked on. Great, her arrival had already been witnessed. She slid into the booth and met Melanie's eyes.

"Hi," Melanie said shyly. "Thanks for meeting me."

She nodded, taking careful note of her involuntary reactions to talking to Melanie again. Considering the last time she'd seen her, she'd been making out with Evelyn, she felt surprisingly dispassionate. After two different rounds of anger and resentment, perhaps she'd exhausted her rage.

"You're working on this side of town now?"

"Yes."

"Do you like it?"

She shrugged. "It's okay. It'll take some time to really get to know the sector. But there are some good guys and girls on the shift." None like Evelyn, but she didn't say that.

"She needs you," Melanie blurted.

She didn't speak. The sadness in Melanie's eyes went beyond what she expected, given the situation.

"You must have heard what happened."

Of course she had. It didn't matter what shift she worked. News of a police-involved shooting spread through the department quickly, not to mention garnering extensive media coverage for several days afterward.

"She has other friends in the department," she said, trying not to think about what Evelyn must be going through right now. At one time or another, every officer thought about what would happen if they ever had to fire their gun. She had always assumed that if it happened to her, Evelyn would be there to help her through it. Now, she wished she could do the same for Evelyn.

"You're her best friend."

"Not anymore." She threw up her hands but forced herself to keep her voice low. Perhaps that was why Melanie had asked to meet her in public, where she knew Kendall couldn't yell. "A best friend doesn't go after my woman behind my back."

"That's not what happened. And if you would stop being an ass and think about it, you'd realize that's not the kind of person Evelyn is."

"*I'm* being an ass?"

"Yes." Melanie sighed. "I'm sorry I hurt you, Kendall."

She scoffed.

"I am. But you know we weren't happy. One of us had to make the decision eventually. So now I'm the bad guy."

Kendall bit her bottom lip to keep from giving in. Melanie was right, of course. The demise of their relationship wasn't one-sided. And truthfully, her bitterness had become more habit than genuine emotion over the past several months.

"And I know that my being with Evelyn hurts you even more. We didn't do it to hurt you. In fact, we both tried to fight it."

She didn't like the thought of them together, talking about her—pitying her. She had always felt as if she were the common cog in their relationship. Realizing that they were actually closer without her bruised her pride. "So, what? You guys are soul mates now."

"Kendall—"

"No. Tell me, Melanie. I need to hear you say the words. Are you in love with her?"

When Melanie didn't answer, Kendall shook her head. "Wow. I guess that's my answer." She didn't need to hear it after all. Melanie's face had registered confusion and then a look of love so strong it stabbed her in the chest. "Have you told her?"

"No."

"You should." She'd never have guessed she would be telling Melanie to profess her love to someone else. But she struggled to recall when Melanie had looked at her the way she looked now while discussing Evelyn. She didn't know if she'd be able to be friends with either of them again, but a part of her still loved them both and wanted them to be happy.

"Maybe you should, too," Melanie said.

"Tell her I'm in love with her?"

"Not exactly. But you do love her and she loves you. Do you really want to throw away five years of friendship?"

She did miss Evelyn. She might have overreacted when she accused her of pursuing Melanie in a predatory manner. She would like to think it hadn't happened that way. But she needed more time before she could forgive what still felt like a betrayal.

❖

Melanie left the coffee shop even more off balance than she'd been for the past two days. She'd been taken aback when Kendall had guessed how deeply her feelings ran, even before she herself was aware of it. But she shouldn't be that surprised. For the past seven years, Kendall had known her better than anyone and was apparently still proficient at reading her.

She'd talked about how Evelyn needed Kendall, well aware of the irony given their recent argument. She hadn't been there when Evelyn needed her, either. She'd been too wrapped up in her own feelings and had lost sight of what Evelyn had just been through. And she didn't like what that said about her as a person. So as she steered her car from the parking lot into the street, she knew exactly where she wanted to go. She turned right, heading away from home.

Ten minutes later, she navigated the old neighborhoods of Belle Meade. She'd always liked driving these streets. The new subdivisions in the suburbs featured rows of cookie-cutter homes set on a quarter of an acre. But when she visited these older neighborhoods with homes on spacious lots, she saw tons of potential. She loved when she got an account on properties like these.

She pulled into the circular drive of the Fisher home, happy to see Evelyn's car parked in front of the three-stall garage. She slid out of the truck and hurried to the door, growing more eager to see her.

After she rang the bell, the door opened and she was a little let down to see Margaret instead of Evelyn.

"Hello, dear," Margaret said, smiling.

"Hi. Is Evelyn here?" She felt like a little kid asking if her friend could come out to play. Judging from Margaret's welcoming expression, Evelyn hadn't filled her in on their fight. Actually, Melanie wasn't certain she was even aware of their shift beyond simple friendship.

"She is. Come on in." Margaret turned and went back inside, leaving her to close the door behind her. As they passed the stairs,

Margaret yelled up them, "Evelyn, you have a visitor." Then she led her into the kitchen. "Would you like something to drink? I've made a nice pitcher of sweet tea."

"No, thank you."

"I was just making a pie for dinner tonight. Sit and keep me company until Evelyn comes down." She circled the island and picked up a rolling pin. A flat oval of dough littered with flour was pressed to the counter.

Before she could pull out the chair, Evelyn entered the room. "No need, Mom. I'm here." Evelyn met her eyes and her heart broke at the thought that she'd caused the wrenching sadness in her gaze.

She glanced at Margaret and then back at Evelyn. She was about to ask if they could go somewhere and talk, but Evelyn beat her to it.

"Let's take a walk."

She nodded, trying for an apologetic smile. She followed Evelyn out the back door onto the patio. As they circled the swimming pool, she fell into step beside Evelyn. She glanced down at Evelyn's arm swinging next to her and wished she were confident enough to take her hand.

"You never told me how things went with your father that night."

"Really well. Actually, we had the first totally honest conversation I can remember in a long time. He finally accepts that I'm going to be a police officer until *I* choose not to be. And I guess I accept that he's going to continue to worry and try to find another career path for me."

"That's great."

"Yeah, he took yesterday off and we played golf."

"I didn't know you golfed."

Evelyn laughed. "I don't. I'm horrible at it. But it was still a nice day." When they reached a chaise lounge on the far side of the pool, Evelyn sat down, leaving room next to her.

"I'm sorry we argued." She said what she should have said two days ago. "And I'm sorry I didn't track you down and make you talk to me until today."

Evelyn nodded slowly. "I should have returned your call."

"Yeah, you should have. I'm okay with us disagreeing, but I don't want to let things go so long without talking about them. I don't believe that's healthy for a relationship."

Evelyn looked up. "You didn't come here to break up with me?"

"Of course not. But I do want to let you know that in the future, if we argue, it's not okay for you to just walk out on me."

"I thought you—you said you didn't want to date a cop."

"Yes, I said that. And it wasn't fair for me to make such a generalization, nor should I carry my baggage with Kendall into a relationship with you. But you didn't stick around long enough for me to realize that. In fact, what you really should have done was stayed and convinced me of it."

"You wanted me to…"

"Fight for me." She smiled. "Old-fashioned, I know."

"I guess a part of me expected this not to work out, even though I very much wanted it to." Evelyn took her hand and rested both of their hands on her knee. "So when you started talking about us as if we were a mistake, I saw that as the other shoe dropping."

"I wouldn't have let you jeopardize your friendship with Kendall if I wasn't serious about us."

"I haven't really done this before—this long-term thing. If that's what we're doing," Evelyn said hesitantly.

She nodded. "That's what we're doing. I love you, Evelyn. So, yeah, I hope it's long-term. But that means you can't avoid me for two days when we argue. We can agree on a mandatory cooling-off period, if that's what you need. But it sure as hell can't be two days. I've been going crazy missing you."

Evelyn smiled. "Let's go back to the part where you said you love me."

Melanie touched her cheek, then stroked down to her neck. She drew her close, and when their mouths were only a whisper away, she said, "I love you."

"I love you, too," Evelyn said. Then she closed the space between them and touched her lips tenderly.

Melanie leaned into her, deepening the kiss and letting all of her emotions from the past few days flood their embrace. Evelyn stretched back on the chaise and pulled her with her, until they lay together, with her nestled close to Evelyn's side, resting her head on her shoulder.

A gentle breeze feathered across their skin, carrying the sweet scent of Margaret's rose garden, the one piece of landscaping that Melanie's crew didn't maintain here. In the distance two birds sang distinctly different songs. She closed her eyes and drank in the feel of the sun on her face and Evelyn's body pressed next to hers. Six months ago, she never would have imagined herself here, but now, she didn't want to be anywhere else.

"I didn't realize our schedules bothered you so much. I supposed I should have, though," Evelyn said after a few minutes.

"It probably shouldn't. It's not as if I think we need to be together every minute. I guess I just worry about the toll it took on my relationship with Kendall." She raised a hand to stop any forthcoming protest. "I don't mean to keep bringing that up, but you work the same shift, so it's a very real concern."

"We rebid in a couple of months. I can change shifts."

"You don't want to do that."

"It's no big deal. I've been on long enough to get good days off, even if I bid for day shift."

"But you love the guys you work with."

"Yeah, they're good guys. But I'm sure I'll eventually feel the same way about whatever shift I'm assigned to." Evelyn stroked the length of her forearm lying across her stomach. "We could have a similar issue as one you had with Kendall, I'll give you that. But you didn't give me a chance to address it before you assumed I would react the same way Kendall did. I would have told you that day that I would rebid."

She shook her head. They'd both been too quick to give up on their fledging relationship out of fear that the other would hurt them first. "I was wrong to make you feel bad about your shift. We can make this work no matter what hours we keep. I would never want you to think you can't have the career opportunities you want because of us."

"If an assignment or promotion comes up that I want, we'll talk about it, whether it means more or less time for us. But as long as I'm in patrol, I'm just as happy on days if I get to spend my evenings with you, to have dinner with you and tuck you in at night." She smiled. "I've been missing those things, too. So, let me be clear, if it's between you and my job, I choose you—every time."

Warmed by Evelyn's words, Melanie rolled to cover Evelyn's body. "You are an amazing woman. And I'm so lucky." She slipped her leg between Evelyn's.

"That's true. But let's not traumatize my mother too much. I'm pretty sure she's keeping an eye on us through the kitchen window."

Melanie chuckled and shifted back to Evelyn's side. She closed her eyes and sighed, immersed in the sensation of Evelyn next to her and the harmony created by two distinct avian melodies.

Chapter Twenty-two

Evelyn sat on the front steps of her parents' house marveling at how her life had changed. She'd gone from enduring serial fix-ups to facing a hopeful future with a woman she loved. Even more strange, that woman had been one of her closest friends for the past five years. But the change in her relationship with Melanie felt natural. And they had already successfully navigated the first bump in the road.

Friday, after they talked, she had left her family's home and spent the night at Melanie's house. Then they spent a leisurely weekend making love, seeing a movie, taking walks, and making love again.

Today, they had returned for Sunday dinner. Her father had filled her mother in on the change in her relationship with Melanie, and today they both treated Melanie like part of the family. Of course, she always had been to some degree, but for Evelyn their kindness felt different—like approval.

In the days since the shooting, she had done the mandatory counseling session and had agreed to return for a couple more voluntary ones next week as well. She'd pretty much come to terms with the shooting. She had done her job, by the letter, and had no qualms about going back out there. Despite what primetime television portrayed, the number of times she would likely fire her gun in the line of duty was pretty small.

But, logic aside, she still had her emotions to deal with, and taking a life had changed her. Despite his crimes, the boy she had shot was still someone's child—she had since learned he was nineteen years old, but she still thought of him as a confused boy. Evelyn had participated in youth outreach through the police department before and had met men who, in spite of violent pasts, had turned their lives around. She didn't believe everyone could, or would, do it, but some had. And she would never know if this particular boy could have.

So, she committed herself to making sure she was stable enough to do her job well, for her safety and that of her fellow officers. Personally, she also wanted to begin her relationship with Melanie in a good place.

She leaned against the porch railing post, tilted her head, and closed her eyes. The sounds of Melanie and her mother in the kitchen making dinner lilted through the window behind her. Her father was in his office, finishing a phone call with a client. So she'd snuck out here in order to take a minute to absorb it all.

She opened her eyes at the sound of tires on the driveway but remained seated as the car parked in the drive behind Melanie's. Kendall circled the front of her car, approached the house, and stopped at the bottom of the stairs. Hope sent Evelyn's heart beating against her ribs, and she fought the desire to descend the steps.

Kendall shoved her hands awkwardly into the pockets of her jeans. "Melanie told me you would be here."

Evelyn nodded, having decided to play this meeting cool until she could determine Kendall's intentions.

"How are you?"

"I'm okay."

"Mind if I join you?"

She inclined her head in an affirmative response. Kendall climbed the steps and lowered herself hesitantly to the step beside her.

"I heard it was a clean shoot," Kendall said.

"Yep."

"Any word on when you'll be back?"

"Tomorrow. I'm cleared, but Stahlman told me to go ahead and take the weekend."

"Have you had enough time?"

"Sure. I'm bored to death sitting around the house."

"Don't bullshit me. Did you talk to a counselor?"

"Department policy."

Kendall nodded.

"How do you like working out West?" Evelyn failed to keep the slight edge out of her voice.

"It's totally different. I've been in Green Hills and Belle Meade a lot of the time. Less crime but a lot more entitled rich people."

She glanced over her shoulder at the house behind her. "Be careful, I come from entitlement."

"You haven't expected privilege a day in your life."

Evelyn smiled. When she spoke again, she didn't hesitate. She would say what she needed to say, and if things didn't work out how she wanted, at least she'd tried. "I miss you."

"Yeah, me, too."

"Do you want to come in for dinner? I'm sure the folks would love to see you."

"Not this time. You, your parents, Melanie...I'm not quite there yet."

"Do you think you will—get there?"

Kendall shrugged. "Probably. We're lesbians, after all. Staying friends after a breakup is what we do."

She laughed. "I'd like that, and I know Melanie would, too."

"I just wanted to check on you." Kendall stood and descended the steps, stopping on the last one. She turned, sincerity shining in her eyes, and met Evelyn's. "If you need to talk or anything, give me a call."

"Thanks." She made a mental note to phone Kendall mid-week and suggest they meet for lunch. She decided to hold off telling her she planned to bid for day shift in a couple of months.

"All right, I'll see you around." When she reached her car, she gave Evelyn a small, somewhat sad smile. "I'm glad you're happy, Evelyn."

She stood as Kendall maneuvered down the drive. Though their truce was tentative, it was definitely a good start. Maybe she would somehow manage to keep her friend and find love at the same time.

"Was that Kendall?" Melanie asked as she came through the front door.

"Yeah."

Melanie wrapped her arms around Evelyn's waist and pressed her cheek against the back of her shoulder. "Are you okay?"

"I'm good." She grabbed Melanie's hands and pulled them more firmly around her. She would fill her in on the details of her talk with Kendall later. For now she just wanted to enjoy being in Melanie's embrace. She turned and put her arms around Melanie's shoulders. "I love you so much."

Melanie smiled and kissed her. "Me, too."

"Do you want to sneak upstairs to my old room and fool around?" she teased, flicking her eyebrows upward.

"I'd love to, but your mother sent me out here to tell you dinner is ready."

"Ah, one of the side-effects of my making up with my father. I'm afraid we'll have to attend more family dinners."

"I don't mind at all."

"Good, because I kind of like the idea of you and my mother in the kitchen making dinner, while my father and I retire to his study." She smiled at the antiquated imagery. "You did say you were an old-fashioned girl, didn't you?" She released Melanie and turned toward the front door.

"I did say that. But not so old-fashioned that I can't picture you and your father clearing the table and doing the dishes after dinner." Melanie swatted her rear as she followed her into the house.

As they stepped into the foyer, Evelyn spun and gathered Melanie against her once more. What began as a quick kiss heated up when Melanie slipped her tongue between her lips. She returned Melanie's ardor, then reluctantly pulled back. "I'll certainly help with the dishes if it means I can get you home sooner."

"If I didn't think it would offend your mother, I'd ask her to wrap our dessert up to go." Melanie smiled, took her hand, and led her into the dining room.

As much as she'd come to enjoy spending time with her parents, she already looked forward to leaving. After all, she had plans to make slow, passionate love to her best friend.

About the Author

Erin Dutton is the author of eight romance novels: *Sequestered Hearts*, *Fully Involved*, *A Place to Rest*, *Designed for Love*, *Point of Ignition*, *A Perfect Match*, *Reluctant Hope*, and *More Than Friends*. She is also a contributor to *Erotic Interludes 5: Road Games* and *Romantic Interludes 1 & 2* from Bold Strokes Books. She revisited two characters from one of her novels in *Breathless: Tales of Celebration*. She is a 2011 recipient of the Alice B. Readers' Appreciation Award for her body of work.

Erin lives near Nashville, Tennessee, with her amazing partner, and often draws inspiration from both her adopted hometown and places she's traveled. When not working or writing, she enjoys playing golf and spending time with friends and family.

Books Available from Bold Strokes Books

Cut to the Chase by Lisa Girolami. Careful and methodical author Paige Cornish falls for brash and wild Hollywood actress, Avalon Randolph, but can these opposites find a happy middle ground in a town that never lives in the middle? (978-1-60282-783-7)

More Than Friends by Erin Dutton. Evelyn Fisher thinks she has the perfect role model for a long-term relationship, until her best friends, Kendall and Melanie, split up and all three women must reevaluate their lives and their relationships. (978-1-60282-784-4)

Every Second Counts by D. Jackson Leigh. Every second counts in Bridgette LeRoy's desperate mission to protect her heart and stop Marc Ryder's suicidal return to riding rodeo bulls. (978-1-60282-785-1)

Dirty Money by Ashley Bartlett. Vivian Cooper and Reese DiGiovanni just found out that falling in love is hard. It's even harder when you're running for your life. (978-1-60282-786-8)

Promises in Every Star edited by Todd Gregory. Acclaimed gay male erotica author Todd Gregory's definitive collection of short stories, including both classic and new works. (978-1-60282-787-5)

Wonderland by David-Matthew Barnes. After her mother's sudden death, Destiny Moore is sent to live with her two gay uncles on Avalon Cove, a mysterious island on which she uncovers a secret place called Wonderland, where love and magic prove to be real. (978-1-60282-788-2)

Sea Glass Inn by Karis Walsh. When Melinda Andrews commissions a series of mosaics by Pamela Whitford for her new inn, she doesn't expect to be more captivated by the artist than by the paintings. (978-1-60282-771-4)

The Awakening: A Sisterhood of Spirits novel by Yvonne Heidt. Sunny Skye has interacted with spirits her entire life, but when she runs into Officer Jordan Lawson during a ghost investigation, she discovers more than just facts in a missing girl's cold case file. (978-1-60282-772-1)

Murphy's Law by Yolanda Wallace. No matter how high you climb, you can't escape your past. (978-1-60282-773-8)

Blacker Than Blue by Rebekah Weatherspoon. Threatened with losing her first love to a powerful demon, vampire Cleo Jones is willing to break the ultimate law of the undead to rebuild the family she has lost. (978-1-60282-774-5)

Another 365 Days by KE Payne. Clemmie Atkins is back, and her life is more complicated than ever! Still madly in love with her girlfriend, Clemmie suddenly finds her life turned upside down with distractions, confessions, and the return of a familiar face… (978-1-60282-775-2)

Tricks of the Trade: Magical Gay Erotica, edited by Jerry L. Wheeler. Today's hottest erotica writers take you inside the sultry, seductive world of magicians and their tricks—professional and otherwise. (978-1-60282-781-3)

Straight Boy Roommate by Kevin Troughton. Tom isn't expecting much from his first term at University, but a chance encounter with straight boy Dan catapults him into an extraordinary, wild weekend of sex and self-discovery, which turns his life upside down, and leads him into his first love affair. (978-1-60282-782-0)

Silver Collar by Gill McKnight. Werewolf Luc Garoul is outlawed and out of control, but can her family track her down before a sinister predator gets there first? Fourth in the Garoul series. (978-1-60282-764-6)

The Dragon Tree Legacy by Ali Vali. For Aubrey Tarver time hasn't dulled the pain of losing her first love Wiley Gremillion, but she has to set that aside when her choices put her life and her family's lives in real danger. (978-1-60282-765-3)

The Midnight Room by Ronica Black. After a chance encounter with the mysterious and brooding Lillian Gray in the "midnight room" of The Griffin, a local lesbian bar, confident and gorgeous Audrey McCarthy learns that her bad-girl behavior isn't bulletproof. (978-1-60282-766-0)

Dirty Sex by Ashley Bartlett. Vivian Cooper and twins Reese and Ryan DiGiovanni stole a lot of money and the guy they took it from wants it back. Like now. (978-1-60282-767-7)

Raising Hell: Demonic Gay Erotica, edited by Todd Gregory. Hot stories of gay erotica featuring demons. (978-1-60282-768-4)

Pursued by Joel Gomez-Dossi. Openly gay college student Jamie Bradford becomes romantically involved with two men at the same time, and his hell begins when one of his boyfriends becomes intent on killing him. (978-1-60282-769-1)

The Storm by Shelley Thrasher. Rural East Texas. 1918. War-weary Jaq Bergeron and marriage-scarred musician Molly Russell try to salvage love from the devastation of the war abroad and natural disasters at home. (978-1-60282-780-6)

Crossroads by Radclyffe. Dr. Hollis Monroe specializes in short-term relationships but when she meets pregnant mother-to-be Annie Colfax, fate brings them together at a crossroads that will change their lives forever. (978-1-60282-756-1)